D1571911

Sanditon *on* Reflection

D B Thomas

Sanditon on Reflection

ISBN 978-1-09837-565-2

Foreword

Jane Austen began writing her last novel, Sanditon, in 1817, wrote 12 Chapters then put it aside and with her death the same year, never finished it. I believe her final unfinished novel requires a proper ending. Of course, no one knows how Jane Austen would have ended Sanditon if she had been able to finish it, but I hope she would have approved of mine.

Sanditon on Reflection begins before Jane Austen's Sanditon does with a young Charlotte and explores the mysteries in her life that come to light over the course of her discovery of who she is and how she finds love and life in Sanditon, the fishing village come English Bathing Spa Town in Regency Era England. My companion book, 'Sanditon HEA Found', available on Booksie at https://www.booksie.com/users/db-thomas-288777 , which was completed in May 2020 is written in step outline format for possible development into a Sanditon Season 2 screenplay following the cancellation of Andrew Davies' beautiful 2019 Sanditon series after one season. I also have, in addition to writing these two books, participated with thousands of fans who have worked tirelessly to convince the TV and film powers that be to produce a Second Season or more to ensure that Jane Austen's HEA story requirement for her last unfinished novel is realized.

Dedication:

I dedicate this work to writers Jane Austen and Andrew Davies; to actress Rose Williams who is the incredible and beautiful Charlotte in Andrew Davies' 2019 ITV/MasterPiecePBS production; to Marjan de Jonge, the painter/artist from the Netherlands who inspired me with her Sanditon related paintings and whose beautiful "Is that all I am to you" Charlotte oil hangs on my wall and who also created the cover and illustrations for this book; to Sanditon Sisterhood members around the world who have worked tirelessly and creatively to get a Second Sanditon Season produced; and last but by no means least, to my beautiful Finnish wife Mervi who put up with my Sanditon writing "obsession" that possessed me in the time of Covid-19.

Acknowledgement and Disclaimer:

This novel is a work of fiction. It builds on and develops characters, themes and story lines from Jane Austen's unfinished final novel, Sanditon, and draws inspiration from Andrew Davies' 2019 one season television production of the same name. References to actions of real individuals and actual events of more than 200 years ago where used are entirely figments of my own imagination. I have utilized no sources other than the two mentioned above except for internet research which was undertaken to try to make the story reflect as accurately as possible the era in which it is set.

Prologue

"Time will explain." Jane Austen - 'Persuasion'
Willingden - 1812

I n her sixteenth year, 18 February 1812, Charlotte Heywood sits quietly in her classroom, her glossy auburn locks curling around her shoulders. The rain is beating against the large window of her classroom and the wind is lashing the trees on this stormy Tuesday morning but she is warm and comfortable. Although she adores her nine siblings, she enjoys the quiet of her class room which is a part of a complex of rooms behind the main house. Charlotte's study time which is four days a week requires her to spend five hours in class with her tutor after morning chores and for part of the afternoon she serves as the teacher of five of her younger siblings teaching them writing and mathematics. Then she has her late afternoon chores.

On a normal day, she would entertain mathematics, history, writing, reading of the classics, French and German. But today, she sits relaxed with a large volume of drawings of architectural delights from all around Europe and a book of Shakespeare's sonnets. She always enjoys her classes, but because it is her birthday, and in celebration of her attaining her sixteenth

1

year, her tutor has allowed her to choose her own lessons for the day. She loves the thought of travel to visit the glorious buildings she craves to see and pours over the drawings as her imagination takes her to exotic locations. She also enjoys Shakespeare's sonnets as she imagines how she might encounter love someday as a handsome man of mystery emerges from the shadows of one of those magnificent buildings. A particular favorite is Sonnet 116.

Let me not to the marriage of true minds

Admit impediments. Love is not love}

Which alters when it alteration finds,

Or bends with the remover to remove.

O no! it is an ever-fixed mark

That looks on tempests and is never shaken;

It is the star to every wand'ring bark,

Whose worth's unknown, although his height be taken.

Love's not Time's fool, though rosy lips and cheeks

Within his bending sickle's compass come;

Love alters not with his brief hours and weeks,

But bears it out even to the edge of doom.

If this be error and upon me prov'd,

I never writ, nor no man ever lov'd.

    William Shakespeare

Despite her love of dancing, Charlotte has grown up as a bit of a Tomboy, able to ride and when she is not being observed, ride astride for side saddle is so impractical in her mind; shoot, garden, care for livestock and even serve as her siblings' nurse in dealing with scratches, scrapes and the odd sprain and even on one occasion a broken bone, and now she is awaking to her own body as she feels the mystery of herself becoming a young woman. She has found herself considering what her future might be and dreaming about the yet unseen face of the man with whom she might share it. Although she has never been further from Willingden than the five miles to Hailsham and never seen the sea despite the nearness of Eastbourne, she is desirous of opportunities to travel. She like the entire family is well aware of her Father's notorious unwillingness to travel away from Willingden, but she knows of her Father's visits to London to "collect his dividends." She resolves to ask him if she may travel with him on his next visit to London. Finding a propitious opportunity as she accompanies him on his early morning rounds of the farm, she asks the question. 'Papa, may I travel with you to London on your next visit?' He looks a bit startled and replies, 'Why would you wish to go to London, Charlotte? It is a dirty place and unpleasant. I can barely wait to leave it for the fresh air and open fields of Willingden! But let me talk to your Mama and then we will decide.' 'Thank you, Papa,' Charlotte replies. 'I so want to see London.'

Later in the morning, as Charlotte walks from her classroom toward the dining room and goes by the drawing room, she overhears a conversation underway. It is her Papa's voice. Charlotte hears, 'Jane, Charlotte wants to accompany me to London, and I understand. She has now sixteen years and of course she wants to see London. But she looks so much like her Mother and I worry that the resemblance might be noticed.' How strangely put to my Mama, thinks Charlotte as she continues on to the dining room.

Two months have passed and Charlotte's excitement is palpable. Her Papa and Mama have agreed to her accompanying him to London. And her sister Anne, two years her junior, will accompany them as a companion for Charlotte while her Father conducts his business in London. Both are over the moon with joy. They depart on a beautiful and warm April day as flowers are springing up in the fields and the woods glow with the beauty of lime green leaves. The discomfort of the roads in terrible condition after the wet winter and spring months are unnoticed by the girls as they contemplate the magic of a visit to London. Charlotte has visions of the well dressed men and women on the streets and the processions of royal carriages all in gold and gilt carrying the rich and mighty of England. They chatter incessantly and the time passes without notice until they arrive in Tunbridge Wells, where they will overnight in the inn before continuing to London on the morrow. Charlotte is amazed at all the people and the buildings that far exceed anything she has ever seen before. They find rooms in the inn with Charlotte and Anne sharing a room neighboring their Papa's. They change and soon Papa knocks and asks them to accompany him to dine. They go down to a large dining area and are greeted, Mr Heywood very familiarly, by the Master of the Inn, a bear of a man, as they are shown to a table. 'Mr. Heywood,' he says, 'wonderful to see you again! Are you on our way to London and who are these lovely young ladies?' 'Yes, we are on our way to London,' Mr Heywood responds, 'and these are two of my daughters, Mr Catchpole. Allow me to introduce Charlotte and Anne.' 'Miss Heywood, Miss Heywood,' he returns, 'it is a great pleasure to meet you,' as both girls curtsy prettily. Mr Catchpole continues, 'I would counsel an early start tomorrow. The roads are in terrible condition as you already know from your journey from Willingden but they are even worse from all the traffic almost to London.' After apprising them of the dinner offerings, Mr Catchpole wishes them a good onward journey and says he will look forward to seeing them on their return journey. They take their meal and then retire for the evening.

Morning comes quickly and they are again greeted by a fine day. Mr Heywood gathers the coachman, carriage and their rested horses from the stable and they set off. It proves to be a "very rough lane" as Mr. Catchpole had warned, the roads are muddy and rutted and it is slow going but the excitement between the girls grows as the spires and buildings of London loom in the distance. Charlotte can barely contain herself as she admires the grand buildings in London and as they pass by Buckingham Palace, she imagines herself entering to attend a ball on the arm of a handsome and mysterious man dressed in splendid fashion. She recalls from her lessons and shares with Anne that this royal palace was earlier called The Queen's House and is the residence of Queen Charlotte, the Mother of the Prince Regent. They continue on to find their lodgings and settle into their rooms for a early night because tomorrow will be a very full day. Papa has promised them a tour of the city which will include a stroll through Hyde Park, the Palace of Westminster and then St. Paul's Cathedral taking in other sights along the way.

They start the morning early with a good breakfast then out into the sunshine they go. Charlotte and Anne marvel at the buildings especially the smart houses, the massive structures standing all around them and the elegantly dressed people they see along the way. Mr Heywood explains the city and talks of royal palaces and the great and wealthy of the city. Charlotte wonders at his knowledge and says, 'Papa, you know so much! Why have you never told us these stories before?' He responds that he was waiting for an opportunity to tell when he could show them what he was talking about. They conclude the day with a stroll through Hyde Park where they see many well dressed people walking arm in arm in the warm afternoon sunshine. In the distance, they see a royal troop of soldiers, resplendent in red, smartly marching to the beat of a drum. Closer on and coming toward them is a splendidly dressed coterie of women and gentlemen in top hats. Mr Heywood suddenly says sharply, 'Charlotte, Anne, we must go now! It is getting late and I must rise early on the morn to conduct my business.' He turns away from the approaching group and when Charlotte and Anne remain fixed staring at the glorious sight of wealth and privilege, he grabs both by their arms and pulls them after him. Charlotte glances at his face and sees a very unfamiliar look of anger, or is it perhaps fear, on his face. 'What is the matter Papa,' she asks? 'Nothing,' he replies, 'come with me; quickly now.' 'Yes Papa,' she and Anne chorus.

Upon their return to the hotel, Mr Heywood orders their meals to be served in their rooms and then they climb the stairs to their quarters. Charlotte is puzzling over her Papa's change in attitude from enjoying the day and talking about the wonders of London, to his sudden decision to return to their inn after encountering the finely dressed group in Hyde Park. He comes to their room to wish them a good night and Charlotte takes the opportunity to ask. 'Papa, what is wrong, why did we have to leave Hyde Park so suddenly?' He looks into her eyes and says, 'Charlotte, I have had to change my plans. We must begin our return journey to Willingden tomorrow just as soon as I conduct my business early in the morning. You and Anne must remain in your chamber and be prepared to depart when I return.' Charlotte protests, 'But Papa, you promised that we should have four days London.' 'Charlotte,' he says in a tone she has never heard from him before, 'I have made up my mind!' 'Yes, Papa,' she replies.

Chapter 1

Wednesday - 18 February 1818 - Willingden

Six years have passed since that sixteenth year birthday celebration trip to London. Charlotte has grown into a beautiful young woman by her twenty-second birthday, although the fact that she is beautiful has escaped her notice though not that of the young men who have made her acquaintance. She continued her studies through her 21st year and has added Latin to her reading language repertoire of French and German. She is a voracious reader of novels as she finds in them the delights of exotic locales, high society and romance otherwise denied her in Willingden.

As her classes have now concluded, she has devoted increasing amounts of her time to helping her Mama with her now 10 younger siblings and serves as teacher and tutor to many of them. She is teaching those old enough riding and shooting as well since she is a superb horsewoman and a crack shot. She has become proficient in helping her Papa manage his accounts and he has turned almost all responsibility for that over to her with the exception of his dividends collection trips to London which he undertakes by himself. She has become her Papa's right hand in managing the Heywood estate and in partnership with her older brother, Benjamin, is fully capable of overseeing all aspects of the farm. With regard to the dividends that her Papa travels to London several times a year to collect, Charlotte has on occasion asked to join him again for a London visit, but the answer has always been no.

Charlotte also has become the talk of Willingden as the partner of choice for the Balls held in the village because of her beauty and grace on the dance floor. The unmarried young men all vie for her attention and she is attracting would be suitors from as far away as Tunbridge Wells as rumors of her beauty have spread. However, she has not traveled further than Hailsham because her Papa has been adamant since their trip to London six years back that they remain close to home. She loves the balls that she can attend and is solicitous of the young and also older men who ask to be added to her dance card. Several have professed their affection to her but she has politely declined any and all advances. She has yet to meet a man who has stirred her affection in return.

Chapter 2

On a blustery March day in 1818 with the blue sky and bright sun promise of Spring which is just a day away but with an edge to the wind that reminds of winter, Charlotte rises early as is her wont. She loves Spring with the coming blossoms, the greening fields and woods and she has determined to take 20 year old Anne, 14 year old George and 16 year old Thomas out into the fields to see if they can scare up some game for the evening meal. They follow the track from the house across the fields and into the wood. They see nothing of game but the smells of warming earth and budding green are delightful and they meander their way back out of the wood and onto the lane that runs to Willingden which is a mile down the road from their family home.

As they approach a bend in the road between the hedges, they hear the sounds of horses at fast clip climbing the steep lane toward the bend. Suddenly, a carriage and four careen round the bend at speed and as it is a very sharp turn, the carriage begins to tilt and while Charlotte and her siblings gape in surprise and shock, it turns over onto its side. The coachman and the footman at the back of the carriage jump for their lives as the horses scream in fear and continue to drag the carriage toward Charlotte and her charges. Charlotte sees a frozen George in front of her, pushes him quickly to the side and then grabs at the reins of the panicked lead horse nearest her. With a firm grip, she holds onto the horse's halter pulling his head down as he drags her along. Thomas grabs the harness of the other lead horse and throws himself onto his back pulling back strongly on the reins. The horses slow and then stop as Charlotte and Thomas talk to calm them.

As the coachman and footman come up to hold the horses, Charlotte runs back to the carriage and calls out. 'Is everyone all right?' There is no sound for a moment and then a very shaken looking gentleman shoves open the carriage door above his head and looks out. 'Are you all right, Sir,' Charlotte asks? 'Yes,' he replies 'but I seem to have injured my ankle. And, Mary, are you all right, My Dear,' he asks of someone yet unseen? Charlotte hears, 'Tom, what were you thinking, directing our coachman to drive so fast on this "very rough Lane"?' She emerges, bonnet askew and directs her gaze at Charlotte. 'Did you stop the horses, Miss?' 'Yes ma'am,' replies Charlotte, 'with the help of my brother Thomas.' 'You should not have done it, it was very dangerous but we are grateful. You have saved us from possible serious injury. Thank you,' the lady exclaims!

The gentleman pulls himself up and out of the carriage and then assists his lady. Charlotte, Anne and Thomas help them to climb down from the overturned carriage. The gentleman says once on the ground standing mostly on one foot as he favors his injury, 'I am Tom Parker of Sanditon and this is my wife, Mary Parker.' 'I am very pleased to meet you, Mr Parker and Mrs Parker,' says Charlotte with a curtsy. 'I am Charlotte

Heywood, this is my sister, Anne and these are my brothers, Thomas and George.' 'Miss Heywood,' Tom Parker replies, 'I wonder if it should be possible to take us to a place where we might rest while my men right the carriage and prepare it for us to continue our journey.' 'Of course,' Charlotte replies, 'please accompany us to our home which is very near by. My Papa will be happy to assist you I am sure. Let us go and find him and bring a cart since your ankle appears to be very painful.' She asks Thomas to run back to the house, alert Papa and bring the cart to transport their unexpected visitors to the house where Mr Parker's injury can be cared for and Mrs Parker can take her rest.

As they wait for the cart, Mr Parker talks to his coachman who tells him that two of the wheels on the carriage have been damaged and will need to be repaired or replaced before they can continue on their journey. 'Terrible news,' Tom Parker replies, 'I have urgent business in Sanditon to attend.' But there is nothing to be done and shortly thereafter Thomas arrives with the cart accompanied by Mr Heywood. They are introduced by Charlotte; Mr Tom Parker and Mrs Mary Parker to her Papa, Mr Stephen Heywood. With the pleasantries concluded, Mr Heywood assesses the situation with the carriage wheels and Mr Parker's ankle. 'It appears that your carriage will require extensive repairs before you can continue your journey,' he says, 'and your ankle will require time to recover. My daughter, Charlotte, will look to your injury upon our arrival back at the house and I will bring some men to help right your carriage and bring it to our barn.' After entertaining some protestations as to the inconveniences caused his rescuers from Mr Parker, the party sets off in the cart back to the Heywood home.

On arrival, Mr and Mrs Parker are greeted by Mrs Jane Heywood and the rest of the extensive Heywood family. Mr and Mrs Parker are invited in; Mr Parker now requiring assistance as his rapidly swelling ankle is becoming more painful to bear his weight by the minute. They are taken to the drawing room where Mr Parker's boot is removed, his ankle elevated and placed on a cushioned footstool. 'I would be obliged if you should send for a Physician,' Mr Parker says. 'His presence is the reason for my and my wife's visit to Willingden. We are in urgent need of a Physician for our Sanditon Sea Bathing Town project and we have come to see if we might procure his services for the distinguished visitors to our town.' 'I fear you are mistaken,' replies Mr Heywood. 'There is no such personage resident in Willingden nor indeed anywhere in the Parish.' 'I beg to differ, Mr Heywood, as I just yesterday morning read in London in the Morning Post and the Kentish Gazette that there is such a gentleman here! Allow me to show you the advertisements I myself cut from the posts,' Mr Parker replies. He opens his valise and pulls out the papers to show them. Glancing over them, Mr Heywood says, 'These advertisements refer to Great Willingden which is several miles off. Let me assure you again, that there is no Physician hereabouts.' Mr Parker replies, 'I wondered at the lane so rough in your neighborhood rather lacking in refinement and certainly not adequate for a town of the size to have its own Physician in residence. I have been led astray by my own lack of attention to geography. But, what am I to do about my ankle which now pains me greatly?'

'As I advised you, Mr Parker, my daughter, Charlotte, who is very proficient in surgical matters, particularly with scrapes, sprains and such, will serve your requirements very well,' responds Mr Heywood. Charlotte steps forward to carefully examine the injured ankle. She gently moves it back and forth and up and down and pronounces it just a sprain, not a break, but serious enough to require several days rest before any lengthy rambles should be attempted. She has some cold well water fetched to soak his foot in and recommends a regimen of regular soaks in cold water for a few days to reduce the swelling and then keeping it wrapped lightly as the swelling subsides. Mr Parker expresses his approbation for Charlotte's treatment saying that his ankle did indeed already feel better with such expert care.

Over the next several days as Tom Parker's ankle heals under Charlotte's care, Mr and Mrs Parker become a part of the large Heywood family. Tom Parker is impressed with the smooth cooperation among the various members of the Heywood family. Mr. Heywood is seen to be a efficient manager of the farm with the help of his older children and his workers who without exception are happy and well treated. The Heywood household is well managed by Mrs Heywood and again, the servants are observed to be well treated and happy. And in particular, their approbation of Charlotte grows by the hour. She is seen to be involved in every aspect of the farm operation from decisions about livestock, the fields, financial matters, education and care of her younger siblings to decisions in the kitchen.

As Mary's affection for the beautiful young woman grows, she begins to think about the benefits of having Charlotte join her in the care and education of her own children. So, on the afternoon of their eighth day in Willingden, Mary says to Tom, 'Miss Heywood would be a wonderful addition to our household. She is well educated and an able teacher who could benefit our own four children. And with her knowledge of finance, she could be of great help to you in managing your Sanditon Sea Bathing Town project.' Tom agrees and they resolve to ask after dinner if Charlotte should be allowed to accompany them to Sanditon as a companion for Mary and a tutor for their children.

Following dinner in the large dining room required to seat the family, Mr and Mrs Heywood retire with their guests to the drawing room. Mr Heywood reports that broken spokes of their carriage wheels and the damage to the axles on the side of the carriage that had been dragged along the road are almost complete. And says, 'My daughter reports that your ankle will soon be in condition such that you will be able to walk on it without undue pain. I should expect that you will be able to continue your journey home in the coming week.' 'Capital news,' exclaims Tom Parker. 'We must move on most urgently despite your excellent hospitality which I fear, we have abused.' 'Not a bit of it,' responds Mr Heywood. 'You truly have been welcome in our humble abode.' Mary Parker then says, 'Mr Heywood, my husband and I have been discussing how we might possibly repay your hospitality.' Tom Parker steps in and says, 'Yes, we should like to invite the whole Heywood family to be our guests in Sanditon. Spring has has now arrived and the beach in Sanditon will soon be beckoning guests. You have been such wonderful hosts and we must reciprocate your kindness.' 'You are very kind, Mr Parker, Mrs Parker, but we cannot accept,' replies Mr Heywood. 'I never travel far from the homestead except for my two or three annual trips to London "to collect my dividends" and spring planting is upon us!' 'Well, then,' replies Mr Parker, 'might you allow your daughter, Miss Charlotte Heywood, to accompany us to Sanditon as a par-tial recompense for your kindness? She would be treated as family. Mary is quite taken with her and we should very much like to have her as our guest. And of course, should she desire a companion, we should be very glad if her sister Anne were to accompany her.' Mr Heywood looks to Mrs Heywood, then says, 'we shall have to ask her. Charlotte now is two and twenty and has a mind of her own. We shall not presume to make such a decision for her. However, Anne must remain with us. She will need to take Charlotte's responsibilities with the children's education.'

Mrs Heywood goes to fetch Charlotte. When they return, Mr Heywood says, 'Charlotte, Mr and Mrs Parker have a proposition for you. Your answer is your own decision and we shall not interfere.' 'What is it,

Papa,' asks Charlotte? 'Mr Parker...,' exclaims Mr Heywood looking to him. 'Miss Heywood,' Tom Parker responds, 'Mary and I should like very much for you to accompany us to Sanditon. You have been wonderful to us and we should see you as a valuable addition to our family. You should serve as a companion to Mary, a tutor for our children and perhaps you could be a coadjutor to me for my Sanditon Sea Bathing Town project. You should dine with us, have your own sleeping chamber and be treated like a member of the family.' Charlotte's eyes begin to shine with excitement. 'Oh, Papa, Mama,' she says, 'could I? I know you need me because there are so many chores and what of my brothers' and sisters' schooling?' 'You shall be missed, Dearest Charlotte,' replies Papa as Mama nods in agreement, 'but you are of age and it is time for you to see and learn more of the world.'

Mr Parker then says, 'Miss Heywood, I should like to tell you now about my Sanditon Sea Bathing Town Project, to which I alluded on the unfortunate day of our arrival and was the purpose of our coming to Willingden in search of a physician, because I may require your assistance as well. I am building a new spa town in the Sanditon fishing village. I believe it will rival Brighton and exceed Eastbourne when finished in terms of attracting visitors for cures offered from sea bathing. The beach is very fine and the town is sheltered from the winds by the headlands surrounding it. We are building now but much remains to be done.' Charlotte responds, 'Oh Mr Parker, I love the thought of it and should very much like to assist you in whatever way possible in realizing your dream.' 'Then it is settled,' says Mr Parker, 'you shall accompany us to Sanditon!'

On the evening before the planned departure of the party to Sanditon, Mr Heywood asks Charlotte to come with him for a stroll through the fields. 'Charlotte,' he says, 'I am very happy for you to see more of the world, but I must caution you to be careful. You have grown up in a small village

15

where you know everyone. That will not be the case in Sanditon where there will be many strangers, many new acquaintances and while some or even all may be good and honorable, some perhaps will not be. I want you to be very careful!' 'I shall Papa,' replies Charlotte, 'but what could happen while I am in the care of Mr and Mrs Parker?' 'There is always the possibility that you could find your trust misplaced in someone,' Mr Heywood responds, 'and further I would like for you to avoid going to London should the occasion arise.' 'Why, Papa,' Charlotte asks? 'It is for your own good,' says he. 'The why of it all will be revealed when the time is come.' 'Yes, Papa,' replies Charlotte.

Chapter 3

Wednesday - 1 April 1818 - Willingden/Sanditon

The morning dawns on the day of departure and all is excitement in the house. Charlotte has arisen early to be sure she has her trunk packed with her necessaries. She goes into breakfast and finds the whole family assembled to send her off. Mr and Mrs Parker are finishing their breakfast and go out leaving Charlotte to say her goodbyes. There are tears and smiles and demands for letters to sent on a regular basis to tell of her adventures in Sanditon. Charlotte promises to be a faithful correspondent. Anne comes to Charlotte and says, 'I shall miss you, Dear Sister.' 'I shall miss you too, Anne,' replies Charlotte, 'but I am confident that you too shall have an opportunity to come to Sanditon and I shall show you the sights.' Charlotte hugs each of her siblings in turn and then her Mama, who looks at her with a hint of tears in her eyes. 'I shall miss you, my Darling Girl, please take good care and write often.' 'I shall,' Charlotte replies. Mr Heywood then walks Charlotte out to the waiting carriage. 'Remember my words, Charlotte,' he says 'and please be careful.' 'I shall, Papa,' she replies as he hands her into the carriage. Then the carriage lurches away as the well rested horses are feeling their oats and ready to run. Out of the yard they go to shouts of good bye and good journey as Charlotte looks back and waves before settling back into her seat with a smile at Mr and Mrs Parker.

The carriage rounds a bend and the sea comes into view. It has been a comfortable three and one half hour journey from Willingden and the early April weather has been glorious with a warm sun and azure sky dotted with cotton boll clouds floating here and there. The sea is a dazzling blue and Charlotte gasps at the sight of it. It is her first ever opportunity to see the ocean for herself and she is smitten with the beauty of it. A breeze ruffles the curtains of the carriage and carries with it a scent of the sea, something of salt and earth, which is delightful to Charlotte's senses. The journey has been filled with a practically non-stop soliloquy from Tom Parker of all he has accomplished and all he has plans still to accomplish in his Sanditon Sea Bathing Town. Mary has glanced at him from time to time with a bit of a frown but has stayed silent. Charlotte has listened as well as she can considering the views out of the carriage window have occupied her attention and the anticipation of seeing the sea, the English Channel, for the first time has almost overwhelmed her. And there is it.

Tom Parker suddenly stops discussion of his accomplishments and says to Charlotte, 'Ah, the sea air! It will complete the healing of my ankle, so ably cared for by yourself for which I am forever in your debt.' He continues, 'Miss Heywood, soon we shall be passing by Sanditon House. It it is the residence of Lady Denham. She is very wealthy and she is my prime investor and accordingly requires much of my attention. I must make regular calls on her to keep her updated on my progress. She is a difficult taskmistress but her fortune and investment in my Sanditon Town are most important! We shall take you to call on her at the earliest opportunity, will we not, Mary?' 'Yes, my Dear,' Mary replies.

Tom continues. 'Lady Denham is very astute, lacking in education but not in intelligence. First as Miss Agatha Brereton, she married a wealthy man, a Mr. Hollis, who was a man of property in the "Parish of Sanditon" and from him came Sanditon House which you shall soon visit. Upon his death a few short years later, she married again, to Sir Harry Denham, again a propertied man of a neighboring Estate and owner of Denham Place located on that Estate. From him upon his death again a few short years later, she gained a title and all of his fortune. It is from this that Sir Harry's fate provides us with a cautionary tale and keeps me forever upon my toes. It was Sir Harry's intention that he should gain Mrs. Hollis' property and fortune though his marriage for his own Denham heirs, but Lady Denham was too clever by far for him because she had kept her Hollis fortune and properties out of his grasp and on his death, she gained his title and fortune! And I would be remiss if I did not mention her nephew Sir Edward Denham and niece Miss Esther Denham, brother and sister who reside together at Denham Place. They are heirs apparent of Lady Denham's estate and as such both require our every effort to gain their favor. There also is the companion of Lady Denham, Miss Clara Brereton, a relative who may also share in Lady Denham's fortune on her passing. There are some signs that she is deeply in Sir Edward's favor. As the future of Sanditon Town could be in their hands as well as it is in Lady Denham's now, we must therefore work assiduously to stay in the favor of one and all.' He stops as his breath runs short. Charlotte considers his words. Yes, Lady Denham holds the fate of Mr Parker and his Sanditon Sea Bathing Town in her hands. She is a woman who has power and knows how to use it. Yes, thinks Charlotte, I shall look forward to calling on her.

The carriage continues on toward Sanditon and Tom Parker points out Sanditon House in the distance and then a short time later Denham Place through the trees. As they come into the village passing by the church, the carriage begins its descent from the hills down into Sanditon. Along the way, Tom Parker calls Charlotte's attention to another house. 'This is the home place of the Parker family. There I was born as were my brothers, Sidney and Arthur and my sisters Susan and Diana. And it was Mary's and my home until recently. But with the Sanditon Sea Bathing Town project, we have built our new Trafalgar House and have lived in it for two years now.' Charlotte asks, 'Shall I meet all of your family in Sanditon?' 'No,' Tom replies, 'our parents are not living. They were taken by the Pock (smallpox). Susan, the eldest is poorly and lives in London with her husband, Wilbur, a solicitor. But you shall soon meet Arthur, the youngest of my siblings, and Diana, our sister, both unmarried who share a house in Sanditon. And at a later time, you shall meet Sidney, my other brother and my partner in the Sanditon Sea Bathing Town who spends most of his time in London at our family home there. He is planning to come to Sanditon soon and you shall meet him then. But I shall warn you now that Sidney is a bit of a conundrum and can be quite sharp in the sharing of his opinions.' Mary interjects, 'But he is a handsome man with a good if unsettled spirit and I am sure you shall enjoy making his acquaintance, Charlotte.'

As Mary makes her comment about Sidney Parker, the carriage pulls up to Trafalgar House. Then as Tom Parker hands Mary and then Charlotte down, three children run out to the carriage, jumping with joy at Mama's and Papa's return, followed by a woman with a baby in her arms. 'What a welcome home we receive, do we not, Mary,' shouts Tom! 'Surely our children have grown more fond of their Mama and Papa in our absence as evidence of our eyes shows us. And here is Diana, my Sister, with our youngest. Miss Heywood,' he continues, 'may I introduce you to my Sister Diana Parker who has been so kind as to oversee the care of our children during our long and mostly unplanned absence.' 'I am very pleased to make your acquaintance, Miss Heywood,' Diana says 'and welcome to

Sanditon.' 'Thank you, Miss Parker, I have heard so much about you from Mr Parker and I am so pleased to meet you,' replies Charlotte. 'And,' says Tom Parker, 'allow me to introduce our children, Elinor, Lucy, Henry and our last born of six months, William.' Surrounded by the three enthusiastic children, Charlotte feels at home at once as a gaggle of children at her feet is her daily regimen in Willingden. As she prepares to enter at Mr. Parker's invitation, Charlotte admires the grand new Parker residence of Trafalgar House which enjoys a pride of place location on the terrace in the heart of new Sanditon Town, set off to the side of the older buildings of the old Sanditon fishing village very near to the beach.

They go in and Charlotte is immediately engaged by the modernity of the place. She admires the elegant furniture and the well decorated rooms that she can see from the hallway. Then Mary who has been occupied with the demands of her long neglected children due to her unplanned absence joins her and says, 'Come, Charlotte, we must get you settled. You will want to unpack your trunk and make an acquaintance with your sleeping chamber.' They go up the stairs and continue toward the back of the house. 'I hope you will find your room suitable, Charlotte.' They enter a commodious room, well decorated and incorporating a large window through which Charlotte can see the sparking sea over the rooftops. 'Oh,' says Charlotte taking in the luxury of the room and the glorious view out the window, 'I have never seen such a beautiful room, let alone, ever thought to occupy one as my own. We children in Willingden all share sleeping quarters, I with my sister, Anne and other younger ones, three or four in each chamber. I shall be very happy to call this my own.'

After Mary leaves her to her own devices, Charlotte stands and looks out the large window in her bed chamber over the rooftops toward the sun dappled sea. She feels as if she is in a dream. This cannot be real, she thinks. She feels a sense of destiny, of being in a place she is supposed to be. But then she is overtaken by a chill, a feeling that there is something or someone waiting to take it all away. She shivers, then shakes it off and says to herself, Courage, Charlotte, you are overwhelmed by your good fortune and are acting like a ninny. It is nothing. She turns away from the window to her trunk and begins to unpack her belongings. She notices a large cupboard opposite the bed and begins to hang her gowns and stow her undergarments in the drawers. It feels like home, she thinks, it feels like I belong here. She reaches the bottom of her trunk and finds a small package, wrapped and tied with a bow. She opens it. It is a book with a note from Anne. Charlotte reads;

Willingden

31 March 1818
My Dearest Sister,

I shall miss you with all of my heart. But I know you must make your way out into the world. This book will help you I hope. I know you love to read and I know at some point that you will marry. I have read and loved this volume called "Pride and Prejudice" by Miss Jane Austen and wanted you to have it. Papa was kind enough to purchase it for me to gift to you when the occasion arose. Now it has. Just know that whatever life deals you, I shall always love you. Be brave, Dear Sister and write to me as often as you can.

Anne

Charlotte feels the prickle of tears as she opens the volume, glances through it and then lays it by her bedside. I shall enjoy your gift, Dear Sister, she thinks as she goes out.

Downstairs, Charlotte sees and hears that all is chaos as the children vie for Mama's and Papa's attention and Baby William wails. Diana is anxious to return to her own bed as her planned one week stay at Trafalgar House had turned into a week plus a fortnight because of Tom and Mary Parker's Willingden mishap. She is telling Mary that poor Arthur has suffered so grievously during her absence despite his being only a short distance away. And she would like to return home to join him as soon as possible. The footman enters whom Tom acknowledges as Morgan and announces the arrival of Mr. Arthur Parker. A rotund man of rosy countenance bounds into the drawing room. 'Tom, Mary', he cries, 'it is so wonderful that you have returned at long last! I was concerned with poor Diana's burden and of course, your unplanned absence. But all is well that ends well. You are home.' Tom turns to Charlotte and says, 'Miss Heywood, allow me to introduce you to my Brother, Arthur Parker.' 'So pleased to meet you, Miss Heywood,' he says as Charlotte curtsies and returns a, 'I'm very pleased to meet you, Mr Parker.' 'You know Miss Heywood,' Arthur says, 'I feel as if I know you! You remind me of someone, I don't remember whom, but it will come to me.' He then goes to sit with the children who proceed to climb all over him. Even Baby William stops wailing. Arthur clearly is a family favorite of the children, Charlotte observes. 'Shall we all go in to dinner,' proposes Tom as Morgan comes in to announce the evening meal.

As the meal progresses, Tom Parker further explains his grand vision for Sanditon. He waxes poetic about his plans for Sanditon saying, 'It is to become destination of choice for the London Beau Monde (rich and fashionable society). When our town is ready, we will attract guests from Eastbourne and Hastings and even Brighton will be eclipsed in our shadow. But we must have a physician in our town to attain the pinnacle of success for our spa town. Why, well, first, any town worthy of its name must have its own Physician because clientele of means require that a man of medicine should always be close at hand. Second, as a beach spa town, there should be someone, and a Physician is preferable, who can dispense appropriate advice regarding sea bathing and diet to improve the body and mind. So, Miss Heywood, I must find my physician. Procuring the services of such a man was the purpose of our visit to Willingden as you know. We shall yet find the man who will help me attain my dream and make Sanditon the first of destinations to those who look to find or rediscover their health.' 'Here, here,' cries Arthur, 'with all our maladies, Diana, we look forward to the realization of our Brother Tom's dream! Do we not?' 'Yes, indeed,' Diana replies, 'but now is it not time to beg our Brother's indulgence and depart for home, Arthur?' 'Indeed it is,' he returns, 'however, Sister, should we not first retire to the drawing room for a glass or two of Madeira to for-tify us for our walk home in the cold of the evening,' looking askance at his Brother as he says it? 'Yes…, yes indeed,' replies Tom.

Chapter 4

Thursday - 2 April 1818 - Morning - Sanditon

Following a restful first night in Sanditon, Charlotte rises early. The household is still asleep so Charlotte determines to walk on the beach, to enjoy the quiet of the morning and to visit the mighty ocean, to see and touch a body of water that falls off the edge of the earth, no opposite shore in sight, and beyond the horizon, washes the shores of exotic lands of which she has only read. She dresses quickly and bundles up against the chill of the early April morning and then lets herself out into the street. It is only a short walk along the terrace to an opening in the dunes whence she descends down onto the beach. A sharp wind whips sand into her eyes but the feel of sand and shingle underneath her shoes, something new and unfamiliar, causes her to stop to remove her shoes and stockings despite the cold. It is low tide and the broad expanse of sand alternating with shingle pulls her toward the water and at last she stands, her unfettered hair flying and her gown billowing in the strong breeze. The sea washes across her bare feet, pulling an involuntary squeal of mixed shock and delight from her lips. Oh, she thinks, I am undone! Never, shall I wish to be anywhere again that is far from the sea. I shall find my life and love here and never shall I live anywhere else.

Charlotte walks back from the waters edge, brushes the sand from her now very cold feet and then drying them as best she can with the helm of her gown, puts her stockings and shoes back on. Then she ascends the path between the dunes back upon to the terrace and walks along the street. She passes a bakery whence wafts the smell of fresh baked bread and pastries. Her stomach protests its emptiness and she hurries on down the way to Trafalgar House. She is admitted by Morgan, the footman and proceeds toward the dining room. There she finds the Parker family at the dining table. Mary jumps up. 'There you are, Charlotte,' she says. 'We were troubled by your absence and when not seeing you come down, I went to your chamber and found it empty.' 'Please accept my apologies,' Charlotte replies. 'I rose early and could not resist going to the shore because I had never before touched the ocean, but I should have left a note.' 'No, no, 'responds Mary, 'it is nothing, but you should never go into the water alone. I realize you would not now because of the cold. But when the water is suitable for swimming in the summer you might and the currents can be quite severe and could sweep you away should you wade too deeply in. Well, now you must be hungry, please join us for breakfast.' Expressing her thanks with a smile, Charlotte fills a plate from the sideboard and joins the Parker family at the table.

'As I was just saying, Charlotte, before you arrived, I have received a letter from my Brother, Sidney,' says Tom. 'With your permission, I shall read it now.' He begins;

London 30 March 1818

My Dear Brother:

I shall soon be returning to Sanditon. I know you have been awaiting word from me regarding financing of the Sanditon Town Project. I hope to bring positive news on my arrival, but I must tell you that I am finding more and more doors closed to me related to your project. There is a strong feeling that the south coast does not require another bathing town and that it will not be able to compete with the likes of Brighton, Eastbourne and Hastings. But I shall endeavor to bring good news. If all goes well, you shall see my arrival in Sanditon one week hence of the post date on this letter.

Ever your affectionate brother,

Sidney

'Well,' says Tom, 'this is good news indeed! We shall look forward to his visit and to hearing his good tidings.' And he says, 'Charlotte, you soon shall have the pleasure of meeting Sidney and certainly he you. But today, I would ask you join me in calling on Lady Denham. I have been remiss in not keeping her, my most precious major investor in our new town, informed of our progress because of our accident in Willingden. She is a fearsome taskmistress and will not book being left too long in the dark as to my progress. Mary, will you be able to join us?' 'Yes,' she replies. 'Capital,' responds Tom, 'this afternoon then it shall be!'

Chapter 5

Thursday - 2 April 1818 - Afternoon - Sanditon

It is early afternoon and Tom has gone out to check on the progress of his workers. He advises Mary and Charlotte that he will not be long away and as soon as he returns, they can proceed to call on Lady Denham. Charlotte awaits his return in the drawing room. She is puzzling to herself about Tom Parker's reaction to Sidney Parker's letter. It was a bit strange she thinks that Tom Parker should react so enthusiastically to the letter. The contents of the letter in Charlotte's mind were not nearly so positive as Tom's reaction to it was. Of course, news of Sidney Parker's pending arrival in Sanditon was cause for happiness, but difficulties reported about finding needed financing seemed decidedly negative to Charlotte.

Mary enters and interrupts Charlotte's reflection. 'Charlotte,' she says, 'we have not had opportunity to talk alone and there are several things I should bring to your attention, I feel, since you will be a part of our family here at Trafalgar House. First, there is the matter of Tom's Sanditon project. I fear that he is over enthusiastic and sometimes unhearing of things he does not wish to hear. His ambition to make Sanditon a bathing town to rival Brighton is all consuming and sometimes blinds him to the difficulties he faces in realizing his dream. He leans heavily on Lady Denham's commitment as a major investor and his Brother Sidney to procure additional financing that he needs. And Tom continually adds to the expense of the project by dreaming up new enhancements. I worry that he is putting our fortune and very livelihood at risk. And speaking frankly, Charlotte, I fear that Sidney is becoming weary of Tom's constant demands on his time. He has his own matters to deal with that Tom ignores just as he ignores our growing debt.'

'And speaking of Sidney,' continues Mary, 'you shall soon meet him. As you have already heard from Tom, Sidney is a man of fair appearance, indeed he is very handsome, and he has his own fortune from his work as a trader of commodities, wines and liquors and from an old childless aunt of whom he was the favorite. He appears as bit of a rake, very much a man about town in London where he resides most of the time and he has caught the eye of many a young lady. But he is a wounded man, his spirit was broken by a young love of many years back before he attained his majority. He and she, a Miss Maria Campbell, had dreamed of marriage, but Sidney's situation at the time was not such as to attract the approval of said young lady's Father. The Father died suddenly of some matter of the heart, leaving a widow who discovered on his passing that his fortune was considerably diminished from what she had thought because of bad habits and failed investments. But young love is what it is and the couple persisted in their dreams of marriage. However, Sidney was suddenly presented with the news when the banns were read that the young woman he had taken to his heart was betrothed to another, an elderly man of considerable fortune. He was heart broken and so I believe he still remains, ten years on. He is very distrustful of young women because of it and I may say can be unfeeling in his words toward them. So I shall caution you now to be on your guard.'

Tom soon returns and requests Mary's and Charlotte's company for the walk to Sanditon House and their call on Lady Denham. As Tom and Mary walk together arm in arm, Charlotte follows behind, mulling over in her mind what Mary had shared with her in the morning. So, she thinks, there is ever a dark side to paradise. Behind the beauty of the place and the smiles on the faces, there hides perhaps something less than the eye perceives. I shall endeavor to remember my Papa's words to be cautious of what I do not know; this is not Willingden after all.

After the best part of a mile's journey along the lane away from the shore, the party of three walks through the grand gates of Sanditon House and then along a winding lane finally rounding a bend where the impressive facade of Sanditon House comes into view. Oh what a grand house, she thinks, it reminds me certainly of the royal and impressive palaces and houses of London and unbidden comes a thought from her daydreams of years past, of that mysterious man, a man yet unseen but a man who will own her heart, perhaps emerging from a house such as this. Do not think of it, Charlotte, she tells herself. You are no longer a child and certainly there is no reason to think of such things now.

They arrive at the door and are admitted by a royally dressed footman who invites them in, shows them to a grand gallery and asks them to wait while he sees if Lady Denham is available for their call. As they wait in the gallery, Charlotte looks at the portraits of unknown men and women, gazes at the crimson flock wall paper and at massive chandeliers hanging from the ceiling. Truly this is the residence of a woman of means, she thinks, and I can see why her patronage of Tom Parker's Sanditon Sea Bathing Town Project is so important.

The footman returns and enjoins them to follow him into the drawing room, a similarly grand room of large proportion with floor almost to ceiling windows looking out over expansive gardens stretching back to groves of magnificent trees. Standing in wait is a mature woman of indeterminate age dressed in a beautiful purple and gold gown. The footman announces Mr Tom Parker, Mrs Mary Parker and their guest, Miss Charlotte Heywood. Without civilities the Lady says, 'Mr Parker, you have been remiss in calling and keeping me apprised of the status of our Sanditon project,' staring directly at him and ignoring Mary and Charlotte. 'Lady Denham,' responds Tom Parker, 'I beg your forgiveness; I was unavoidably detained on my return from London by an accident along the way that resulted in an injury to my person which required rest and recovery before I could continue my journey onward to Sanditon.' 'If that be the cause of it,' she responds, 'could you not have posted me a letter advising me of your situation?' 'I beg your pardon, My Lady, it is unforgivable that I did not do so, but I was very indisposed and I hope you will forgive me.' 'Harrumph,' she huffs as Tom Parker hastens to move the conversation off of his lack of civility. He continues, 'You of course know my wife, Mary, but allow me to introduce to you our guest, Miss Charlotte Heywood.' Charlotte curtsies. 'Whence she came,' responds Lady Denham, 'I don't believe I am acquainted with the name Heywood?' 'She was my savior in Willingden where we had our accident, was she not Mary,' replies Tom, 'and her attentions to my injury were essential to my quick recovery allowing me to be here today, My Lady!'

'Come forward, Miss Heywood, and allow me to look at you,' demands Lady Denham! Charlotte steps forward thinking, she is indeed formidable. I fear for poor Tom Parker or anyone else who dares to cross her. 'Well,' Lady Denham says, 'you are not unpleasant to look at and quite presentable but does your family have a fortune with which to gain you a husband, with a Title perhaps? What is the occupation of your Father?' 'He is a gentleman farmer, Ma'am,' replies Charlotte. 'That will not do, Miss

Heywood, that will not do at all! You should not expect to find a husband here!' 'Indeed I do not,' Charlotte replies. 'I am not in search of a husband, not here nor anywhere. And when I do marry, I shall not marry for money nor Title, but for love.' 'Balderdash,' responds Lady Denham, 'of course you are here to find a rich man. You appear a sensible girl and why would you not wish to marry well?' She continues, 'My companion and poor relation, Miss Clara Brereton will attend you and Mrs Parker while I discuss my investment with Mr. Parker,' gesturing as she speaks toward chairs on the other side of the room. 'Hawkins,' she calls out to the footman at the door, 'Fetch Miss Brereton here forthwith!' 'Yes, my Lady,' he replies with a bow and goes out of the room returning shortly thereafter with an attractive young woman who appears to be of Charlotte's age.

'Miss Brereton,' Mary says, 'allow me to introduce my guest, Miss Charlotte Heywood.' Mary then says 'I shall leave you to get acquainted,' and retreats to a chair nearer the table where Lady Denham appears, from Charlotte's perspective, to be remonstrating forcefully with Tom Parker. Miss Brereton says with the beginnings of a smile, 'You have met my Great Aunt then, Miss Heywood? What do you think of her?' Charlotte hesitates for a moment and then replies, 'She is quite firm in her opinions, I believe,' then stops. Miss Brereton's smile broadens and then she says, 'Please call me Clara and yes, you may speak your mind with me. I know my Great Aunt is of strong opinion and she always speaks her mind even when we should hope that she would not.' Charlotte returns a smile of her own saying, 'Thank you, Clara, and please call me Charlotte.' 'We shall be friends,' says Clara. 'Have you been long in Sanditon and how do you like it?' 'One day only,' Charlotte replies, 'and already I love it here! I am very partial to the beach and the ocean which I had never before seen.' 'Then you must also try sea bathing,' Clara says, 'although the water is very cold now, still it is wonderful and it is the main attraction for Mr. Parker's new Sanditon Town.'

Hawkins enters again, and announces Sir Edward Denham and Miss Esther Denham. An elegantly dressed pair enter and Sir Edward makes a bee line toward Charlotte and Clara leaving Esther standing alone. 'Miss Brereton,' he asks, 'who is your lovely companion?' Then turning his attention to Charlotte, he continues, 'I have not had the pleasure.' 'This is Miss Heywood, a guest of Mr and Mrs Parker,' replies Clara. 'Enchanted,' says he, looking into Charlotte's eyes as he takes her hand and raises it to his lips. Charlotte responds with a curtesy and a 'Pleased to make your acquaintance, Sir Edward,' quickly pulling her hand out of his grasp. Miss Denham who in the meantime has walked up to the group says, 'Edward, please introduce me,' giving him a sharp and Charlotte thinks disapproving look at the same time. Introductions are made and then Lady Denham calls all of them over to where Tom Parker stands looking very much like a disciplined school boy in Charlotte's estimation. 'The next time I see you, Mr Parker, I shall look forward to a more positive report on the status of construction, Mr Sidney Parker's progress in finding more funds and an increase in the numbers of paying guests for the coming Summer,' she says. 'Now,' she continues, 'it is time for my afternoon rest so please see yourselves out, but I would have a private moment with Miss Heywood if you please!' The party files out and after the doors are closed, Lady Denham says, 'Miss Heywood, I saw you with Edward and I shall caution you to not encourage him. He is not to be trusted with young women and further, he must marry for a fortune. He has very limited wealth of his own; he hopes to inherit from me as my heir, but I have no plans to depart this earth anytime soon. He therefore is not a man for whom you should set your cap. You cannot bring him a fortune and he cannot offer you one. He certainly will ply you with approbations and wonderful civilities but he is not to be trusted. Do you understand me?' 'Yes My Lady,' replies Charlotte, 'but you need not concern yourself. Sir Edward is a man of fair appearance, but he does not suit my temperament, Good Day.'

Clara meets Charlotte outside the drawing room and walks her to the door. 'We should walk, tomorrow, if it suits you and the weather is fine,' Clara says. 'That will suit me very well, thank you,' replies Charlotte. 'Then I shall call for you at Trafalgar House tomorrow in the early afternoon,' Clara concludes. As Charlotte walks out to where Tom and Mary Parker wait, she thinks to herself, your advice, Papa, was very wise. I thank you for raising my attention to look behind the faces and words of my new acquaintances. She hears Tom Parker talking to Mary saying, 'I must bring Sidney with his good news to Lady Denham as soon as he arrives. Lady Denham is quite impossible to satisfy but I am sure Sidney's good news will improve her temper.' Charlotte thinks again, oh how is it that such enthusiasm can be had from a letter which seemed to me to carry very little in the way of news that can satisfy Lady Denham. But perhaps Mr Tom Parker's enthusiasm will be rewarded on his brother's arrival.

Chapter 6

Friday - 3 April 1818 - Sanditon

The following afternoon, as promised, Clara Brereton calls for Charlotte at Trafalgar House. Charlotte has helped Mary with the children all morning and has quickly become a second Mama in the family as far as the children are concerned. The older children, Elinor, Lucy and Henry vie for her attention and approbation just as they do with their Mother. But now it is time to join with Clara for the promised walk that Charlotte has very much been looking forward to. She and Clara go out onto the Terrace and walk toward the new apartments and other buildings along the Main Street of the growing town. As they walk along, Clara tells Charlotte about her life in Sanditon. 'I am three and twenty,' she says, 'and I have been Lady Denham's companion for the better part of two years. She is difficult at times to deal with, but I am only a poor relation and I count myself very blessed that I have a place to live that is comfortable and the company for the most part tolerable. And the sea and air and open spaces quite suit me after the dirt, sickness and crowding of London whence I came and was born and raised.' Charlotte's attention is captured at that moment as they come upon a new building under construction and she admires the new row of handsome houses and apartments. Then she turns back to Clara and asks, 'Do you have relations still in London?' 'Yes,' replies Clara, 'I have my Mother and two younger sisters who depend on the small income that I receive from Lady Denham. My Father is dead.' 'Oh' says Charlotte, 'I'm sorry!' 'No, don't be, my Father fell at the Battle of Waterloo almost three years ago and an Uncle has helped as much as he can but we are accustomed to our poor situation. We are fortunate that my Great Aunt, Lady Denham, has taken me in and keeps us from the workhouse.' They continue their walk and turn toward the beach and as they pass down the street, they encounter a older woman accompanying three finely dressed young ladies walking in the opposite direction. Charlotte notes that one of the young ladies is of exotic complexion. 'Do you know who those young ladies are,' she asks Clara? 'Yes,' Clara replies, 'they are Mrs Griffiths, a Governess, and her three charges. Mrs Griffiths is a long time resident of Sanditon and runs a boarding house for young ladies. The exotic young lady, Miss Georgiana Lambe, is from the WestIndies, I understand, and she is a very wealthy heiress. The other two are sisters, Victoria and Rose Beaufort who are daughters of an officer who serves the East India Company and is seldom at home.'

They continue on and as Clara and Charlotte descend to the beach, they encounter Arthur and Diana Parker. 'Good Day to you, Miss Heywood, Miss Brereton,' says Arthur. 'Are you out for a constitutional on this fine day as we are?' 'Yes, indeed,' replies, Charlotte. 'Well,' he says, 'we must continue on as I fear the cold wind and the dampness of the air will cause my rheumatism to make itself known and so we must find our way home and sit by the fire until the chill leaves my bones; don't you agree, Diana?' 'Oh yes, Arthur,' she replies, 'we must make all haste. Good day!'

As they continue their walk, Clara smilingly says, 'Arthur and Diana Parker are full of imagined illnesses and they are always in search of improvement, but they shall never find it because the problem is in their heads, not their bodies. And while I speak of the Parkers, Miss Heywood, I suppose you have not had the pleasure of Mr Sidney Parker's acquaintance?' 'No, I have not yet, although I am told by Mr Tom Parker, that he will be arriving here early in the week coming.' 'Then, I am timely to warn you, Charlotte, that he is a man not to be trusted. Do not mistake me for he is a most comely man, a man I could almost call beautiful, but you should be on your guard against him. He can be charming; indeed perhaps he will make you most happy to have his approbation, but he is man of moods who will take you under his spell and then turn on you with no civility, none! I myself have experienced his moods; he can change from one moment to the next without warning. Do not fall under his spell for if you do, you will regret it!' Charlotte and Clara continue on in silence for a space as Charlotte mulls over in her mind Clara's words. That is the second warning I have received about Mr. Sidney Parker she thinks, first Mary and now Clara. Well, I shall have to meet this enigma and see for myself. Their stroll concluded, Clara walks Charlotte back to Trafalgar House, wishes her Good Day, which Charlotte returns with thanks and Good Day and they exchange promises to see each other again soon. Charlotte then goes in to the mayhem of a house alive with the noise of children and enterprise.

Chapter 7

Saturday - 4 April 1818 - Morning - Sanditon

Next morning over a breakfast of kippers and poached egg, Tom Parker raises the topic of his Brother Sidney's visit. 'If Sidney is true to his word,' he says, 'he will be here tomorrow. And this coming Friday, six days hence, we shall entertain our first substantial ball of the season. By the by, Charlotte, I should very much like for your attendance at the ball. Do you enjoy dance?' 'Oh yes,' replies Charlotte, 'I am very partial to dance, indeed, it is one of the great pleasures of my life.' 'Then you shall go,' replies Tom. Mary then asks, 'Charlotte, have you gowns and dance boots with you suitable for a ball and dancing?' 'Yes, replies Charlotte, 'I have a gown and boots suitable for Willingden but perhaps they are not of a standard for such a grand ball as is here in Sanditon.' 'Then we must remedy that and perhaps to that end, we can borrow from Miss Esther Denham or Miss Clara Brereton. But we shall sort it out. My husband, the projector of Sanditon Town must be secure in the knowledge that his coadjutor can put her best foot forward in blue boots of the latest fashion if such can be found,' Mary concludes with a smile.

'Very good,' says Tom. 'And I am informed that Lady Denham will join us tomorrow for tea. She has concerns about the pace of work on our houses and apartments and of commitments to occupy them over the coming summer. She has so many spies about, you know,' he says, 'and I believe that some of my workmen are complaining of I know not what, but such twaddle is reaching her ears. All will be well though because Monday, Sidney will be here and I can put Lady Denham's fears to rest.' Charlotte smiles her agreement, but thinks to herself, here it is again, unbridled optimism, but we shall see.

After breakfast and a time with the children, Charlotte and Mary retire to her chamber to look over the contents of Charlotte's cupboard for her first Sanditon ball appearance. Mary says, 'These gowns perhaps are a bit past the fashion of the day and your boots will not do. We shall visit the cobbler to see if we may procure those dance boots for you and, given the short time before the Ball, call first on Miss Denham to see if perhaps she might have something suitable for you to wear. We shall also visit the modiste and see about commissioning work on a gown of the latest fashion for future balls.' Much ado about nothing, Charlotte thinks, but she knows that Mary is doing her best for her and she smiles her thanks.

Chapter 8

Saturday - 4 April 1818 - Afternoon - Sanditon

In the afternoon, Mary and Charlotte walk to Denham Place. It is another fine day for early April, and the looks and smells of Spring are all around. As they approach the house, Charlotte notices the grounds appear to be unkept and wonders at that especially since the grounds at Sanditon House are so immaculate. They arrive at the door and are admitted by a servant and shown to the drawing room. As they wait for Miss Denham, Charlotte sees the state of the room with peeling wallpaper, faded drapery and furniture coverings and again wonders about the state of affairs between Lady Denham and her relations. Miss Denham enters and Sir Edward, who appears to be in his cups, follows her into the room. He leers at Charlotte as he almost stumbles into her and raises her hand to his lips in a clumsy attempt at gallantry while ignoring Mary and slurs a unintelligible greeting. 'Leave us, Edward,' Miss Denham says to him, 'we shall talk again later.' Sir Edward glowers at her then blearily turns and weaves his way out of the drawing room 'My apologies,' Miss Denham says, 'for Edward's half-seas-over state, but I am pleased to welcome you, Miss Heywood, to Denham

Place, humble though it is. We had no time to get acquainted yesterday at Sanditon House.' 'Thank you,' Charlotte replies.

Mary speaks up and says, 'As you know Miss Denham, Miss Heywood is newly arrived in Sanditon and has as yet not had time to prepare her wardrobe for the coming Ball. She will be visiting the modiste to remedy that, but it will not solve the immediate issue of the Ball this week coming. I thought to suggest that we might impose on your kindness for the loan of an appropriate ball gown.' 'Certainly, I shall be very pleased to be of service. I have several gowns which are suitable for a young woman, which I no longer am at five and twenty, but the material is very fine and with some slight modification, I think we might fit you out very well for the Ball. Please follow me.' They trail Miss Denham into her dressing room where a servant retrieves several gowns at her direction. Charlotte's eye is immediately captured by a simple white gown with a plain dark blue ribbon around the bodice. She says, 'Oh, I love this one' as she touches the smooth fabric. Esther picks it up and says, 'Yes, it is of the finest muslin and I believe it will be quite suitable for the Ball with little modification necessary to fit since we are of similar stature. You may have it, Miss Heywood, not as a loan but as a welcome gift to Sanditon.' 'Oh, I could not,' replies Charlotte, ' it is too much.' 'Fiddlesticks,' says Miss Denham, 'and please call me Esther. We shall not be strangers in our small town.' 'Thank you, Esther,' replies Charlotte, 'and please call me Charlotte.' 'Well,' Mary says, 'we have a accomplished our goal today and Esther, I am in your debt. Shall we see you at the Ball?' 'Yes,' responds Esther, 'I shall see you there.'

Charlotte and Mary say their good byes and depart. As they walk back toward Trafalgar House, Mary offers, 'Sir Edward was the usual unpleasant toff if not a bit more so because of drink, but Esther was a surprise. I believe she likes you.' 'She was of very pleasing of temper indeed,' Charlotte replies, thinking of the yet unknowns about Lady Denham's relations.

Chapter 9

Sunday - 5 April 1818 - Sanditon

Charlotte finds that everything slows down on a Sunday in Sanditon. No, it is not like the farm where there are cows be milked, pigs and chickens to be fed and crops to be harvested no matter what the day. It is a day to attend church and spend the rest quietly at home or in taking outings to the beach or to the paths along the cliffs. So after a bounteous breakfast, the whole family walks to church where they are welcomed by The Reverend Mr Hankins. Charlotte looks around at many unfamiliar faces and wonders who they are and who she will find as friends among the assembled faces as she becomes more acquainted with the townsfolk. The Reverend Hankins delivers a sermon about loving your neighbor as yourself and then they go out to enjoy the day.

In the afternoon, Tom reminds Mary and Charlotte that speaking of loving thy neighbors, Lady Denham will be joining them for tea later in the afternoon and then begins to play with the children while Mary and Charlotte sit and talk about the coming week. Mary says, 'There is much to get done, Charlotte. 'We must get your gown ready and I hope we can find you some new dance boots. I would have preferred if the ball had not been so soon after your arrival, but we shall persevere. Also, I would suggest that you should be prepared for perhaps a bit of incivility again this afternoon when Lady Denham calls. This is unlikely to be a social call on her part for it never is. She certainly will take Tom to task for something or other and she does not beat around the bush about it.' 'Well,' Charlotte replies, 'my Papa is quite direct in his approach when something at issue needs to be resolved so I shall not find offense in her approach I am sure.' Mary smiles and says, 'Perhaps you will be of assistance to Tom then in more than his papers and his bills. He is quite at a loss in dealing with Lady Denham. I believe he fears her and she knows it. You have courage that he does not and perhaps that will be of help to him in his dealings with Lady Denham.'

The appointed hour for tea arrives and Lady Denham is as good as her word arriving on the minute. She is announced and stalks regally in to join Tom, Mary and Charlotte. 'Ah, Miss Heywood,' says she, 'it is good to see you again. Esther told me you and Mary called on her yesterday. I am pleased that you did so soon after your arrival in Sanditon. Esther was quite happy to see you, but now to business,' she says as the tea is brought in. 'Mr Parker, it has been brought to my attention that work is not progressing as it should and I have been given to understand that this state of affairs is due to you. What have you to say for yourself? And you told me at our meeting of a few days ago, that you were expecting positive news from Mr Sidney Parker. I should like to know what that news is? Have you heard from him?' 'No, not yet,' replies Tom, 'I expect Sidney in the coming week.' 'Well,' Lady Denham replies, 'Mr Sidney Parker's news or lack of it does not explain my news that work is slowing on construction of the apartments we need for our coming summer guests that you have told me to expect. Can you tell me why that is?' Tom stutters, 'Well, My Lady, it is a conundrum I am dealing with. I am having problems with timely deliveries of materials. I assure you that I am addressing it.' 'Well, you had better be,' Lady Denham shoots back. 'I assure you that I shall have more than words for you if your representation to me about the success of our Sanditon project falls short.' 'All will be as I promised, My Lady,' Tom says, 'do not worry!' 'I always worry when my money is involved, Mr Parker, and you will do well to not forget it,' she snaps! She then rises and says 'I must be going but Miss Heywood, I should welcome your call anytime it is convenient. We shall chat about your future here in Sanditon.' She goes out and when the front door closes, Mary asks, 'Tom what was she talking about concerning slowing construction and what were you talking about in response about problems with deliveries?' 'There is nothing to concern yourself about, Mary,' he responds, 'it is just the effect of weather at this time of year.' Charlotte thinks to herself, hmmm, Lady Denham is not one to be trifled with and I hope Mr Sidney Parker does indeed come with that news Tom is hoping for.

Chapter 10

Monday - 6 April 1818 - Sanditon

Charlotte awakens to the sounds of a gale shaking the house and shrieking under the eves. The portents of Sidney Parker's arrival today, she wonders to herself as she prepares for the day. We shall see what the day brings with the storm. Mary has advised the previous evening that they will visit the cobbler today in search of those blue boots and the modiste to modify the Ball gown that Esther has given her. She goes down to breakfast and finds Mary and the older children at the table. 'Where is Mr. Parker, this morning,' Charlotte asks? 'He has gone out to inspect the buildings,' Mary replies. 'He is concerned that the strong winds could cause some damage.'

Just then a loud crash is heard, followed by a shout of pain, and Mary and Charlotte jump up and run toward the front door. Tom Parker is standing in the open door with the wind and rain whipping about him as Morgan is on his knees with blood pouring down his face.' 'What has happened,' Mary cries? 'It was the door, when it was opened, the wind slammed it into Morgan's head,' replies Tom. 'What can we do? There is only the apothecary and he perhaps is still snug in his bed.' Charlotte exclaims, 'Let me look at the wound!' They take Morgan into the kitchen and seat him at the table. 'I need clean cloths and some hot water,' says Charlotte, as she presses her hand against the wound to slow the flow of blood. The requested items are soon brought and Charlotte carefully washes the blood away enough to see the wound.' 'Yes, she says, 'this will need stitching to close the wound.' Looking to Mary, she continues, 'I will need a needle and thread and some whiskey.' Mary leaves and returns with her sewing box as Tom procures the requested whiskey then Charlotte says to Morgan, 'I'm sorry, Mr Morgan, but this is going to hurt. Drink some of this whiskey.' Morgan takes a large gulp and then another of the whiskey. Then after washing the wound and pouring some whiskey into it, Charlotte begins stitching the wound closed as Mary and Tom look on in amazement. After finishing her work, she suggests that Morgan keep the would as clean as he can and occasionally clean the area with whiskey and let her know if he experiences any signs of anger around the wound. He looks at Charlotte with gratitude, rises and leaves as Mary suggests he rest for a while. Mary asks, 'Charlotte, where did you learn how to do that?' 'I read it in a book,' she replies.

> '[Sewing] fills up the interstices of time... It accords with most
> of the indoor employments of men, who... do not much like to
> see us engaged in anything which abstracts us too much from
> them. It lessens the ennui of hearing children read the same story
> five hundred times. It can be brought into the sick room without
> diminishing our attention to an invalid.'

> Letter from Mrs Trench to Mrs Leadbeater, May 1811

Afternoon arrives with no sign of abatement of the howling gale and the rain comes in waves bucketing down on the town. 'Surely, Sidney will not attempt to travel to us today,' Mary remarks to Tom as they sit together in the drawing room waiting for their afternoon tea. 'Yes,' Tom replies, 'it is probable that tomorrow will bring a better day to travel. In any case, I have much to do, bills to sort and plans for our construction to ponder.' Charlotte, remembering Mary's earlier comment about helping Tom with his bills speaks up. 'I wonder if I might be of assistance,' she asks? 'I often help Papa with the papers and bills in Willingden.' 'Could you, Charlotte,' responds Tom? 'I am most disorganized because of the press of business and my unexpected accident in Willingden.' They walk over to a work table covered haphazardly with missives, some open, some not and papers of various kinds with no apparent organization. Charlotte looks at the disorganized pile and says, 'First Mr Parker, with your permission, I shall look through everything and place the papers into piles which will be easier for you to review and take appropriate action on.' Tom exclaims his appreciation. 'Oh, if you would, Charlotte, I should be very grateful for your help.'

Charlotte begins her work as Tom returns to sit by Mary and soon, she has organized the table and calls to Tom, 'Mr Parker, here you are. I have made piles of everything so that you will have an easier time of reviewing. I would like to call your attention to two letters, which are demanding payment and by the dates, the due dates for payment have passed. One is from a London Bank and the other refers to building materials ordered by a Mr Stringer and there is a note from him attached.' Tom glances in Mary's direction then rises and comes over to the work table. 'Yes,' he says quietly, 'I have been waiting for Sidney to bring me news of financing he is pursuing in London and certainly will manage payment of them soon. Mr. Stringer is my building foreman. He is a son of Old Stringer, a vegetable farmer and sometime brick mason who is one of my workmen, and he has hopes of bettering his station though his work on my Sanditon Town. But Mr Stringer worries above his remit with regard to payments, which are my domain. You shall meet the ambitious young man in good time.' Mary speaks up and says, 'Tom, Charlotte and I had planned to visit my seamstress, Mrs Smith, today to make adjustments to Charlotte's ball gown and to see if the cobbler might have blue boots for her, but the rain and wind have made that plan untenable. We shall go tomorrow.' 'By all means,' replies Tom, 'we shall want our guest to put her best foot forward at the Ball. There will be many young men in attendance, and I am sure that Charlotte's dance card shall be full to her and our approbation.'

Chapter 11

Tuesday - 7 April 1818 - Sanditon

Charlotte awakens to wind and scudding clouds but at least, she thinks it appears the weather may be improving, certainly over the previous day. After breakfast, Mary says 'Well, as the ferocity of the rain and gale has abated somewhat, perhaps we should go now, Charlotte,' and they are soon on their way to the modiste with the gown.

On arrival at the shop, 'Smith's Modiste', a smiling, rosy cheeked woman bustles to the front of the shop as they enter. 'Ah, Mrs Parker,' she asks, 'what may I do for you and your young and if I may say, beautiful, companion today?' 'Well, Mrs Smith,' Mary replies, 'allow me to introduce our guest, Miss Charlotte Heywood, newly arrived from Willingden just this week. As you know, we are having our Ball this Friday coming. We have procured a gown for her but it will need some adjustment for a proper fit.' 'Yes,' replies Mrs Smith, 'I am very busy now as a consequence of it, but if the adjustments to Miss Heywood's gown are not extensive, I shall be able to deliver it back before the Ball. Let us retire to my sewing room at the rear and see what we need to do.' The three women walk to the back of the shop where Mrs Smith directs Charlotte behind a screen to put on the gown. She does so then steps out from behind the screen. Mrs Smith gasps, 'My Dear Miss Heywood, you are a vision indeed. There is very little I will need to do to this gown. It fits you perfectly and perhaps only a little adjustment at the neck line is necessary to make it a truly bespoke gown.' 'Wonderful,' Mary says, 'you will have all of the men at the Ball smitten, Charlotte.'

As Charlotte looks at herself in the mirror, Mrs Smith continues to stare at her. 'You know, Miss Heywood, you look remarkably like a young lady whose gowns I had a hand in making in London many years ago when I was a seamstress in the shop of my dear departed husband, a tailor who held a royal warrant to the Court of King George III. I do not remember her name, but suffice it to say that you could be a sister although that cannot be since I left London several years before the turn of the century.' 'Well then,' says Mary with a smile, 'Charlotte certainly will be the belle of the ball. And in the coming days before Summer, we would like to commission a new gown or two for Miss Heywood's use.' This was followed by additional discussions about materials, colours and decorations and then concluded with agreement on future dates for fittings.

Agreeing that the gown will be ready the day before the ball, Thursday, Charlotte and Mary take their departure and walk down the street a few doors before arriving at the cobblers. They go in to find that there is only one pair of blue boots in the shop and they are a perfect fit for Charlotte. 'What good fortune,' Mary cries. 'You shall indeed be the belle of the ball, Charlotte, light on your feet and a vision for all the young men in your beautiful gown and new boots.'

Chapter 12

The following morning, the wind is still blowing strongly if giving signs of slowing and the rains have diminished to occasional showers with the sun teasing the ground here and there though breaks in the still angry clouds. Charlotte determines to brave the elements and after breakfast and a quick conversation with Mary about the day, she declares her intention to walk to Sanditon House to call on Clara. Mary protests that she should not walk alone but Charlotte mollifies her with a promise to go straight there and to not dally on the way back. Charlotte goes out to the sound of Tom's complaints to Mary about Sidney not arriving as expected the previous day. She arrives at Sanditon House with no difficulties along the way, is admitted and finds Clara there with Esther.

'So good to see you,' Clara says to Charlotte. 'And have you been properly introduced to Miss Denham? I fear that proper introductions were not made when you first called here several days ago,' she adds. 'Yes,' replies Charlotte, 'I called on Esther Saturday last.' A servant appears and says, 'Miss Brereton, Lady Denham requires your presence!' 'I must go, but

I shan't be long, I don't think, please stay and I shall return as soon as I am able,' says Clara and takes her leave. Esther asks, 'Have you had the opportunity to have the gown fitted, Charlotte?'

'Yes,' she replies, 'yesterday Mary took me to the seamstress. I was fitted and your gown will require only minor adjustments and I shall have it tomorrow. And I purchased a new pair of dance boots as well.' 'Wonderful,' replies Esther with a smile, 'we shall endeavor to survive the suitors on the day then.'

Charlotte smiles back at Esther and then says, 'I am very curious about the townspeople here and would feel more at home if I could but understand the folk hereabouts. We are few in Willingden and there are no great houses nor people of large fortune there like there are here in Sanditon. Mr Tom Parker told me the tale of Sanditon on our journey here from Willingden, but I would know more if you are willing.' Esther replies, 'Well, the Parker family with whom you came here is a family of long history, I know not how long, but they have a country estate in the Parish a mile or two out from Sanditon proper very near to Sanditon House. 'Yes, I saw it,' replies Charlotte, 'when I come into Sanditon with Mr and Mrs Parker from Willingden a few days back. But there was very little said about it; only that they had left it in the care of a man upon their move to Trafalgar House two years ago.' 'Yes,' replies Esther, 'the family is a bit of a mystery, the parents both died of the Pock (smallpox) I am told and Tom Parker as the eldest son inherited the main of the fortune. Susan, the eldest of the family, whom is never seen hereabouts, lives in London I am given to understand. The others, Diana and Arthur have fortune enough to keep them in comfort, and Sidney is a tradesman who is well established in the cotton and wine trade and has a substantial fortune of his own. Diana and Arthur live here in a house they share. Sidney lives in London at the family home in Holborn. I know little else about them except I have heard rumors that Tom Parker is on the road to debtors prison for his spendthrift ways and Sidney Parker is a man of unstable temper. There is a tale that he was jilted by a young lady many years ago and he still is something of an outlier for it. I should warn you to be on your guard with him.' Hmmm, Charlotte thinks to herself, my third warning now about Mr Sidney Parker. I shall be on my guard but I shall see for myself when we meet.

Esther continues, 'I can be more certain of the history of which I am a part. My half brother Edward is one and thirty and I am five and twenty. We are brother and sister of different Mothers, wife one and two of Sir Harry Denham's younger brother's marriages. There is little to tell beyond that. Edward and I are poor; Lady Denham has in her hands the lands, the house in which Edward and I reside, Denham Place, and the fortune that is a part of the Denham legacy as she does from her first husband Mr. Hollis whence came the bulk of her fortune. She has gained fortunes, extensive lands, two estates and a Title through her marriages and is the iron fisted matriarch of Sanditon. As for Clara, she is a poor member of the Brereton family of London and is a niece of Lady Denham who brought her to Sanditon two years ago to become her companion.' 'Yes,' replies Charlotte, 'Clara told me of her connection to Lady Denham and of her coming to Sanditon.'

Clara returns at that moment, apologizing for her delayed return. 'Lady Denham is in a temper this morning. It was a very slow process with her toilet because she kept pacing around. She is very angry at Mr Tom Parker. She was upset when she returned from her call on him Sunday last not having received the assurances she had hoped about the slowing of work on the town and she wonders why it is always such a chore to get a straight answer from him. And still three days later, she has not seen either of the Parker brothers. I fear Mr Parker is in for another pummeling when Lady Denham next calls at Trafalgar House or he calls here as he must.' Charlotte remembers the jumble of paper and unpaid bills on Tom's work table that she had looked at and organized for him just two days prior and thinks to herself, I cannot be surprised nor completely unsympathetic to Lady Denham's concerns. I hope he is, but perhaps Mr Parker is not fulfilling his obligations to her.

'Well, I must be walking back to Trafalgar House,' Charlotte announces. 'Mary will be expecting me.' Clara responds, 'I hope you will forgive my discourtesy for disappearing during the main of your visit.' 'Think nothing of it,' replies Charlotte. 'Your first obligation is to Lady Denham. We shall see you at the Ball on Friday, I hope.' 'Yes, certainly,' Clara says with a smile. 'I shall be there as will Lady Denham. She never misses a Ball. Balls are a great source of gossip and excitement and still she on occasion will accept an invitation onto the dance floor. I have been told that in her younger days, her beauty and prowess on the dance floor were her pathways to favorable marriages to two men of fortune.' Money and marriage for it, muses Charlotte; I wonder if either is the key to happiness. Esther then speaks up, 'I too must be going, perhaps we shall walk together, Charlotte?' 'Oh that would be wonderful,' cries Charlotte, 'we can brave the wind and rain together.' They both say their goodbyes to Clara and take their leave.

Chapter 13

s Charlotte and Esther walk back out onto the road from Sanditon House, the wind begins to buffet them almost as if the gale which had abated somewhat during the morning had lain in wait for them and now had come out of hiding to show them its strength. Soon Charlotte and Esther are holding on to their bonnets and skirts for dear life as they bend to the merciless wind. They are just at the point of turning back to Sanditon House when they hear the sounds of horses and carriage. Heads down against the wind, they hear rather than see the carriage pull to a stop near them. A melodious man's voice calls out, 'May I offer you transportation to your destination, ladies?' Charlotte looks up, straight into the most beautiful pair of eyes she has ever seen. Her heart skips a beat as she wonders who this can be. His head is bare, no doubt his top hat has been stowed away because of the wind, and his dark hair shines with moisture. He seems to have been soaked through from rain in the open phaeton but appears none the worse for it. In fact, Charlotte thinks to herself that she has never seen a more appealing man in her life.

'Yes, Sir,' Charlotte responds. 'We have but a short way ahead of us but because of the wind and the rain, we shall welcome a quicker journey to our destinations.' Esther speaks up, 'Mr Parker, your arrival is indeed welcome. My companion, Miss Charlotte Heywood, and I were on our way from Sanditon House when this abominable wind and wet came up to challenge us. Miss Heywood is newly arrived in Sanditon and is a guest of your Brother Tom and Mary.' 'It is a pleasure to see you again, Miss Denham and a pleasure to meet you as well, Miss Heywood. Sidney Parker at your service.' He steps down and then hands his passengers into the phaeton. Once they are safely settled, he coaxes the horses into motion and then asks where he may take them. 'I shall appreciate your dropping me at Denham Place,' says Esther. 'And I shall be going to Trafalgar House,' replies Charlotte. Esther continues and asks, 'Are you in town for the Ball this coming Friday, Mr Parker?' 'No,' he says, 'I have not much interest in Balls. I find them vexing and full with irritating and fulsome conversation.' 'But do you not like to dance, Mr Parker,' questions Charlotte? 'Dance is a chore, a civility with which of course I must comply but I cannot say that I find it of any interest otherwise,' he responds. Charlotte thinks, yes a man to grace any woman's dance card who does not wish to dance other than to meet an obligation. I cannot fathom it but I have been warned of him and I'm sure I shall learn more of his mind while he is here in Sanditon.

After dropping Esther at Denham Place, Charlotte and Sidney continue on to Trafalgar House. On arrival, Sidney hands Charlotte down and then turns his phaeton over to a stable boy. They approach the front door together, ring and are admitted by Morgan. He has a bandage on his forehead and Sidney remarks on it asking, 'What has happened to your head, Morgan?' 'I was struck by the door, Mr. Parker. Day before yesterday as I was admitting Mr Tom Parker, the wind took the door and gave me quite a wack. Miss Heywood was my surgeon, saving me from the loss of considerable blood. I am today feeling quite well, thanks to Miss Heywood.' 'Very good, Morgan,' he says 'and where did you learn your surgeon skills, Miss Heywood?' 'From a book, Sir,' Charlotte replies. Sidney looks at her quizzically with a bit of a smile or was it a frown Charlotte asks herself.

They continue on into the drawing room where Tom and Mary are sitting beside the fire. Tom jumps up, saying 'We expected you yesterday, Sidney, wherever have you been? I must talk with you immediately!' Mary interrupts, 'Tom, Charlotte and Sidney are both wet through and will need hot baths and a change of clothes. Please give Sidney time to recover from his journey before you talk with him.' Sidney replies, 'Thank you, Mary. It was a difficult journey in the gale and I had to make a unplanned stop in Hailsham because of the ferocity of the storm. But I shall stay at the hotel because I have two friends from London arriving to join me. I shall see you tomorrow, Tom, and we shall talk.' 'But Sidney, my discussion with you is of the utmost urgency,' presses Tom. Sidney responds with a sharp edge to his voice, 'Tomorrow, Tom! Now I must go to the hotel and get out of these wet things.' Mary says, 'We shall look forward to your presence tomorrow Sidney and would welcome you to join us for breakfast. And it seems you have met our guest, Miss Charlotte Heywood, and tomorrow you shall become better acquainted.' Sidney bows to Mary and Charlotte and takes his leave. Mary turns to Charlotte. 'What did you think of Sidney,' she asks? 'Is he not as I said, very pleasing to the eye?' 'Yes,' Charlotte replies with a light blush colouring her face, 'Mr Parker is quite good to look upon.' 'But now,' replies Mary with a knowing smile, 'we must get you into a hot bath before you catch your death of cold.'

In the evening after Charlotte retires, she finds sleep to be an elusive quarry. She thinks of the three warnings she has gotten from Clara, Esther and Mary as well. Who is this Sidney Parker with those beautiful eyes?

Unbidden, her mind wanders back to the daydreams of her younger years, to the man of mystery with the unknown face who would find her heart. Has she seen the face of that man now she asks herself? You don't know him she muses, you cannot consider a handsome man with beautiful eyes anyone with whom you wish to become of close acquaintance until you know what is in his heart. Have patience, Charlotte, have patience and as she begins to drift off to sleep, she remembers her Papa's warnings before she left Willingden about being careful with people whom she does not know, to be cautious of placing her trust in the hands of strangers. As her eyes close, she resolves to do just that.

Chapter 14

Thursday - 9 April 1818 - Morning - Sanditon

Charlotte opens her eyes to sunshine streaming through her window as a pair of beautiful eyes fades slowly in her memory like the gale of yesterday has from the day she is awakening to as she stretches in the luxury of her own bed. She still has not gotten used to sleeping in a bed by herself because as far back as she can remember, she has shared a bed with her sister Anne and a room with Anne and two other siblings. But she tells herself that she can become accustomed to it with a smile. Today is the day when I shall receive my gown for tomorrow's ball. I wonder if Sidney might ask for a dance despite his aversion to it as he told Esther and me and who might be those two friends from London he mentioned yesterday? Will they also be fine gentlemen who view dance with no approbation? Hmmm, we shall see.

Charlotte goes downstairs and into the dining room where she finds Mary, Tom and Sidney at the table. Sidney has Henry in his lap and is finding eating difficult as Henry seems to be insisting on his full attention. Tom's face is flushed and he appears to be angry and stays silent.

Mary glances up, notices Charlotte and invites her to sit. 'Good Morning, Charlotte,' she says. 'I hope you slept well!' 'Indeed, I did, Mary, thank you,' replies Charlotte. I...' 'Well,' Tom interrupts, 'Sidney we shall talk later!' He rises from the table and stalks out of the dining room. Mary says, 'Please pardon Tom and his lack of civility this morning.' Charlotte looks toward Sidney and then says, 'No, I am sure he has much on his mind with the building and tomorrow the Ball,' noticing as she says it a flash of anger or irritation on Sidney's face. He says, as Henry continues to enjoy the comfort of his Uncle's lap, 'I soon must return to the hotel, Mary. My friends from London, Lord Somerset and Mr Nisbet should arrive today and Tom wants me to call on Lady Denham with him as well. So I must be on my way.' He rises, places a protesting Henry down with a pat on the head and a promise to see him again soon and says 'I bid you Good Day, Mary, Miss Heywood,' then bows and leaves the room soon followed by the sound of the front door closing.

Following the entry of the governess to take the children, Mary says, 'I'm sorry for Tom's lack of civility, Charlotte. I do not know what happened this morning but Sidney came early and he and Tom argued over something before I came down. He and Sidney sometimes quarrel. They are so different and I fear Tom never stops thinking about his projects and never lets Sidney forget his obligations although I'm sure he never does. But it is a cause of vexation between them. And perhaps now is a good time for me to tell you a little more about Sidney. He is not his best self at times as he was not with you this morning and there is a reason which I earlier made you aware of.'

Mary continues, 'After his heartbreak, Sidney began roughhousing and drinking and finally when he would not listen to reason nor return to Sanditon, his father indentured him to a trader of long acquaintance, a

Mr Lambe, who was master of a cotton and sugar estate in the WestIndies and Sidney sailed there with him. I think Mr Lambe treated Sidney more like a son than a indentured man and did not require Sidney to complete his contract. In fact, Mr Lambe made Sidney his plantation overseer and over time, as Mr Lambe's health declined, Sidney took over more and more of his master's personal responsibilities.' 'Oh,' Charlotte interjects, 'when I walked with Clara a few days ago, we saw a Mrs Griffiths with three young ladies walking in the street one of whom Clara said was a heiress, a Miss Lambe, from the WestIndies.' 'Yes,' replies Mary, 'Miss Lambe is the daughter of the same Mr Lambe of whom I have spoken who was Sidney's benefactor. Miss Lambe's Mother is dead and Miss Lambe is the only living issue of Mr Lambe. Upon his death, his will made Sidney her guardian until she reaches her majority which now is two years hence. As her guardian, Sidney returned to London with her a year or so back. In addition to his obligation to Ms Lambe, since his return, Sidney has continued with the cotton trade with connections he made in the WestIndies and London as Mr Lambe's estate overseer and also has engaged in the wine trade on the continent to become a successful London wine trader in his own right. And the elder Parkers who died of the Pock (small pox) during travel to the continent before Sidney's return from the Indies also left him a small sum to which Sidney has added substantially. A distant aunt also left him a substantial sum as well. But I fear despite his success and his efforts to fulfill his obligations to the family and to Ms Lambe, Sidney remains a lonely and wounded man as a consequence of the failed romance of his youth. He sees all young women as not to be trusted and frivolous.' Charlotte says, 'But surely he cannot believe that!' 'I believe he does,' replies Mary.

As Charlotte sits quietly with Mary mulling over in her mind the conundrum of a wounded, brooding and perhaps jaded man with the handsome, successful and debonair appearance of a "Beau Brummell" gentleman that she sees in Sidney, Morgan comes in and announces a caller, Lady Denham. She bustles in and demands without civilities, 'Where is Mr Parker?' Mary responds, 'I understood that Tom was on his way to call on you today, Lady Denham.' 'No, not him, Mr Sidney Parker,' she snorts! 'Mr Tom Parker did call on me with another nothing report on the value of my Sanditon investment and said his brother Sidney was supposed to join him with me and report on his progress of gaining additional investors. But he did not appear and Mr Tom Parker was unable to tell me why.' Mary responds, 'My husband left here this morning with words as to his plans to meet with you today and Sidney made plain his intention to join him when he left here several hours ago. I can not think what could have happened.' 'Well, you can tell him for me that I expect to hear from them both together by tomorrow morning and certainly before the Ball latest or I shall begin steps to withdraw my investment from Sanditon Town.' She turns and storms out. 'What could have happened, where could Sidney be,' Mary says mostly to herself as she exchanges glances with Charlotte? 'Perhaps, Mr Sidney was delayed by the arrival of his London visitors,' offers Charlotte. 'Yes, that must be it,' replies Mary. 'I shall go to the hotel and see if I can find him and we also must go and collect your ball gown, Charlotte!' 'I shall accompany you now,' says Charlotte, 'if I may.' 'Yes indeed you may,' returns Mary. They ready themselves and go out.

Chapter 15

Mary and Charlotte walk arm in arm along the street the short few steps to the hotel from Trafalgar House. They come upon Mrs Griffiths who is all a flutter. 'Oh my ladies, have you seen one of my young ladies along your walk. She has quite disappeared.' 'To which young lady are you referring, Mrs Griffiths,' Mary asks? 'Miss Georgiana Lambe,' she replies. 'Mr Sidney Parker is out searching for her right now. She was to go to the haberdashery for just a few minutes to buy some odds and ends and she has not returned since her departure over four hours ago. I am quite beside myself and Mr Parker is very angry with me!' Oh Mr Parker, Charlotte thinks to herself, you do, like Atlas, indeed "carry the weight of the world on your shoulders." She speaks up, 'Mrs Griffiths, I have not had the pleasure of your acquaintance, but I am Charlotte Heywood and I saw you and Miss Lambe on the street the other day. We will be sure to be alert for Miss Lambe and do our best to bring her to you should we locate her.' Mrs Griffiths profusely expresses her thanks and hurries off down the street.

Mary says to Charlotte, 'Well, we must pick up your gown and as Mrs Smith's shop is located in the old part of the town, we shall have opportunity to look for Miss Lambe along the way.' They conclude their walk to Mrs Smith's small shop and admit themselves to the jingle of a bell above the door. Mrs Smith hurries out to meet them and says, 'I am so behind in my work because of the demands for gowns and adjustments for the ball tomorrow and here I have in the back a young lady who has demanded that I produce a new gown of the finest silk for her for the Ball. I have been cutting and sewing for the bulk of the morning but she is very demanding and I have gotten nothing else done and still I have four gowns to make adjustments to besides hers. I am overburdened.' She pauses for breath and then continues 'But I have your gown ready, Miss Heywood, yet I would like for you to try it before you go to be sure that you are satisfied.' At that moment, a call is heard from the back room, 'Mrs Smith, where are you?' 'Oh bother,' says Mrs Smith, 'I must go back, she is so demanding of this gown.' She turns toward the back room and gestures for Mary and Charlotte to follow.

They enter the room after Mrs Smith and there is Miss Georgiana Lambe, draped in swaths of shimmering turquoise blue silk. She looks at them and says, 'Who are you,' with a smile and challenging look? Mary says, 'Miss Lambe, you know very well who I am and this is Miss Heywood. Mrs Griffiths is looking for you as is Mr Parker.' Miss Lambe exclaims, 'Mrs Parker, I told that silly woman I was in need of a ball gown. She would do nothing about it. I brought this silk all the way from the WestIndies and I shall have a new gown for the ball tomorrow. So here am I! You may so advise her if you wish and Mr Parker too. Now, please allow Mrs Smith to get back to her work or we shall be here all night.' Mrs Smith sighs and goes to get Charlotte's gown. Charlotte puts it on and comes out to where Mrs Smith and Mary wait to inspect and Miss Lambe can see her. Miss Lambe says, 'I see I shall have some competition on the dance floor tomorrow,

Miss Heywood. You may call me Georgiana.' 'Thank you,' replies Charlotte, 'and you may call me Charlotte.' 'Well Miss Lambe,' says Mary, 'we must be going and we will advise Mrs Griffiths and Mr Parker when we see them that you have been found.' Charlotte changes back into her street clothes, takes the packaged gown and they go out.

On the way back to Trafalgar House, they stop by the hotel and ask for Mr Sidney Parker. They are told that he is not in his room as his key is on the hook, so Mary asks for quill and paper to write a note and she leaves there on a message for Sidney advising that Miss Lambe has been located at Mrs Smith's having a ball gown made and then they go back out onto the street again to continue toward Trafalgar House. They arrive at Trafalgar House in time to meet a departing Sidney and Mrs Griffiths and advise them both of Georgiana's whereabouts. 'That silly girl,' exclaims Mrs Griffiths, 'how dare she go off like that without a how do you do!' Sidney lets out a long breath and then grates, 'Mrs Griffiths, you are not to let her wander about without escort.' 'Yes, Mr Parker, it will not happen again, I assure you,' responds Mrs Griffiths. 'I shall walk to Mrs Smith's now and escort Georgiana back to her quarters.' Charlotte speaks up, 'Mr Parker, I'm sure Georgiana did not intend to cause you grief, she is young and wanted simply to have a new gown for the ball.' Sidney looks at her and says, 'This matter is not your concern, Miss Heywood. I am her guardian and must ensure her safety and well being. I thank you and Mary for find-ing her and letting me know. Now I must join my friends Lord Somerset and Mr Nisbet lately arrived from London whom I have kept waiting whilst I searched for Georgiana. Good Day,' turning on his heel as he says it and stalks away in the direction of the hotel. And there is the man I have been warned of, thinks Charlotte, unfeeling, short tempered and arrogant in his attitude. And he said nothing about keeping Tom or Lady Denham waiting for the expected conversation of the future of financing for the Sanditon Sea Bathing Town.

Chapter 16

The day of the Ball dawns with a beautiful blue and cloudless sky more inclined to feel like a summer day than Mid-April. This may be a Friday to remember, Charlotte, she thinks to herself as she prepares for the day. She goes down to breakfast to hear Tom telling Mary that he will soon go out to the hotel to meet Sidney and they will go together to call on Lady Denham. He wishes Charlotte and Mary good morning and goes out. Mary says, 'It is such a warm and beautiful day that I believe the children will enjoy a walk on the beach this morning. We shall return in good time to prepare ourselves for the ball and I have taken the liberty of ordering a bath be prepared for you this afternoon, Charlotte, on our return.' 'Thank you, Mary,' Charlotte replies, 'That will be very well indeed!'

The children run like gazelles on the beach, shouting, jumping and laughing in the bright sunshine while baby William gurgles his joy in his Mother's arms. It is indeed a beautiful day to be by the sea, thinks Charlotte, and Tom Parker's appreciation of the difficulties to successful completion of his project may not be appropriately recognized but his dream of a sea

73

bathing town here is indeed a worthy one in my estimation. As they continue on down the beach, they encounter Mrs Griffiths and her charges, Victoria and Rose Beaufort and Georgiana Lambe. Civilities are exchanged then they join together and continue on down the beach.

Georgiana joins with Charlotte, slowing the pace until they lag behind the rest of the group, and then says, 'Sidney was so angry with me last evening at Mrs Griffiths. He came in and ordered Mrs Griffiths to keep me confined unless she or someone trustworthy can accompany me. I wonder if you might call at Mrs Griffiths on occasion and ask me to join you for a walk. I cannot abide being treated like a child and I shall not be! If Mr Sidney Parker thinks he is going to run my life from dawn to dark for two more years until I reach my majority, he is mistaken.' 'Of course I shall,' replies Charlotte. 'Mr Parker was angry with me as well yesterday when Mary and I saw him and Mrs Griffiths and reported that we had found you. I don't understand why he should be so…, so difficult!' 'He considers me a burden on his time,' Georgiana replies, 'and I am a young woman as well and for him that is reason enough for his dislike. But, to a happier topic, Mrs Smith has promised that my ball gown will be ready this afternoon in time for the ball although she had to work all night she told me, to make such assurances. I saw that you looked very well in your gown at Mrs Smith's so neither of us shall want for dance partners I am sure.' 'Does Mr Parker dance,' asks Charlotte? 'He told me that he does not enjoy dancing and I am uncertain as to whether I believe him or not. Who does not like to dance?' 'Mr Parker can dance and dance very well when he must, but he must be prevailed upon to do so. He sees it as more of an obligation than a pleasure,' replies Georgiana. 'In my opinion, Mr Parker would avoid balls altogether if he did not see the possibility that his avoidance would give offense to important personages,' she concludes. Well, Charlotte thinks, we shall see then what the ball brings and what indeed it will show of Mr

Sidney Parker's resolve to be non-compliant with the wishes of the ladies at the Ball. I should imagine that he will look very well in dress for a ball and likely will be welcome on the dance card of any lady.

Chapter 17

Friday - 10 April 1818 - Afternoon/Evening - Sanditon

The afternoon of the Ball arrives. Following her return from the beach, Charlotte had luxuriated in the hot bath, delightfully scented with jasmine oil, that Mary had promised, and then dressed in her now bespoke gown from Esther Denham and made hers by Mrs Smith. Mary's maid assists her with her hair and her flowing mane of auburn waves are captured with several pins on the top of her head. She puts on her new blue dance boots and then looks at herself in the mirror wondering if she will do for the Ball? The maid compliments her appearance and then leaves her chamber soon to be replaced by Mary who comes in dressed beautifully in her own gown. Mary gasps, 'Charlotte, you are beautiful and a vision in that white gown. I shall not be surprised to see a crush of young men in your direction at the Ball. Please come down stairs when you are ready. Tom and Sidney have returned from meeting with Lady Denham and are waiting for us in the drawing room,' she concludes with a smile as she goes out. Charlotte feels a flutter in her stomach on hearing that Mr Sidney Parker is here at Trafalgar House. What will be his opinion of me, will he find me pleasing to his eyes, she ponders as she goes down to meet her party.

Charlotte enters the drawing room followed by Mary to find Sidney and Tom engaged in a heated conversation. She catches just a few words about bill payments before Sidney and Tom realize her presence and stop their conversation. Both look in her direction and Tom Parker speaks. 'How well you look, Charlotte. You certainly will be putting your best foot forward at the Ball tonight. Don't you agree, Sidney?' Sidney's look lingers on her but he does not respond to Tom's question instead replying with a simple, 'Good Evening, Miss Heywood.' Mary says, 'Perhaps we should be going. Tom, you must be there to welcome the guests.' 'Yes,' Tom replies, 'we must get to the assembly hall a bit early it is true. I expect a large turn-out.' He offers his arm to Mary and they go out. Sidney does not offer his arm, instead bowing and indicating the Charlotte should proceed him out of the drawing room. So Charlotte thinks, he wishes to maintain his distance. So be it.

On arrival at the assembly hall great room, a large gathering is already present. Across the room, Charlotte recognizes Sir Edward and Esther Denham. Beautifully gowned women and well dressed men circulate around the large open floor with chairs spaced around the perimeter. A team of musicians, tuning their instruments, occupies one end of the room. Tom moves to the center of the floor and in a loud voice, gains the crowd's attention over the noise of the babble. The crowd quiets as he raises his voice further and welcomes the attendees to the ball and invites everyone to enjoy themselves on and off the dance floor. The musicians begin to play and soon the floor is a swirling kaleidoscope of colour and fashion. Charlotte stands with Mary and Sidney as Tom makes his way back to them. At that moment, two gentlemen appear and Sidney immediately goes to greet them and escorts them back to the party. 'Tom, Mary, Miss Heywood,' he says, 'allow me to introduce you to Lord Somerset and Mr Nisbet, two friends of long acquaintance who have joined me from London.' Appropriate civilities are exchanged all around, and then the arrival of Lady Denham escorted by Clara Brereton is announced. Tom quickly excuses himself to go welcome Lady Denham and escort her and Clara to a seating place of honor appropriate to Lady Denham's station. Their arrival is soon followed by Mrs Griffiths and her three charges. Georgiana is resplendent in her new blue silk gown and her arrival is noted by more than one as she runs over to Charlotte as soon as she sees her. She ignores Sidney and greets Charlotte enthusiastically saying, 'What do you think of Mrs Smith's handiwork, Charlotte? Is it not beautiful? I should not have had it had I depended on Mrs Griffiths' charity,' giving Sidney a challenging look as she continues, 'nor would I have had I depended on my guardian to do his duty in meeting my requirements.' Charlotte glances at Sidney who says nothing but she notices that he quickly turns his head away. Was he staring at me, she asks herself? She resolves to keep Mr Sidney Parker under close observation this night.

Tom turns to Mary and says, 'I must ask Lady Denham to dance but first shall we take a turn around the floor, Mary, before duty obliges me to leave your side?' Mary replies, 'Yes, Tom,' then turns to Sidney and says, 'Sidney, will you not ask Charlotte to dance? She is our guest and she will have many young men asking for her presence with them on the dance floor. I see Mr Stringer looking this way and there will be many others. I suggest that you use your lucky acquaintance with Charlotte that any and all young men here would love to have and take her out onto the dance floor now.' Sidney frowns almost imperceptibly at Mary's words which Charlotte catches but then he turns to her and asks with a bow, 'Miss Heywood, may I have this dance?' Charlotte looks into his handsome but unsmiling face thinking I would prefer not to be a burden of duty for Mr Parker, but it is a Ball after all and I will no doubt be seeing much of him here in Sanditon. She takes his offered arm and they move onto the floor with Mary and Tom to ready themselves for the next dance.

As the couples align themselves to begin the dance, Charlotte sees that Lord Somerset has found Esther as a partner and Mr Nisbet has done the same with Clara. She sees Georgiana has a dance partner on the floor as well and notes with surprise that it is Arthur whom she had not seen arrive at the Ball. This is wonderful she thinks. My new acquaintances are all engaged for the dance and appear very amiable, but for me, in the arms of the man with the beautiful eyes who seems to feel no approbation for either dance or for me. The music begins to play and as they dance, she sees immediately that Mr Sidney Parker is a wonderful dancer, handling all of the turns and intricate steps with grace and ease. She thinks for a man who professes to have no approbation for dance, it certainly seems that dance suits him very well. And as they swirl and turn together on the crowded floor, Charlotte feels something she has never experienced before, little tremors when their bodies touch and a feeling of soaring excitement at the same time. This is a contradiction, both the most comfortable and the most uncomfortable place I have ever been in she thinks. And when they face each other, she finds herself unwilling to look into those beautiful dark eyes looking down at her but unable to look away. What is this, Charlotte, she asks herself as suddenly she finds herself covered in goosebumps followed by a thought that sends a blush to her face. Charlotte muses, I wish this dance would never end, but end it does and then she finds herself strangely unwilling to move away from Sidney and it seems to her that he is very slow to release her from his hold as well.

As he walks her from the floor, Charlotte thinks, I hope he will ask me for a second dance and she feels a sharp disappointment when he does not and simply says, 'Thank you, Miss Heywood,' then leaves her standing beside Georgiana and Mary who have also left the floor and walks across the room to where Mr Nisbet and Lord Somerset are standing. 'How did you find him,' Georgiana asks? 'He is a wonderful dancer,' Charlotte replies. 'I am surprised that someone who claims dance not to be of interest is so very proficient at it.' Mary comments, 'Sidney is a man of many talents and a man who, in my opinion, will make the woman who captures his heart the most loved and happy of women.' Georgiana interjects, 'He is too prideful and unwilling to change his opinions, I think, to make a woman a good husband. I know that from my life under his thumb. I grant you that he is a man of many talents but he is lacking in civilities toward young women. You will see, Charlotte. Do not trust him. He will break your heart if you do!' And here again I hear and see the conundrum of Mr Sidney Parker thinks Charlotte.

Charlotte's reverie about Mr Parker is interrupted by the appearance of Lord Somerset in front of her. 'Will you do me the honor of dancing with me, Miss Heywood,' he asks? Charlotte accepts and he escorts her onto the dance floor. As they dance, he says, 'I must say that you are very beautiful. I was struck by your beauty when I first saw you. Are you familiar with the personage of the Duchess of Kent? She is a very high ranking and influential member of the Prince Regent's Court. And I must say that you and she are very alike in appearance. The resemblance is almost uncanny.' 'No, Lord Somerset,' Charlotte replies, 'my family has no relations of whom I am aware in London. I was born and raised in Willingden and have not but one time and that many years ago, ever to set foot in London. But I understand that you and Mr Nisbet are friends of long standing with Mr Parker?' 'Yes, Mr Nisbet and I are friends of long acquaintance. We were classmates at Oxford. Mr Nisbet is of a very wealthy family engaged in weaving of fine muslins, calicos and chintzes with spinning factories in the Midlands and also the production of steam machines. My family has connections primarily in cotton through stocks in the East India Company. We first met Sidney when he came to London about five years ago representing a Mr Lambe who was engaged in sugar production in the WestIndies and cotton trade from the Americas. Sidney was representing Mr Lambe in efforts to dispose of his property in the WestIndies as his health was declining and he wished to return to England. Mr Lambe had freed his slaves but that had earned him the anger of fellow plantation owners and he was in fear for his daughter, a young woman of mixed blood who is Mr Lambe's only living offspring. Then Sidney returned to London again just over a year ago with Miss Lambe in tow. He had been made her guardian by Mr Lambe in his will just before his death at the hands of an unknown assassins. You should know as well that Sidney was with Mr Lambe on the night of that cowardly attack and narrowly escaped death himself as he fought the assassins off but he was wounded in his unsuccessful effort to save Mr Lambe.' 'How awful for Georgiana, and Mr Parker too,' exclaims Charlotte! 'You know that Georgiana is here tonight. You have made her acquaintance before?' 'Yes,' Lord Somerset replies, 'I am aware that she is here tonight. Sidney is very protective of her, too much so in Miss Georgiana's estimation,' concludes Lord Somerset with a smile. 'Well,' he says, 'may I have a second dance, Miss Heywood,' accompanying his request with a gallant bow? 'Perhaps we can give Mr Parker cause to come to your rescue as I believe he is smitten with you.' 'Yes, gladly,' Charlotte replies as she takes his arm to move back to the dance floor. As they dance, Charlotte is thinking, you are a puzzle Mr Sidney Parker. You are a man of many coats, some coarse, some fine but you have a heart even if you choose not to show it, a man who would lay down his life for another. I must know him better.

The Ball runs long into the evening and Charlotte finds no shortage of dance partners, including Mr Nisbet, Tom Parker, Arthur Parker, a Mr Stringer, who requests a formal introduction through Tom, and even The Reverend Mr Hankins whom she notices seems to linger in Mrs. Griffiths' presence and finally by Sir Edward who is quite charming as he appears to be sober on this particular night. However, the partner she wants and hopes to see approach and request a second dance seems to have disappeared. Where, she thinks, did he go? She had enjoyed that one dance with Sidney Parker more than any she could remember so despite the gaiety of the evening, Charlotte cannot help but to feel that her evening is incomplete. Then as the evening draws to a close, the last dance is called and Charlotte is lost in her thoughts, suddenly there he is, at her side. 'Miss Heywood,' he says, 'may I have this dance!' Caught out in her thoughts and with surprise that her wish should be granted, Charlotte feels a glorious blush rising up her neck to her face. Unable to look into those eyes, she replies, 'Yes, Mr Parker,' accepting his arm as they walk onto the dance floor and the music begins to play. It is a waltz and thinking of the closeness to come, Charlotte feels, unbidden, the beginnings of another blush. And as Sidney pulls her into his arms to begin the dance, there is something of excitement and yes, comfort in being in those arms. She can feel his eyes on her and slowly, irresistibly, her eyes are drawn upward to his. Yes, this is joy, this is happiness, this is the feeling I shall always wish to have when I am married she thinks as the dance ends and slowly they part. Sidney walks her back to a gathering where Mary and Tom are standing, thanks her for the dance then excuses himself and walks away. Mary says, 'Charlotte, you and Sidney dance so well together! You know that I never in my life have seen him dance with anyone more than once. I believe that you have bewitched him.' Charlotte laughs a little with embarrassment and says, 'Oh Mary, I am sure that he was just being polite,' whilst secretly hoping to herself that this is not the case at all.

Chapter 18

Saturday - 11 April 1818 - Sanditon

The following morning comes with a cloudless sky and a hint of the warmth to come later in the day. Charlotte feels a surge of excitement as she goes down the stairs to breakfast and then a pang of disappointment as she sees that there is no Sidney at the table. 'Good Morning, Charlotte,' says Mary, 'You slept well I hope.' 'Yes, indeed,' she replies. 'I was exhausted from the Ball.' 'It was a great success,' announces Tom. 'Sidney's friends Lord Somerset and Mr Nisbet perhaps are interested investors, if we can bring them in, and Lady Denham was very pleased by the success of "her" ball and by the presence of possible additional investors. I think Sidney and I have quite redeemed ourselves in her eyes. But today, we have a special treat in store. The waters have been judged warm enough for sea bathing; yes, it is early in the season; but we shall today take you to try one of the wonders of Sanditon, our sea bathing machines, will we not Mary?' 'Yes,' Mary replies, 'and I have invited Miss Brereton and Miss Denham to join you, Charlotte, and Arthur and Sir Edward will join us as well. 'Will not Sidney be there too,' asks Charlotte?' 'No,' replies Mary, 'unfortunately Sidney has business to conduct with Lord Somerset and Mr Nisbet.' Charlotte accepts that with a sigh of disappointment. I would very much have liked to see him today she thinks and thank him for his civility to me at the Ball.

In the afternoon, Charlotte sets off with the party from Trafalgar House to be joined as they walk by Arthur and Diana. 'I did not see you at the Ball, Diana,' Charlotte says. 'Oh I was there,' she replies, 'but I did not dance. I have been feeling poorly and Arthur as well, but once he saw Miss Lambe, he became irrepressibly animated despite his condition and managed to hold his own on the dance floor with Miss Lambe and others. I do believe he will need the attention of a Doctor though if he keeps ignoring my advice. I think Tom still entertains the thought of gaining a Physician for Sanditon in spite of Lady Denham's disapprobation because of the cost but, if so, he will be very welcome.' They continue on to the beach where they meet the rest of the party already standing near the bathing machines.

Following a brief explanation of what to expect while in the machine, Charlotte enters one with Clara where they remove their gowns and undergarments and don head to toe flannel bathing costumes which they find hanging in the bathing machine compartment. By the time the horses have pulled them into the calm after the surf, they are ready to try the water and descend the steps into what proves to be freezing water which elicits screams from them both. Clara, teeth chattering, says, 'What do you think of sea bathing, Charlotte?' 'Wonderful,' Charlotte replies as a icy wave washes over her head, 'but I should think that it is not quite the season for it. We did bathe in the stream on our farm in Willingden and I have no doubt of the benefit to health of a dip in the sea, but I believe this is overly brisk.' Both quickly scurry back up into the bathing machine, waving as they go to Mary and Esther who are standing on the steps of the bathing machine next to them and have not descended into the water. On reentering the bathing machine, two servants wait to help them remove their heavy wet flannel costumes before drying and wrapping them in thick woolen blankets then handing them steaming cups of tea. 'I believe that the tea is the best part of sea bathing today,' laughingly says Clara. 'Yes, I agree,' replies Charlotte. 'By the way, I saw that Mr Nisbet and you were partners on the dance floor last night.' 'Yes,' Clara replies, 'he was quite gallant and I hear very wealthy as is Lord Somerset. Your Mr Sidney Parker has some excellent friends in my estimation.' 'My Mr Parker,' Charlotte replies with a blush, 'whatever do you mean for I am barely acquainted with him?' 'Oh Charlotte, I saw you entranced in his arms on the dance floor and others remarked on it as well including Lady Denham who wondered aloud how long it would be before you and Mr Parker were betrothed. Mr Parker is quite well to look upon as I am sure you will agree and he is wealthy unless he shall be bankrupted by his involvement with his brother Tom.' 'Yes,' Charlotte admits, 'Mr Parker is very good to look upon and he is a wonderful dancer.' Clara's smile broadens in time with a glorious blush on Charlotte's part.

The bathing party parts ways after climbing back up from the beach and Charlotte walks back to Trafalgar House with Tom and Mary accompanied by Diana and Arthur. They go in to find Sidney waiting for them. Charlotte goes to him intending to express her appreciation for the evening at the Ball. She says, 'Mr Parker, thank you for your wonderful civilities at the Ball.' He looks at her coldly and then up over her head as he bows stiffly and says, 'Thank you, Miss Heywood,' then turns and walks over to Tom. Charlotte asks herself, what have I done? He was so warm and friendly at the Ball. Was I too forward in expressing my approbation to him? I don't understand him and perhaps I shall not want to.

Chapter 19

Sunday - 12 April 1818 - Sanditon

The next day, following another sermon from The Reverend Mr Hankins, this time about the wages of sin, Charlotte is approached by Sir Edward as she leaves the church and walks with the Parker family back toward Trafalgar House where they plan to gather for a meal. 'Miss Heywood,' he says, 'I wonder if I might ask you to remain behind your party so that I might have a word with you?' Charlotte replies, 'I would prefer that you call on me at Trafalgar House. It might be misconstrued if we should be seen walking together in conversation' as she hurries to catch up the Parker family. 'I have no reason to detain you, Miss Heywood,' offering her his arm as he says it which Charlotte declines , 'but I noted that you and Clara shared a bathing machine yesterday and I wonder if you talked about events at the Ball.' 'To what events are you referring, Sir,' asks Charlotte as she picks up her pace to close with Tom and Mary? 'Well, Clara was engaged quite a lot with Mr Nisbet at the Ball and seemed quite taken with him and if I am not mistaken, she accepted more than two sets (4 dances) from him.' 'Oh, I am sure you are mistaken,' replies Charlotte, 'but in any case, I am not at liberty to share any confidences that Miss Brereton might share with me. Now, if you will pardon me, I must hurry to catch up to Mary and the children.'

As she rejoins with the Parker family, Charlotte thinks about her encounter with Sir Edward. What interest does he have in Clara I wonder? She certainly would not be the wife for him. He needs money to go with his title and as Lady Denham told me, a suitable bride for him requires that she come with a substantial dowry. As Charlotte ponders Sir Edward's motives, Mary drops back to walk beside Charlotte as she comes up and says, 'Was Sir Edward being forward with you, Charlotte? I was almost on the point of sending Tom back to fetch you when you left his side. He does not have the best reputation and I should not wish for you to be seen associated with him.' 'I advised him that if he wishes to talk with me, I should prefer he call at Trafalgar House,' replies Charlotte. 'He seems to have an interest in Clara's affairs; I don't know if it is because he is taken with her or if he per-haps sees her as a competitor for Lady Denham's affection and fortune. But in any case, I told him I would not share any confidences that Clara might share with me with him.' 'Well,' replies Mary, 'do be on your guard around him and never let him get you alone!'

Chapter 20

Monday - 13 April 1818 - Morning - Sanditon

Charlotte rises early intending to see if she can be of assistance to Tom and after breakfast, follows him to his work table. 'How may I be of assistance to you today,' Charlotte asks? 'Let us sort my post, he replies, 'and then would you like to accompany me see some of the work being done on my town?' 'Oh yes,' she replies, 'I should like that very much!' They go out after the work is done and walk down the street to the new construction underway. Mr Stringer comes toward them and says 'Good Morning, Sir and Miss Heywood.' 'Miss Heywood, thank you for honoring me with a dance at the ball this last Friday evening.' 'It was a pleasure, Sir,' she replies. 'Well then,' Tom says, 'why, Mr Stringer, has not more progress been made to complete these apartments we see here before us?' 'Well Sir,' he says, 'we are having trouble procuring the supplies of wood and brick and mortar that we need. I sent you a note with the last communication I received from our supplier indicating that he had not been paid and is demanding payment before providing any further materials.' 'Yes, yes,' replies Tom with irritation in his voice, 'please advise him that the funds are on the way!

We must have these buildings done and ready for guests before summer.' 'I shall, Sir, but when shall I tell him to expect your payment,' responds Mr Stringer? Tom ignores the question and says, 'Look Charlotte, are not these apartments fine, of the highest quality. I'm sure the London Beau Monde will find them suitable and probably exceeding that to be found in Brighton or certainly Eastbourne!' 'I'm sure, Sir,' replies Charlotte. 'Well,' says he, 'let us return to Trafalgar House and the paperwork, Charlotte.' 'With your permission,' Charlotte returns, 'I have promised to call on Miss Georgiana Lambe at the earliest opportunity and since we are near, I shall do so.' 'Of course, Charlotte,' Tom replies. 'I shall see you back at Trafalgar House then.' Charlotte and Tom say their goodbyes to Mr Stringer who offers to walk Charlotte to Mrs Griffiths' boarding house door. She thanks him saying it is just a few steps and therefore it is not necessary. They each go their separate ways.

Charlotte continues on to Mrs Griffiths' door. She rings and is admitted. Mrs Griffiths says, 'I am glad you have come, Miss Heywood. Georgiana is in a temper and will not come out of her chamber. She has been out of sorts since the ball and she will not tell me what the problem is but I sense that she is very angry with Mr Parker.' Mrs Griffiths escorts Charlotte to Georgiana's door and knocks to no answer. Mrs Griffiths calls out and announces, 'You have a visitor Georgiana…, Miss Heywood.' After a moment, the door opens and Georgiana peers around the edge then opens it wider to admit Charlotte. 'Mr Parker is unbearable,' she bursts out as soon as the door closes. 'He came to me at the ball after several dances and said that I was being too forward with the young men with whom I was dancing, making a spectacle of myself. He may be my guardian but he is not my Father and he has no right to treat me like a child as if he owned me. I shall not stand for it. I am an heiress and I have many thousands of pounds and I shall not be a slave to him nor to his opinions. He forced me to leave the Ball early and escorted me himself with Mrs Griffiths and those Beaufort sisters back here. That Ball was the first opportunity since he dragged me here from London to enjoy myself and Sidney took it upon himself to ruin it for me,' she concludes bursting into tears.

Ah thinks Charlotte to herself, now I know why Mr Parker was nowhere to be seen until the end of the ball when he came to me for the last dance of the evening. She responds to Georgiana's outburst by opening her arms to her and she comes into her embrace. Charlotte says, 'I know that Mr Parker can be harsh and I do not understand him myself. He is changeable like the weather here on the coast, one minute calm and clear and the next with gale and storm. But I do not think he means ill by his actions toward you. He takes his responsibilities as guardian very seriously and I think his heart is in the right place, to keep you from harm, although perhaps his civility toward you suffers a bit because of it,' hoping as she says it that this is indeed the case. 'Perhaps I can call on you a few times a week and Mrs Griffiths will allow me to walk with you to the benefit of us both!' Charlotte continues, 'I too am a newcomer to Sanditon, a bit of an outlier like you, and perhaps we can become friends to the benefit of both of us as newcomers here.' 'Oh yes,' Georgiana cries with a smile as she dries her tears, 'that will be lovely.' 'May I then invite Mrs Griffiths in to see if we can gain her approval,' Charlotte asks? Georgiana frowns then says, 'Well, I suppose we must!'

Charlotte goes out and calls for Mrs Griffiths who quickly appears with a bit of trepidation written on her face and they both return to Georgiana's chamber. 'Mrs Griffiths,' Charlotte asks, 'I wonder if you would approve of my calling on Georgiana from time to time to take her out for strolls with me? It would be good for her health and temper and Georgiana has told me that she would enjoy taking the sea air with me.' A smile lights up Mrs Griffiths' face. 'Oh would you,' she asks hopefully? 'I'm certain Mr Parker will approve. Georgiana, would this plan meet with your approbation?' 'Oh yes,' cries Georgiana! 'Then it is done,' says Mrs Griffiths with a sigh of relief. 'I shall call for Georgiana tomorrow in the afternoon,' accepts Charlotte receiving a radiant smile from Georgiana as she says so. Charlotte then says her goodbyes and takes her leave.

Chapter 21

Monday - 13 April 1818 - Afternoon - Sanditon

Charlotte returns to Trafalgar House and after removing her bonnet and cape, goes into the drawing room. As she enters, Sidney is saying that he will be leaving for London in the morning. 'Ah, Charlotte, you are back,' welcomes Tom. Sidney nods brusquely. 'Please pardon the intrusion,' Charlotte replies. 'I shall join Mary and the children if you can tell me where they might be.' 'Baby William is with the nurse and I believe that Mary is entertaining the other children in the kitchen,' Tom says, 'but please tell us how your call on Miss Lambe went. Was she well?' 'Yes, she was Mr Parker, but she expressed a preference to get out more to walk and take the air as she is feeling unduly confined,' replies Charlotte glancing at Sidney at the same time. She notices a frown beginning to form between those beautiful eyes and hastens to add, 'And I volunteered to be her companion and Mrs Griffiths approved subject, of course, to your approbation, Mr Parker, which Mrs Griffiths was sure would be forthcoming.' 'I shall talk to Georgiana and Mrs Griffiths later this afternoon,' Sidney responds, 'and determine whether or not my approval for your offer to act as Georgiana's companion will be granted. My ward has proven over and over that she will take advantage of any opportunity to betray my trust and I must be certain that she will not betray yours.' Mary comes in as Sidney is finishing his statement and says, 'Sidney, Charlotte is not a child and there is no need to insult her as you just have done. She is quite competent as both Tom and I can vouchsafe and I do believe that you can trust Charlotte to take excellent care of Miss Lambe just as we trust her with our own children.' Sidney's face flushes and then he says, 'My apologies, Miss Heywood, for my choice of words. I had no intention to insult, I assure you. But Georgiana is no child and I must have a word with her to be sure she understands that your word carries the weight of mine in my absence.' He then turns to Tom and says, 'I shall leave tomorrow and be gone for a week back to London to catch up with some business matters and I shall see what I can do with the banks to extend your loans as we have discussed. Goodbye, Mary, Miss Heywood...,' he says as he bows and leaves the room.

Mary and Charlotte leave Tom to his papers in the drawing room and go into Mary's sitting room. Mary smiles sympathetically and says, 'I'm sorry about Sidney's behavior, Charlotte. I believe he is determined to keep you at arms length. I watched him with you on the dance floor at the Ball where I believe he quite forgot himself and became the charming Sidney we all know he can be. He was quite taken with you as I told you at the ball. I had never seen him dance twice with any woman 'til you since Maria. He is attracted to you and I believe that has frightened him and now he is trying to push you away. Don't let him, Charlotte. He is a man worth having and if you win his trust, I believe you will own his heart.' Well, thinks Charlotte, first a warning from Mary about Sidney and now encouragement to pursue him. Hmmm! We shall see.

Chapter 22

The unseasonably warm weather of mid-April has continued 'til it almost feels like full summer and Charlotte awakens to the early morning warmth with little beads of sweat at her temples. Today we shall surely take advantage of the sea to cool ourselves, she thinks. She heads downstairs to find the three older children begging Mary to go to the beach. 'Yes,' Mary laughs, 'we shall go today to enjoy the water.' 'Wonderful,' says Tom, 'but I shall have to remain here. I am expecting a delivery of brick and building materials and I must be here to sign for them and Sidney will be coming by with Lord Somerset and Mr Nisbet.' 'Will you accompany us, Charlotte,' Mary asks? 'With great pleasure,' Charlotte replies. 'Will we make use of the bathing machines, Mary,' Charlotte asks? 'No,' Mary responds, 'not with the children. We shall not swim but will allow the children to cool themselves while we watch from the shore.' All is made ready, and off the three children, Mary and Charlotte go.

They arrive at the beach which is crowded with walkers, children and people on horseback enjoying the fine day and walk for a while to find a place to call their own. A favorable spot found, Mary and Charlotte spread a blanket, remove Spencers and shoes then sit to watch the children. There is a strong but warm breeze blowing and the children are running and jumping with excitement as they approach the breaking surf. Elinor and Lucy run to the water's edge where the waves are breaking and try the water. They squeal and run back from the breaking surf but Henry runs deeper in and turns to wave back at his sisters. As he does so, a wave knocks him down and as he struggles to stand, he is pulled deeper into the water. Charlotte and Mary run to the waters edge and call to him. He tries again to stand and again a wave knocks him down. He begins to cry and Mary screams for help. Charlotte quickly pulls her morning dress off over her head and clad only in her white cotton chemise, runs into the surf toward Henry. She is surprised by the force of the water and a strong current against her legs. But she moves deeper into the water to reach Henry. She grabs him, pulls him to her then shoves him toward the shore where he reaches shallow water and stands.

Charlotte tries to follow as Henry runs out of the surf onto the sand to a waiting Mary coughing and crying. But her now water heavy chemise impedes her movements and she finds herself pulled deeper into the water where she can no longer find her footing. She struggles to disentangle her legs from the water logged chemise but finds it an impossible task as she finds it increasingly difficult to keep her head above the water. She tries to take a breath and inhales water instead. Now she is tiring rapidly and choking on the briny seawater. The thought crosses her mind that she is going to drown. Was this the chill of premonition that I felt when I first arrived at Sanditon? Is this the place where I am to die rather than find my life? She manages to get her head above the water one more time and then is pulled under again. I am to die today she thinks as she sinks deeper and deeper into the water.

Suddenly she feels a pair of strong arms wrap around her and she is pulled to a broad chest. Is this a dream; is this what dying is? But then her head comes out of the water and she can see the shore and a frantic Mary but she cannot breathe, she is choking and cannot catch her breath. Stop it, stop holding me so tightly for I cannot breathe. Who is this holding me in an iron grip? She feels herself being laid down on the beach and hears shouting. Now she cannot open her eyes, she cannot see, but who is shouting so loudly, who is it begging her to breathe? Stop it, I am not deaf, just let me rest, please let me rest. She tries again to breathe and then comes a cough and she feels like half of the ocean pours from her mouth and nose. And now comes a breath, not of water, but of air, blessed air. And slowly, ever so slowly her eyes open to find themselves looking into those same beautiful dark eyes that she first met on the cliff tops with Esther several days ago, those same beautiful dark eyes that haunt her dreams.

Yes, it is Sidney Parker who held her in his arms, who rescued her from the sea and now looks into her eyes not with anger or disapprobation but is it perhaps rather with anguish and fear? 'Charlotte, he cries, 'Charlotte..., Miss Heywood, are you alright?' Charlotte struggles to sit up and then realizes that she is almost naked because her waterlogged white chemise is molded to her body and nearly translucent. 'Oh, Mr Parker,' she says, 'please pardon the state of my clothing. Is Henry safe?' 'Yes, he is,' replies Mary, who Charlotte now realizes is standing off to the side with the three children. 'You have saved him, but I thought that we had lost you in the saving.' Mary continues, 'If it had not been for Sidney's presence, you would have been lost to us.' Charlotte looks back to Sidney. 'Thank you, Mr Parker,' she says, 'I owe you my life. Why did you come to the beach? I thought you were to meet with Tom.' He replies, 'Yes, but Tom advised me that Mary and the children were at the beach and I thought to come and say goodbye before I leave to London. I did not expect to find you here,' he says as a bit of colour rises to his cheeks, 'but allow me to help you to a bathing machine where you may wait until Mary can procure some dry clothing for you to change into. They proceed to the bathing machine which is nearby and Sidney hands her up the stairs into it. Mary joins her.

After satisfying herself that Charlotte is unhurt, Mary explains, 'Sidney is going back to Trafalgar House to find himself some dry clothing and will direct my maid to bring you some dry clothes here.' She smiles. 'I do believe Sidney came to the beach before he left not to say goodbye to me and the children as he said, but to see you again before he left for he had not joined us on the beach but was standing at a distance away observing us, no, not us, observing you, My Dear. You know he was begging for you to breathe when he carried you from the sea. I have never seen such anguish in his face, nor heard it in his voice. He has been caught out again; he can control his mind but not his heart. You attract him like a moth to a flame.'

Chapter 23

Charlotte awakens the next morning in her chamber none the worse for her near drowning. As she stretches cat like in the luxury of her bed, she thinks over Mary's words, like a moth to the flame. She remembers those strong arms holding her tightly to a broad chest and then what Mary had said about Sidney begging for her to breathe. Could that be as Mary had said? She cannot imagine that strong man, that man with the beautiful eyes, begging for anything. He can be so cold and abrupt and yet if what Mary had said is true, he had come to the beach to see me, even from afar, before leaving to London. Could it be that he does have some small affection for me? Then she remembers how she must have looked to him as he carried her in his arms up onto the shingle, her hair tangled about her face and head and her wet chemise plastered to her body and translucent from the water. She blushes at the thought of it; of Sidney looking at her almost naked. What did he think of me she wonders as she rises to meet the day?

As she goes into breakfast, Tom jumps up from the table and runs to her. 'Miss Heywood,' he says, 'I can never thank you enough for saving

Henry, almost at the cost of your own life. I'm sorry I was not here yesterday when you returned from the beach to thank you. Before Sidney left for London, he told me of your narrow escape and Mary said if it had not been for your quick thinking, Henry would have been drowned.' Charlotte responds, 'I was closest to Henry and I did not think, I just ran to him. I'm happy we were able to get him quickly out of the water and hope that the experience will not cause him to fear it. But I admit, I myself was unprepared for the power of the sea. The current was so strong and not having grown up by the sea, I did not have proper respect for it. I shall certainly be more cautious going forward with myself and of course the children. And Sidney..., Mr Parker; he was the real savior. I certainly would have drowned if not for him. I shall be forever grateful.' 'Oh my dear,' Mary cries, 'Sidney would never have forgiven himself or me if that had been the case. I am sure of it. Oh, and I almost forgot, Sidney did say before he left that you have his approval to escort Georgiana when she wishes to go out.' 'Then,' replies Charlotte, 'I shall call on her this afternoon and see if I can be of service.'

Chapter 24

Afternoon comes and Charlotte walks the few short steps to Mrs Griffiths' Boarding House and finds Mrs Griffiths with Victoria and Rose Beaufort. The young ladies are practicing at the pianoforte, as one sings and the other plays. Mrs Griffiths welcomes Charlotte and asks, 'Miss Heywood, do not the sisters sing and play beautifully? They take turns at the pianoforte and at singing and I cannot tell the difference in skill at pianoforte or voice.' 'Yes,' Charlotte replies, 'they will indeed be welcome in any parlor or drawing room. But I wonder if I may visit a while with Georgiana and perhaps go for a walk with her if she so desires?' 'Oh yes, Miss Heywood, Mr Parker called yesterday and after talking with Georgiana for a bit, came down and advised me that you would be calling and that I am to put Georgiana in your hands whenever you call if it is your wish to take her out. She is in her room and I believe at this moment is writing a letter. Please go up at your convenience.' Charlotte thanks Mrs Griffiths. She then goes to Georgiana's room and knocks. She hears Georgiana call out and ask who is there and when Charlotte announces her presence, the door quickly opens. 'Would you like to go out,' Charlotte asks. 'Yes,' replies Georgiana, 'the heat is stifling in my chamber and I have a letter to post.' They go out and as they leave, they meet The Reverend Mr Hankins who is just arriving. 'I have some sheet music that Mrs Griffiths has asked me to bring for the Beaufort sisters to practice and did you know that Mrs Griffiths has a beautiful singing voice,' he says in passing as he is admitted.

Georgiana and Charlotte walk a few steps down the street then Georgiana giggles and says, 'Mr Hankins seems to be increasing his calls on Mrs Griffiths by the day. He is here at every opportunity and I wonder if he may have some interest in making Mrs Griffiths into Mrs Hankins. Well, we shall see. But I do need to post this letter to London.' They go to the Rose and Crown posting inn and arrive just in time to get Georgiana's letter into the mail bag as the mail coach is preparing to depart. After posting Georgiana's letter, she and Charlotte determine to take a turn on the Cliff.

As they walk along, Charlotte asks Georgiana about her life in the WestIndies before Sidney brought her to London. 'It is a long story,' Georgiana warns, 'but if you wish to hear it, then you shall! I caution you that some of my story is as it was told to me since I was born on the 4th day of July 1799. My father was David Lambe. He was the only son of a Father who was the scion of a wealthy family which had large sugar interests in Antigua. The family had a plantation on the island and hundreds of slaves. My Father, who was born on the plantation in 1751, had married a young woman of notable family in England in his 18th year and they had returned to Antigua to set up a household and raise a family. They were very much in love, but they were not blessed with children. Four children there were, but all died soon after birth. Although my Father was very caring, his wife, Sarah, that was her name, was deeply saddened and overtime her health declined until she died, in 1788 as I remember. When his own Father died a year or two later, my Father inherited the plantation. But he was a unhappy man. He was beset with concerns; the sugar trade was declining in the aftermath of the loss of the American colonies, unrest among the slaves was growing and his great friend, Horatio Nelson, who was the Senior Naval Officer in the Leeward Islands of which Antigua is a part had left in 1787.' 'Admiral Nelson, the victor of the Battle of Trafalgar,' interrupts Charlotte? 'Yes, the very same man,' replies Georgiana. 'My Father was a lonely man,' she continues, 'and sometime between his wife's death and my birth, he found consolation in the arms of a slave, my Mother. He determined to free her and then he married her. I am the result of that union.' 'Was your childhood a happy one,' Charlotte asks? 'Yes,' replies Georgiana, 'I was a Princess..., well, I lived like one and I had a very happy childhood. Although I was surrounded by slavery, I did not know it but as I grew older, my Mother began to tell me about her life as a slave before my Father freed and married her and that there were thousands of people like her who were slaves with no life other than to be worked to death. She also had begun to open my Father's eyes to the horror of slavery and by the time Sidney arrived in 1808, my Father had resolved to free all of his slaves.'

'Sidney,' Charlotte says, 'so he became a part of your life then? 'Yes,' Georgiana replies, 'I was but nine years when Sidney came and he very soon became like a older brother to me. And my Father, well, Sidney became the son he never had. He became my Father's right hand and he learned so quickly that soon he could handle everything on the plantation, and the accounts and the trade connections. But Sidney was a conundrum too. He was a man who came with his own devils. He could be charming and kind but sometimes he would find a dark place to dwell especially when he partook of drink. During those times, he could be cold but even then he was never unkind to me or my Father. And he supported my Father in his determination to free the slaves on his plantation in 1816. When my Father announced his decision to do that to honor my Mother's wishes; she died in 1812; he was met with threats from other plantation owners who saw his decision as a danger to their profits already under pressure from competition from the former colonies. Why they demanded to know should they free slaves for whom they had paid good coin and then have to pay them again to work. But with Sidney's support, my Father pressed ahead with his plans. Then one day, as my Father and Sidney were returning from a meeting with the Governor of Antigua, they were set upon. My Father was seriously injured and Sidney was wounded as well but together they fought the attackers off and Sidney carried my Father home. My Father lived for a week and during that time, he asked Sidney to be my guardian, and when he agreed, a solicitor made the agreement a part of my Father's will. Sidney's wounds were not serious and he soon recovered and when as he was able, he determined that we should leave Antigua because it would not be safe for me to remain there. So he settled the estate according to the directions of my Father's will by giving the freed slaves ownership of the plantation and we set sail for England disembarking in London a year and a half ago; December 1816.'

Georgiana continues, 'And speaking of London, it was so cold, dirty and grey when we arrived. I left the sun and the warmth of the island where I was born and came here to this rainy, dark and unfriendly place and after our awful journey of five weeks across a dangerous and stormy sea; I hated it. And Sidney became his unfeeling self after we landed in London and did not care to hear my complaints nor accede to any of my requests or demands. I did not understand him, why he changed from someone I loved as a brother to a aloof martinet and he would not share anything with me, not decisions he made for both of us, and he began going out in the evenings with those toff friends of his Lord Somerset and Mr Nisbet and coming home in his cups.' 'Where did you live in London after your return,' asks Charlotte? 'At the Parker house in Holborn,' replies Georgiana. 'It is a fine house; I have no complaints on that score, but Sidney confined me to it and forbade me to leave it without him. I knew nothing of London and had no friends and no way to make acquaintances with any and for most of six months, until Summer came last year, I was locked away at the London house only seeing Sidney and his arrogant brother, Tom, and on one occasion, Mary with whom I have no complaint.'

Charlotte asks, 'When and why did you come to Sanditon, Georgiana?' She replies, 'I think Sidney feels that London is too fraught with possibilities for me to become attached to someone who wishes to marry for a fortune. When we began attending the balls in London last year, of course I was bombarded with professions of love and even proposals of marriage from young and old men of title who wished to enhance their fortunes. It is well known in London circles that I shall come into a fortune on my twenty first birthday, and I think Sidney worried that I would be carried away by someone's profession of love. But he should know better. I am not stupid and I wish to marry for love. I do not need and never will need money because I am well provided for by my Father. I will never put my fortune in the hands of someone whom I do not love, but Sidney does not trust me, or perhaps he knows the lengths that the privileged in London will go to to feather their own nests. And perhaps that is a reflection on him, on his own experience with that witch, Maria Wickham, the woman who broke his heart by jilting him in his youth to marry for wealth and whom he came across at a Ball that he escorted me to last year. I think she was flirting with him, teasing him and in the presence of her doddering husband too. He changed even more after that chance meeting, and not for the better. He has since become the man you know which perhaps he has always been, the one who keeps women at arms length, the one who cannot believe that a woman can be trusted to know her own mind nor her own heart, the one that believes a woman cannot be trusted to love even when she says the word. I say again, Charlotte, you cannot trust a man who himself cannot trust for he will forever be looking for evidence to prove his point.' As Georgiana and Charlotte conclude their walk at Mrs Griffiths' door, Charlotte thinks, so this is the man I feel in my heart, the one who comes to me in my dreams. What now am I to do, indeed, what now will be the outcome of my obsession with the man with the beautiful eyes? They say their goodbyes and Charlotte promises to call again soon for another excursion as Georgiana expresses her appreciation for the day and future opportunities to escape the confines of Mrs Griffiths' boarding house.

Chapter 25

A fortnight has passed uneventfully. Charlotte has discovered the library and today she sits there reading. She has befriended Mrs Whitby, the proprietress of the library, and when she is not needed by Mary or Tom and has no calls planned, she finds sanctuary there where she has access to a variety of books including history, novels, the classics and poetry. And although she has just completed her first full month in Sanditon, she feels as if she has always been here and cannot imagine being anywhere else. She has written to her Willingden family and they to her and all is well so she has no immediate plans to visit there. She is hoping that sister Anne will come although she thinks she will probably have to go and fetch her unless she can prevail on Papa to detour through Sanditon when he makes his trip to London to gather his dividends in the Summer. But Charlotte is content. The weather has warmed substantially as Spring has progressed and Tom is hoping that the coming Summer will be warm and pleasant, unlike the previous two, for the visitors he hopes for to fill his apartments and houses. Sidney had returned a few days ago; his stay in London had proved longer than the week he had planned; but he had brought wonderful news to Tom. The bank had extended the terms of his loan and had raised the loan amount. Tom is euphoric. He has been able to make up his arrears to his suppliers and his workers and he can now see his way clear to completing necessary construction to have his bathing town ready for the expected influx of visitors. It appears that the future of Tom's bathing town is bright.

As Charlotte completes that thought, a shadow falls across the open book lying in her lap. She looks up to see Lord Somerset standing near. 'Lord Somerset,' she says, 'I did not know you were in Sanditon.' 'Good Day to you, Miss Heywood,' he responds with a bow. 'Mary told me you were here. I wonder if I may have a word with you?' 'Yes, of course, Lord Somerset,' she says, 'did you arrive with Mr Parker?' 'No,' he replies with a smile. 'I came along with Francis..., ah Mr Nisbet, for a short visit. Francis wishes to call on Miss Clara Brereton and I plan to call on Miss Esther Denham.' 'But that is not the reason I am here, Miss Heywood,' he says. 'There is a matter of some urgency I wish to bring to your attention in hope you that you can assist me as I am greatly concerned about my friend, Sidney. I would like for you to talk to him about danger to him from some recent financial steps he has taken.' 'You wish me to talk to him,' replies Charlotte with surprise! 'I do not know Mr Parker well enough that he would make me privy to his financial matters. Why do you not bring your concern to him directly or to Tom?' 'I believe Sidney will listen to you because he sets great store by you,' he responds. 'Sidney let slip in a moment of perhaps one glass too many that he thinks you quite the most beautiful woman he has ever had the pleasure of acquaintance. I never before have heard him say anything about a woman that might imply affection. But to the matter at hand. Sidney personally guaranteed to the bank Tom's loans and I am concerned by it. Tom Parker is in serious trouble with the banks in London and private investors will have nothing to do with him so if Tom Parker does not make a success of his bathing town and make it quickly, the banks will call in his loans and that could mean ruin for Sidney as well as Tom.' 'Well,' answers Charlotte, 'perhaps I should talk to Mary first. Then if she also is not aware of the precarious state of Tom's finances, I can gain her advice about what to do.' 'I shall leave the matter in your capable hands to handle as you see fit then, Miss Heywood,' Lord Somerset concludes as he bows, wishes Charlotte good day and leaves. From light to dark in a moment, now what shall you do, muses Charlotte? I don't wish for Sidney Parker to think badly of me because I am prying into his business affairs. What might his reaction be to my involving myself in his financial matters, I do not wish to consider. But I shall talk to Mary for her advice at the earliest opportunity.

Charlotte returns her book to Mrs Whitby and leaves the library as it is time to go back to Trafalgar House to join Mary to dine. It strikes her that this might be a opportune time to broach the subject brought to her attention by Lord Somerset to Mary. As she walks down the street, she is approached by Sir Edward who appears again to be in his cups. 'Ah Mish Heywood,' he slurs, 'you are looking exceptionally well today. Might we walk together for a bit,' at the same time taking her arm unbidden! 'No,' cries Charlotte! 'I am on my way to Trafalgar House now,' as she struggles to retrieve her arm from Sir Edward's grip. As she continues to try to release herself, Charlotte hears a familiar voice behind her. 'Miss Heywood, may I be of assistance?' She turns her head and sees Sidney Parker whose face is suffused with anger. 'Release Miss Heywood at once, Sir Edward, or I shall not be responsible for the consequences.' Edward looks at Sidney and says, 'This is not a matter for you to be concerned with, Parker,' releasing Charlotte's arm as he says and then takes a off balance swing at Sidney who blocks it then pushes him away. As Sir Edward staggers away down the street, he says, 'I shall not forget this, Parker. Mark my words.' Sidney ignores him, turns to Charlotte and asks, 'Are you alright, Miss Heywood?' 'Yes,' she replies, 'thank you, Mr Parker, for your assistance. Sir Edward had no evil intent I am sure, but I am glad you were near by.' 'Well,' Sidney replies, 'let me walk you to Trafalgar House which I left but moments ago and put you into Mary's hands.' They walk together the short distance and once the door opens, Sidney excuses himself and walks off down the street. So, thinks Charlotte, it appears that I have a champion in Mr Parker. And I shall have to be more cautious around Sir Edward.

Charlotte goes into the drawing room and finds Mary and Tom. Mary says, 'Charlotte, you just missed Mr Stringer. He was here with Tom discussing some construction plans and as he left, he asked if he might call on you here. I said that I would have no objection, but that whether he should call on you or not was a matter for you to determine.' Tom speaks up. 'Mr Stringer is again trying to climb above his station. I have only the highest regard for his skills, but he is the son of a vegetable farmer and stone mason. He has no fortune nor any hopes of ever attaining one. He can not be encouraged to harbor hopes of gaining the hand of a gentleman's daughter.' Mary says, 'Mr Stringer is a fine young man who will make some young woman a wonderful husband and as I said, it is Charlotte's decision whether to encourage him in his interest or not.' Tom snorts his disapproval and leaves the room.

'Mary,' Charlotte says, 'I don't wish to be uncivil but I hardly know Mr Stringer and I do not wish to encourage him. He is good looking and ambitious and I am sure will find a young lady that suits him but that young lady shall not be me.' 'Then I shall discourage him,' replies Mary, 'at the next opportunity. But have you seen Sidney since his return? He was just here you know with Tom and Mr Stringer. I saw that when Sidney overheard Mr Stringer's request, he seemed to be less than pleased,' she concludes with a smile. 'I just saw Mr Sidney outside, Mary,' Charlotte says. 'He rescued me from Sir Edward who was feeling his drink. Sir Edward tried to strike him but Mr Sidney brushed him off and he staggered away. But Sir Edward did threaten him.' 'Well, it seems that you are finding multiple suitors here, Charlotte, some less attractive than others,' Mary replies.

'Mary,' continues Charlotte before her courage fails her, 'Lord Somerset asked me to talk to Mr Sidney about his finances. I don't believe that it is any of my concern, and I hesitate to say anything to you but I feel I must before I should even think of approaching him.' 'What is it,' Mary asks? 'Well, it is about Tom's loans,' replies Charlotte. 'Lord Somerset said that Sidney guaranteed the loan increases with his own fortune and it seems the loan extensions and the increased amount would not have occurred without Sidney's guarantee.' 'What,' cries Mary, 'I had no idea that there was trouble with financing. This explains those rumors that Lady Denham talked about and problems with materials and workers because of not being paid. I shall talk to Tom,' who chooses that moment to walk back into the room. 'Tom,' Mary challenges, 'did you know that Sidney had to guarantee your loans with his own fortune to gain the increase and the loan extensions?' 'No, I did not,' he replies, 'but it is of no matter because my Sanditon bathing town will become a raging success and now I am considering additional amenities including a hospital to come with the Physician I have yet to find.' Yes, thinks Charlotte, I must talk to Sidney. He is in greater danger than he knows and he must take a stronger role in managing the finances before he is bankrupted.

Chapter 26

The following morning after breakfast, Charlotte is advised that she has a caller. She comes into the drawing room to see Mary and Mr Stringer. 'Miss Heywood,' asks Mr Stringer, 'I wonder if I might call on you from time to time and perhaps on occasion engage you in a walk along the shore or the cliff with of course a proper escort?' 'Thank you, Mr Stringer,' Charlotte replies. 'I certainly value your friendship but I have no wish for our relationship to advance beyond that.' Seeing the disappointment in his face, Charlotte hastens to add that she highly values his friendship and admires his work on Tom's new bathing town. As she is talking, Sidney walks in to hear her words. He looks at Stringer and then at Charlotte with a penetrating gaze that brings a blush to her face to Charlotte's immense chagrin. She sees that Mr Stringer also is looking between Sidney and herself and her blush deepens to crimson. Oh what is it that I may not hide my feelings as I wish she thinks. Now my conversation with Sidney about Lord Somerset's concerns will be even more difficult. Mr Stringer thanks Charlotte for receiving him and Mary as well then takes his departure as Sidney stands looking between Mary and Charlotte.

'Sidney,' Mary says, 'Charlotte needs to talk to you. She has already discussed with me so I am aware.' Sidney looks confused. 'Well,' he says, 'what is it, Miss Heywood?' 'Mr Parker,' Charlotte replies, 'Lord Somerset came to talk to me yesterday. He asked that I talk to you about your guarantee of Tom's loans to gain the additional funds needed and the loan extensions.' 'Why would he do that, not talk to me but to you about my affairs?' 'That I do not know, Mr Parker, but he did and I have shared with Mary because I was not sure of the propriety of doing so, but she thinks I should. Lord Somerset believes your fortune is at risk because of Tom's money problems.' 'Miss Heywood,' he says angrily, 'this is between Tom and me and is not your concern!' Mary says, 'Sidney, Miss Heywood has done you a favor in bringing this to you and to me. I was not aware of Tom's money problems and that all the doors to financing are closed to him except for what you were able to do with your own funds. You must not allow him to continue to spend money that we do not have.' 'What would you have me do, Mary,' Sidney asks? 'We must have a talk with him, Sidney,' Mary replies, 'and have it today.'

Morgan comes in and announces that a young boy has delivered a note for Miss Heywood and is waiting for her response. He gives the note to Charlotte who takes the opportunity to ask him about the state of his head wound. 'Oh, Miss Heywood,' he replies, 'thank you for your concern. All is well and since you removed the thread last week, it has healed to hardly show a scar.' He bows and retreats to wait by the door. Charlotte opens the note and sees it is from Georgiana and quickly reading through it, finds that Georgiana is asking her to come to Mrs Griffiths in the afternoon to walk with her. 'Mary…Mr Parker, Georgiana has invited me to take the air with her this afternoon and if you do not need me, Mary, I will reply in the affirmative.' 'By all means, Charlotte,' Mary replies, 'please do. I can manage very well without you this day.' Charlotte quickly jots a note for Georgiana

116

and puts it into Morgan's hands. Sidney says, 'Miss Heywood, if I may, I will accompany you to Mrs Griffiths this afternoon as I need to have a word with Georgiana.' 'You wish to walk with us then,' Charlotte asks? 'No,' he responds, 'I shall not impose myself on either you or Georgiana during your walk. I shall just have a quick word with her and then let the two of you be on your way. And I shall have a word with Lord Somerset and Tom,' he says, looking at her intently at the same time. Oh Mr Parker, Charlotte thinks, you do give me pause when you turn those beautiful eyes on me, whether in anger or approbation.

Chapter 27

Saturday - 2 May 1818 - Afternoon - Sanditon

A fternoon comes and Charlotte finds herself walking the few short steps to Mrs Griffiths' Boarding House in the company of a man she finds always engages her attention to the detriment of any other. I would walk with you longer should you ask me, Mr Parker, she muses, but Sidney wishes her good day at the door of Mrs Griffiths', bows and continues on down the street toward the hotel, apparently having changed his mind about having a word with Georgiana. Hmmm, she thinks, was his walk with me to see Georgiana just a pretense to accompany me rather than a need to see Georgiana? I hope so. Charlotte looks after him for a moment then turns, rings and enters.

Upstairs, Georgiana greets her with joy. As soon as the door closes behind, 'Charlotte,' Georgiana says, 'you remember that letter I mailed a few weeks ago, when we walked.' 'Yes,' replies Charlotte. 'Well,' continues Georgiana excitedly, 'today I received a reply. It is from one of my London suitors, but this suitor is the one with whom I wish retain a relationship. He is coming to Sanditon to see me.' 'And who is this suitor,' Charlotte asks, 'and when is he coming?' 'He will be here on Monday, two days hence,' Georgiana replies. 'What is his name,' Charlotte asks, 'and is he an acquaintance of Mr Sidney Parker?' 'Yes, he is,' replies Georgiana. 'But I have no wish for Sidney to know of his name nor of his visit. As I already told you on our previous walk, Sidney does not wish for me to have any male acquaintances who he thinks might be after my fortune and as he is my guardian, he will not wish for me to receive this caller here in Sanditon. Will you call for me Monday at the noon hour so that I may meet him?' 'I do think you should tell Mr Parker about this visit, Georgiana,' replies Charlotte. 'He is after all responsible for your welfare as your guardian.' 'Please, Charlotte,' cries Georgiana, 'Sidney will ruin the visit. I have not seen Charles, Charles Porteus, that is his name, since last summer and I must see him without interference from Sidney. You will be with me and therefore there can be no inference of scandal nor impropriety. Please....!' 'If I agree,' responds Charlotte, 'I shall only do so if you allow me to tell Mr Parker after your visit with Mr Porteus.' 'Yes,' returns Georgiana, 'if you must, but he will punish you and me for it.' 'Have you agreed a location to meet,' asks Charlotte? 'Yes,' responds Georgiana, 'he wrote that he will look for me along the road before Sanditon as he prefers not to come into town. I thought to wait on the road near Sanditon House until his arrival and then we shall walk toward the cliffs overlooking the sea.' 'Well then, I still believe it would be best to involve Mr Parker in this meeting but if you are determined that you shall not, then I shall accompany you, Georgiana, to ensure your safety and propriety,' answers Charlotte. 'I shall call for you as you asked and take you to him.'

Charlotte says her goodbyes to Georgiana with another promise to see her on Monday and escort her to her "tryst" with Mr Porteus and goes out. As she walks slowly along, she thinks to herself that I wish I had not agreed to that but I have. And now, I see that I have taken on an obligation that may put me at odds with Sidney and I do not wish to be the object of his disapprobation. And I have no knowledge at all of this Mr Porteus. What if he proves to be a fortune hunter as Sidney Parker believes all those London suitors to be! Then I shall have put Georgiana at risk by my actions. Lost in thought, she hears the sound of gaiety which pulls her from her reverie. She looks up to see Mr Nisbet and Clara arm in arm. They notice her at the same time and Clara calls a greeting. 'Good Afternoon, Charlotte,' she says. 'You of course remember Mr Nisbet.' 'Yes,' returns Charlotte, 'with pleasure'. 'Francis, you remember Charlotte from the ball,' continues Clara. 'Of course, I remember the lovely Miss Heywood,' he says. 'I had the immense pleasure of dancing with her and would have asked for a second dance had I been able to reach her through the crush of potential claimants for a turn with her on the dance floor,' he says with a smile, 'and I did note, Miss Heywood, that our very own Sidney Parker took to the dance floor with you more than once with something of enthusiasm I had never before seen from him.' Charlotte responds with, 'I am sure Mr Parker was only being polite, Mr Nisbet.' 'Not a bit of it,' he replies. 'Sidney does not play at politeness, it is not his forte in my experience. He tells it as he sees it and his actions reflect his approbation or lack of it. No, Miss Heywood, you have him in thrall and a good match you are too. My congratulations on your conquest.' Charlotte blushes at his frankness and Clara whom Charlotte looks up to see is watching her closely, smiles and says teasingly, 'Why Charlotte Heywood, I do believe you are a bit in love with that man. Can it be?' Charlotte feels her blush deepen as she finds herself at a loss for words to respond to that fraught question.

'Well,' sighs Clara, 'I must be getting back to Sanditon House. Lady Denham will be looking for me and I shall have to pay for my absence if I linger here much longer. Good Day.' Mr Nisbet says, 'It was wonderful to see you again, Miss Heywood. I expect we shall be more in acquaintance in the future as I believe Sidney will have you on his arm on a regular basis before too long should that meet with your approbation, perhaps in London as well as here in Sanditon. I believe there is a grand ball in London soon at which his attendance is required. It is the Duchess of Kent's annual masked summer ball. It is quite the event, a bit pagan if I may say so, but held a respectable time after the May Day, I believe on 22 May this year, to avoid crossing the Church. It is a must event for the London Beau Monde should they be lucky enough to gain an invitation and I pray that I shall see you there.' He bows and walks off with Clara as Charlotte considers; well, if that be the case, I then shall have the second visit of my life to London perhaps to a ball on Sidney's arm? I wonder what my Papa would say? Perhaps I should write and inform him if such invitation should be forthcoming given his reluctance to allow me to visit London. I still remember his face in Hyde Park six years back now when he dragged Anne and me back to our lodgings after encountering that well dressed group of London aristocracy. It is a puzzle that I should like to solve.

Chapter 28

Monday - 4 May 1818 – Morning - Sanditon

Following a restful Sunday, Monday dawns with rain beating down on the roof. Well, thinks Charlotte, this is not auspicious for Georgiana's and my rendezvous with Mr Porteus. Perhaps he will not come or will be delayed, but we shall see. She goes down to breakfast and finds Tom, Mary and Sidney at the table. They greet her and Sidney surprises by rising and pulling out a chair for her. Once he has seated her and returned to his place, he says to Tom, 'Will you and Mary attend the Duchess of Kent's Masked Ball?' Tom responds, 'Of course, Mary and I must attend. It is a command performance. The Duchess is very close to the Prince Regent and it would be the height of imprudence to ignore her summons, would it not, Mary?'

Without giving Mary a chance to respond, Tom continues, 'It is also a great opportunity to promote our Sanditon Bathing Town. The wealth of England is on display and many potential investors and customers of our town will be in attendance. It is the perfect opportunity to gain both and I shall expect to see you there, Sidney, to promote our town and Arthur and Diana as well. Our Sister Susan will no doubt wish to be in attendance too, although her ill health may well prevent it. And Charlotte, you must come with us. You will be a great addition to our party and no doubt attract even more attention to our mission to promote our bathing town.'

Turning to Sidney, Tom asks, 'You surely will wish to have our beautiful guest on your arm, will you not, Sidney?' Perhaps a conversation for a later time, thinks Charlotte as she sees another frown begin to form between those beautiful eyes across the table from her but to her surprise Sidney says, 'I shall be pleased to escort Miss Heywood to the Ball if that is acceptable to her.' 'Of course, Mr Parker,' replies Charlotte, 'I shall be pleased to accompany you.' Now there is no doubt that I shall go, thinks Charlotte, but I must write to Papa tonight for his advice. He was most adamant that I avoid London for what reason I yet do not know.

Chapter 29

In the afternoon, the clouds have parted and a welcome sun is sharing its warmth as Charlotte walks with Georgiana along the road out of Sanditon toward the area near Sanditon House for Georgiana's planned rendezvous with Charles Porteus. As they walk in companionable silence, Charlotte is worrying over her role in facilitating a meeting that she thinks could put her at odds with Sidney and that is something she does not want. She was very excited in the morning when it was agreed that Sidney would escort her to a grand London ball although she tried very hard not to show it. She also is happy with Mary's foresight in ordering two ball gowns from Mrs Smith when they had gone to have the gown Esther had given her fitted for the Sanditon Ball. The gowns had been delivered just a few days ago. But there is another worry nagging her as well, her Father's request; no almost demand that she avoid traveling to London. The why of it must be resolved she thinks.

As Charlotte and Georgiana continue to walk and approach Sanditon House, they meet the London coach on its way into Sanditon. It does not slow and Georgiana excitedly waves for it to stop. It does and they look inside, but Georgiana says with disappointment, 'He is not here.' She asks the coachman if a passenger had alighted earlier and he replies that there was and he had left the coach about a half mile up the road. Thanking him, Georgiana excitedly says to Charlotte, 'That must be him,' and grabbing her hand begins to walk at a very fast pace up the road. 'Slow down, Georgiana,' Charlotte laughingly says, 'if it is him, he will wait for you. I do not think he shall start his journey back to London on foot. And you will have the better part of four hours before the coach begins its return journey to London.' But Georgiana hardly slows her pace and as they round a bend, Georgiana spots a well dressed young black man at rest under a spreading oak. He sees Georgiana and Charlotte at the same time, jumps up with a shout of joy and runs toward them. 'Georgiana,' he cries, 'I thought I should never see you again,' as he doffs his hat and offers a sweeping bow. Georgiana, taking his hands in hers, says, 'Perhaps you would not have if I had remained hidden away for yet another year and more by my guardian until I attain my majority, but he has released me from time to time into the care of Miss Charlotte Heywood whom you see here beside me. Charlotte, allow me to introduce Mr Charles Porteus.' 'Miss Heywood,' he says with a bow, 'it is a pleasure to make your acquaintance.' 'Likewise, Mr Porteus,' Charlotte replies. She continues, 'Shall we walk yonder path? It will take us toward the sea and some beautiful views from the cliff tops? I shall follow a few paces behind to allow you to become reacquainted without my hearing.' Both Georgiana and Charles happily agree and they set off. They wind their way along the path with Charlotte trailing along behind, hearing snatches of laugher and excited talk. Eventually they emerge onto a headland from which they can see Sanditon in the distance. The wind is strong but warm and they continue until they find a grassy area that is somewhat sheltered from the wind and seat themselves.

126

'So, Mr Porteus, how long have you known Georgiana,' Charlotte asks? 'Please call me Charles, he says, 'and I have known Georgiana all of my life.' 'What,' Charlotte asks, 'how can that be?' 'Well,' he replies, 'I was born and grew up in the WestIndies, on Georgiana's Father's plantation, in fact. Mr David Lambe was a fine man. He freed his slaves and his will gave his plantation to those freed slaves less than two years ago.' 'Yes,' Charlotte responds, 'Georgiana told me about that.' 'Well,' continues Charles, 'I am the son of a slave whom Mr Lambe freed many years before that and was given a small holding on the plantation. This was before Georgiana was born and I knew her as a baby although when she was born, I was but two years of age. My mother was her nurse and I played with Georgiana as a child. Another thing you should know is that I was born a free man because of the kindness of Georgiana's Father. When he died and Sidney Parker decided to take Georgiana to London, I followed as soon as I could and disembarked in London about six months after Georgiana and Sidney did.'

'You know, Mr Parker then,' asks Charlotte? 'Oh yes,' replies Charles, 'but I must say that we are not great friends.' I don't believe he cares about Georgiana's welfare as he should. Before Sidney left London with Georgiana to come here, he left her locked up alone in the Parker London house with only the servants for company many a night as he went out to carouse the evenings away with his friends. He would be very unhappy should knowledge of my visit with Georgiana in Sanditon come to his attention. He believes I am not to be trusted or better said, he believes that he cannot trust Georgiana with me. Why I wonder, since she and I have known each other longer than he has by far and we are almost like Brother and Sister, although I admit that perhaps we should like to be more than that but we are not lovers, Miss Heywood.' 'Please call me Charlotte, Charles,' responds Charlotte, 'and perhaps Georgiana or I should inform Mr Parker about your visit. Surely he will understand your circumstance and then you can meet openly without subterfuge?' 'I believe Sidney is a good man,' replies Charles. 'He became like a son to Mr Lambe, but he has darkness in him and it can emerge quickly like the arrival of a summer storm. He is unwilling or unable to trust and is quick to judge fault. I warn you not to put your relationship with him, if you have one, Charlotte, into the breach because Sidney will turn his guns on you.'

The hours fly by and almost before any of the party are aware, it is time to walk back to the road so that Charles can catch the London coach on its way out of Sanditon. They arrive on the road in good time and after a short wait, the heavily loaded coach pulls to a stop in response to Charles' wave. He asks for passage, but the coachman returns, 'I'm sorry, but my conveyance is full. You shall have to wait for tomorrow's coach to find passage. I suggest you pay at the post inn tomorrow before we arrive to ensure that you will have a place. Failing that, you shall have to find other means of reaching your destination.' He then slaps the reins against the horses' flanks and the coach pulls away. 'Oh this is a disaster,' cries Georgiana, 'what are we to do? Sidney will almost certainly see Charles or hear of his visit if he must find lodging in Sanditon for the night. That cannot be. Charlotte, what are we to do?' 'Well,' replies Charlotte, 'I still believe that nothing good will come of keeping Charles' visit a secret from Sidney. Yes, he may be angry at the knowledge but I believe that he will be more so if we try to hide Charles' presence or his visit from him.' 'But I cannot bear it, if Sidney forbids Charles to visit me, when he learns of it,' cries Georgiana. 'I am sure he will not,' says Charlotte, 'but I think the best way forward is to see if we can find lodging nearby. Perhaps I can prevail on Clara to find a place for Charles to lay his head for the night at Sanditon House then we can find Mr Parker and tell him of the circumstance. I cannot believe he will not be sympathetic to you, Georgiana, when he knows that there is no subterfuge involved.' 'Well,' replies Georgiana, 'I suppose there is nothing else we can do but still I believe that Sidney will be very angry and perhaps focus that anger on you, Charlotte.'

With a possible way forward agreed, the three young people set off for nearby Sanditon House. They arrive at the door and ring for entry. The footman allows them in and they walk into the grand foyer and ask for Miss Clara Brereton. The footman begs them to wait while he goes to see if she can receive them. After a short time, Clara emerges from a door and comes toward them. She greets Charlotte who reacquaints Clara with Georgiana and then introduces her to Charles. Charlotte continues, 'Clara, Mr Porteus needs lodging for the night as he was unable to procure intended passage on the London coach this afternoon. I wonder if Lady Denham would object to Mr Porteus having a room here for the night?' 'Not at all,' Clara replies. 'There are several rooms above the carriage house any one of which will provide a comfortable overnight accommodation for Mr Porteus. I shall ask Hawkins to escort him to a room and he is welcome to take sup at our butler's table as well.' 'Oh thank you so much, Clara,' says Charlotte to which Georgiana and Charles add their profuse words of gratitude. 'Also Clara, do you suppose you could send someone tomorrow to purchase Mr Porteus' passage on the London coach?' 'Yes, of course,' she replies. 'One of the servants will be making the trip to the butcher tomorrow and he can purchase a place on the coach for Mr Porteus.' 'Then we have the matter sorted,' says Charlotte, 'and now perhaps we should be making our way back to Sanditon as the hour is growing late.' All is happiness and light as Clara walks them back to the front door whence goodbyes are said all around and wishes exchanged between Georgiana and Charles to soon meet again, perhaps on the morrow if an opportunity should present itself.

As they prepare to go out, the door to the drawing room opens and Sidney and Tom Parker emerge. Sidney looks at Charlotte and Georgiana with the beginnings of a smile on his face, then notices Charles half out the door behind them. The smile twists into a grimace of fury and he takes rapid strides toward them. 'What is the meaning of this, Charles,' he grinds out in a low angry voice? 'Georgiana, what is he doing here,' he says glancing angrily between her and Charles . 'Miss Heywood, did you assist in this meeting,' he demands? Charlotte looks into those beautiful, now stormy eyes, and says, 'Yes, Mr Parker, I accompanied Georgiana for purposes of propriety and safety at her request to meet with Mr Porteus, and Georgiana or I were going to tell you of the visit at the earliest opportunity.' 'The opportunity should have been taken before the visit, Miss Heywood,' he snaps. 'But you would not have allowed it,' cries Georgiana. 'No, I would not have,' Sidney growls. 'Georgiana, Miss Heywood, you both have betrayed my trust. Georgiana, you shall not see Charles again.'

'We have not,' shoots back Charlotte who is getting angry despite her best efforts to keep calm in the face of Sidney's accusations. 'You would have been told and I can say that there was not the least impropriety in this visit. Had we not run into you this afternoon, you certainly would have been informed of Mr Porteus' visit at the next opportunity. Georgiana has told me that Mr Porteus is of long acquaintance and that you know him as well from the WestIndies. So I do not see any reason for your disapprobation of his visit.' 'You may not, Miss Heywood,' Sidney snaps, 'but I do. She is my ward and I must ensure that she is not sought out by fortune seekers.' 'I can assure you, Mr Parker,' Charlotte replies, 'Georgiana is safe in my hands and I do not believe Mr Porteus is a fortune seeker. He almost is family which you well know.' 'That is beside the point,' he replies, 'and Charles, I do not want to see you in Georgiana's company again, do you understand me?' Charles steps up to Sidney and replies, 'Sidney, I am a free man and I shall be where I please, when I please. Do you understand me?' Sidney clinches his fists, turns away from Charles and back to Georgiana and Charlotte and growls, 'Now, I shall see the two of you home, and tonight I shall have a private word with you, Miss Heywood.' Turning to Tom who is watching the exchange with an air of bemused detachment, Sidney says, 'We shall have to revisit the outcome of our meeting with Lady Denham tomorrow.'

Sidney, Charlotte and Georgiana go out as Georgiana manages a quick wave to Charles before the door closes behind them. 'Georgiana,' Sidney says, 'if I cannot trust you, I shall have to further limit your excursions. I had believed that I could trust Miss Heywood,' glancing at her as he says it, 'but she has today proved that I cannot.' 'That is so unfair, Sidney,' Georgiana replies, 'to me and to Charlotte, especially to Charlotte. She did not know far in advance of my planned meeting with Charles and she insisted that I should inform you of it which I fully intended to do. However, you seem unprepared to listen nor to give me any freedom to pursue friendship let alone love so I see no reason why I should inform you of anything. In two years, I shall have my freedom from you and your restrictions and I shall do exactly as I please.' 'Be that as it may,' replies Sidney, 'you now are my ward and you shall do as I require.' 'Do not impose the pain of your treatment by Maria Wickham on me, Sidney,' Georgiana shouts. 'I shall not stand for it!' Charlotte sees Sidney go pale at those words and feels a surge of sympathy for him until he shouts back at Georgiana, 'You shall do as you are told,' and stalks off ahead leaving Charlotte and Georgiana to trail behind him. 'I told you, Charlotte, that Sidney would be unreasonable and unsympathetic,' cries Georgiana. 'Now you see the man that he is, uncompromising and untrusting. That is why I cannot and shall not confide in him and why I shall escape him as soon as I can. My one and twenty birthday cannot come quickly enough.' The demons of Sidney Parker still haunt him, thinks Charlotte. What is to be done?

Night comes to Trafalgar House. It is quiet in the drawing room after supper with Tom, Mary, Sidney and Charlotte each in their own thoughts. Sidney suddenly speaks up. 'I had thought to have a private word with you this evening, Miss Heywood, but I believe that Mary and Tom should hear as well. Miss Heywood, your escorting of Georgiana to a meeting with Charles Porteus was reckless and unauthorized and I believe you have betrayed the trust I put into your hands as her companion.' 'Sidney,' says Mary in a shocked tone, 'what a awful thing to say to our guest. You must beg her forgiveness. Charlotte is a most trusted friend of mine and she never intentionally will put anyone in her trust in any danger.' 'Thank you, Mary,' responds Charlotte gratefully. 'Mr Parker, I assure you that Georgiana was never in any danger. But she could be if you persist in trying to keep her from friends and acquaintances, especially Charles whom she has known since her childhood. She will make her escape from you one day and that could put her in real danger. She is much safer if she has some freedom and companions, friends like me who care for her whom she can talk to and share her wants and needs. She is your ward and I understand your worries and obligations to her, but she also is a smart young woman who has a fortune and she will have her own way, whether with your approbation or without. So, in my opinion, you shall have to change your own behavior toward her.' Sidney does not reply but just stares at her. What is he thinking, Charlotte asks herself? There is much going on behind those beautiful eyes that I cannot see but I wish I could. I should so enjoy your approbation, Mr Parker, Charlotte thinks to herself, but I shall not sell my soul for it; not yet.

After retiring to her bed chamber for the night, Charlotte sits to write to her Father;

———

Sanditon

4 May 1818

Dear Papa:

I wish to let you know of a development here in Sanditon. To my current knowledge, I am to accompany Mr Tom and Mrs Mary Parker and Mr Sidney Parker, who will escort me to the Duchess of Kent's masked ball, in London a little more than two weeks hence. I know you have said that I should not visit London and perhaps, now you can explain the why of it to me. I should very much like to attend such a wonderful sounding ball as it has been told to me by Mr Tom Parker and others, but I remain concerned that I should do so without your approbation considering the demands that you have made of me in the past to avoid such visits, including on the day of my departure with Mr and Mrs Parker to Sanditon. And still I remember my visit with you in my sixteenth year when you demanded a early departure from the one London visit that you allowed me, a demand that I yet do not know the reason for.

So, Papa, I look forward to your reply about your reasons so that I may make the right decision about going to the ball. Also, please consider if perhaps Anne could be spared to join me in Sanditon before too long. I should enjoy her company and I dare say that, as I have, Anne should enjoy a stay here in Sanditon very much.

Please give my love to Mama and my brothers and sisters.

I remain

Your loving daughter

Charlotte

Chapter 30

Thursday - 14 May 1818 - Sanditon

It has been been more than a week since Charlotte posted her letter to Willingden and she is hoping for a reply any day because travel to London is but four days away. Sidney has been avoiding her, Charlotte thinks, since the evening when he accused her of being untrustworthy. They have seen each other on occasion at Trafalgar House and about town, but Sidney has remained aloof and shown only the civility due a stranger rather than a friend or family member. So in Charlotte's mind, she has fallen in his estimation although he has not interfered nor changed his approval for Charlotte to escort or meet with Georgiana as the situation has demanded. But he has not forgiven me thinks Charlotte. And it seems that nothing has changed about Tom Parker's plans that he, Mary, Sidney and she should attend the Duchess of Kent's Masked Ball. Mary is making sure that Charlotte will take with her all the necessaries to put her best foot forward at the ball and Tom is waxing poetic about the success he anticipates at the Ball in procuring additional investors and visitors to occupy his houses and apartments in Sanditon for the summer. All is going according to plan, except Charlotte has yet to hear from her Papa. She does not feel comfortable going against his wishes for her to visit London but she does feel that she must go unless she hears from him a reason why she should not so as not to disappoint Tom, she tells herself, but I wish to go in absence of a good reason why I should not.

Charlotte has just returned to Trafalgar House from a walk on the beach with Georgiana and the three older Parker children who have taken to Georgiana as they have to Charlotte. The energetic children run into the drawing room ahead of Charlotte and Georgiana and greet their Uncle Sidney and Mama Mary who it appears have been having a conversation over tea. They look up and smile at the obvious joy and excitement of the children just back from their excursion into the sunshine and fresh air. Sidney stands and looks at the smiling and obviously happy face of Georgiana and then turns those beautiful eyes on Charlotte with an expression I haven't seen before, Charlotte thinks, what is it, is there a hint of softness, even perhaps the beginnings of a smile behind those eyes? Charlotte offers her own tentative smile back. Mary says, 'I see you have returned with your charges none the worse for wear, Charlotte. Perhaps you shall need a rest, to recover yourself from them.' 'No,' replies Charlotte, 'but I wish to leave the children with you now so that I may walk Georgiana back to Mrs Griffiths.' 'Miss Heywood,' interjects Sidney, 'I shall do that if I may. I need a word with Georgiana and this will be a perfect opportunity to do that. Please remain here with Mary. I believe she has a post from Willingden for you.' 'Oh, thank you, Mr Parker,' smilingly replies Charlotte. 'I have been so looking forward to hearing news from home.' She turns to Georgiana and says, 'I hope you will excuse me from my duty, Georgiana,' who smiles in her turn and says, 'Yes, Charlotte, I shall try to bear your absence with equanimity,' as she and Sidney go out.

Mary picks up a letter from the table beside her and puts it into Charlotte's hands. 'I shall attend to the children,' she says, 'and give you the opportunity to read your letter in peace.' She goes out leaving Charlotte alone. The address is in Papa's hand, Charlotte sees; what will he say she wonders as she opens the post and begins to read;

Willingden

Monday 11 May 1818

My Darling Daughter:

I was pleased to receive your post of 4 May and I thank you for it. Please forgive the lateness of my reply, but I had several matters to address before I could respond.

First, with regard to your plans to attend the Duchess of Kent's Masked Ball, I cannot forbid it. You are no longer a child and you must find your way in the world without interference from your old Papa but there are some things in our past that visits to London give rise to. I am not at liberty to tell you what those things are as much as I wish I could. However, suffice it to say that the Duchess has some acquaintance with me and our family. She will wish you to call on her before you attend her Masked Ball and you must do it alone. When you arrive in London, please have a message delivered to her. She will respond and also send a carriage for you upon the agreed time. I regret all of the mystery but it is very important that you do as I instruct, my beautiful child, and please say no more than necessary to your hosts, the Parkers, to accomplish your call.

But now to Willingden; all is well with us. The animals are healthy and the crops are progressing well. The weather has been favorable to now and we hope for a summer that will make up

*for the cold of the previous few. With regard to your request to
have Anne join you in Sanditon, I have talked to Mama and she
believes that we can spare Anne beginning in July, perhaps for the
rest of the summer months. We have talked to her about it and of
course, she is prepared to go now but she will have to wait a little
longer.*

*I hope you enjoy your visit to London but please be careful,
be ready for anything, because life can deal you surprises at a
moment, both good and bad.*

We love and miss you,

Papa

Charlotte puts the letter down and sits with knitted brows for a
bit thinking, now the mystery of my London avoidance is deepened, not
diminished. What is this and shall I find the mystery diminished or deepened further when I call on the grand personage of the masked ball, the
Duchess of Kent herself. Why should she demand a call by me, a country gentleman's daughter, and what will Tom and Mary Parker and Sidney
think of what they surely shall see as an impertinence by me, my Father or
the both of us. As Charlotte puzzles this over, Sidney returns and comes
to sit opposite her. He says, 'Miss Heywood, I have decided to take your
advice with regard to Georgiana and accordingly, I have determined to
bring Georgiana with us to the Masked Ball. Do you approve?' 'Oh yes,
Mr Parker,' she replies. 'Georgiana will be over the moon and you will be
fully restored to her good graces!' 'That will be well,' Sidney replies with
a smile, 'but I prefer that I should be fully restored to yours if you will
allow it, Miss Heywood,' looking steadily into Charlotte's eyes as he says it.
Charlotte smiles back hoping she will not blush, but thinks, oh I shall allow

it Mr Parker, why should I not? You are the one I find in my dreams most of all and if you should find me in yours, all the better.

Chapter 31

The day of departure to London arrives and the party sets off in fine weather. The journey to Tunbridge Wells is uneventful and the group spends a restful overnight in a comfortable inn. They continue the next morning, Tuesday, and arrive in London at the Parker residence in Holborn in late afternoon. They are greeted by the servants, headed by the butler, Mr Collins, and ushered into the house as trunks are unloaded and carried to the appropriate bed chamber. Charlotte is excited to be in London again for the second time in her life as memories of her one and only visit in her 16th year with Anne and Papa come back to her. She also is very impressed by the Parker's well appointed house. She and Georgiana will share adjoining bed chambers which is pleasing to her and Georgiana. After they settle in and have the opportunity to refresh themselves a little, all are called to tea where they sit and plan the days ahead. Georgiana begs their indulgence after tea saying that she is tired and wishes retire to her bed chamber early. She goes out.

Then Tom says, 'Ladies, Sidney, we shall have much before us to accomplish before our Grand Masked Ball just three days hence. I shall call on the banks and see to the status of my loans with Sidney, and we shall see what we can discover about guests at the ball whom we may approach to gauge their interest in investing or purchasing our apartments and houses in Sanditon.' Sidney frowns and says, 'Tom, I am not certain that we should call on the banks, especially if it is to approach them to increase the amount of your loans or to seek new funds. We are quite overextended already and I suggest we let sleeping dogs lie.' 'Balderdash,' replies Tom. 'Our bankers will undoubtedly be very pleased to provide whatever funds we need to complete my grand plan. I don't believe you have been enthusiastic enough, Sidney, in your representations to them on your recent calls. I shall remedy that while we are in London for the Ball.' Charlotte watches as Sidney grimaces and then says, 'I shall not accompany you on your calls, Tom. I was here just a few weeks back and the banks were not receptive to advancing further funding and I fear, if you should ask for more, they might determine to call in your loans viewing your request as a sign that their current loan amounts are at risk. Remember our conversation of nearly three weeks ago after our call on Lady Denham when I warned you of this possibility. I did not tell you then, but those words of warning came directly from Lord Somerset who has close ties to the London banks,' glancing at Charlotte as he speaks. 'The banks must have confidence in this project and at present, they do not. I think you should better spend your time trying to gain new investor interest and summer takers of houses and apartments while we are here for the Ball rather than seeking increases in your outstanding loans.' Tom sputters, 'I am quite certain that my calls will be very welcome.' 'I do not think so,' replies Sidney, 'and, I shall not accompany you.'

Breaking into the pregnant silence as Tom sits red faced while glancing back and forth between Mary and Sidney, Charlotte says, 'Mary, with your permission, I should like to send a note to a personage here in London letting her know of my arrival. My Papa in his last post to me has asked me to do so.' Mary responds, 'May I ask to whom?' 'Well, I know this may sound presumptuous, but he asked me to let the Duchess of Kent know.' Mary gasps while Tom's head jerks around to stare at her and Sidney's eyes widen ever so slightly. Now what shall they think of me, Charlotte asks herself, as she sits under the gazes of three pairs of eyes. Mary says, 'If that is what your Father has asked of you, we can hardly deny you the opportunity to do so, but I fear you will face rejection even of delivery of the note. The Duchess is a close confident of Queen Charlotte and the Prince Regent himself.' Tom speaks up with a gleam in his eye. 'Does your Father have the acquaintance of the Duchess, Charlotte?' 'I know not,' Charlotte replies. 'Well,' Tom says, 'you must send your note today. The Lady is a leader of "The Ton" (Regency high society) and as such her influence is without limit. If we can gain her support, all will be well with my Sanditon project. Please take pen to paper and compose your message then we shall see what response it brings.' He calls Collins and after Charlotte completes her writing, sends him out with instructions to see it delivered to the Duchess' Town residence on Grosvenor Square in Mayfair.

Chapter 32

The day dawns bright and clear just two days before the ball. It looks to be a busy day. Mary tells Charlotte and Georgiana that she wishes to use the day to ensure that all will be ready for the rapidly approaching ball. There are baths to take, jewelry to look through and new capes to buy of the latest fashion. Mary tells Charlotte that she will never see a grander ball than the Duchess of Kent's and they all must look their best. Charlotte wonders at the seriousness of the preparations but considers that she knows very little about the requirements of the aristocracy as the daughter of a country gentleman and so she wholeheartedly jumps into Mary's planning and preparations. Georgiana who also is looking forward to the ball, takes Charlotte aside when Mary leaves them for a moment and says, 'I attended several balls in London with Sidney before he brought me to Sanditon, and I can tell you that your Willingden balls and even the Sanditon Ball that we attended are as nothing compared to a London Ball. But Sidney and I were not extended an invitation to the Duchess of Kent's Masked Ball last year, so I can tell you nothing about it except that invitations to it are highly sought after. So why I wonder this year did Tom Parker receive one? He talks as if invitations to this ball are a part of his life but I can assure you that they are not.'

Mid morning comes with a caller at the door. A finely liveried man enters the drawing room where Charlotte, Georgiana, Mary, Tom and Sidney are taking morning tea. He identifies himself as a representative of The Duchess of Kent and begs to speak to Miss Charlotte Heywood. Tom rises and asks for the purpose of his visit and the caller says that he is not at liberty to divulge that other than that he is to deliver a note to Miss Heywood, wait for her response and then follow Miss Heywood's instructions. Tom sits back down with disbelief evident in his face and Charlotte rises. 'I am Charlotte Heywood,' says she. The caller bows deeply to her and says, 'Allow me to present this to you, Miss Heywood,' offering her a letter addressed to Miss Charlotte Heywood in a fine feminine hand and embellished with a red seal. Charlotte extends her hand to take the proffered letter thinking as she does so back to her Father's letter and his instructions. What is this Papa, could you not have told me more? She looks around the room taking in varying expressions of interest mixed with disbelief on the faces of her companions, as even the usually ebullient Georgiana is silenced by this display of regal formality and Sidney seems to be lost in his own thoughts as he looks at her. Charlotte remains standing, opens the letter which is embellished at the top -The Duchess of Kent- and reads;

20 May 1818

Grosvenor Square 1

Dear Miss Heywood

I request your presence at your earliest convenience. If you are able, please accompany my servant who has put this note into your hands and come with him back to my residence forthwith. You are to come alone. There is a lady waiting in my carriage for your comfort and propriety.

I look forward to making your acquaintance.

Susan

⸺⸱⸱⸺

Charlotte turns back to the waiting party and says, 'If you will pardon me, I have been summoned to the Duchess' presence and I am to go now.' Mary objects and says, 'Charlotte, we cannot allow you to go unaccompanied.' Charlotte replies, 'The Duchess has demanded just that, that I come alone. But she has sent a companion from her house who is waiting outside in the carriage. I must go.'

After a not too long journey from Holborn, the carriage bearing Charlotte pulls up in front of a grand house on Grosvenor Square in the early afternoon. Charlotte has enjoyed the ride in the sumptuous carriage and the company of the young lady from the Duchess' house, Lydia, who accompanies her. During the ride, Charlotte has been mulling over the whys of an invitation from this grand personage and what possible connection her Papa could have with her. She is unable to puzzle anything out that makes sense to her. Then the carriage door opens and Charlotte looks out to a handsome man who is extending his hand to help her down. With a shock, Charlotte sees that it is none other than Lord Somerset. What is he doing here, she asks herself? 'Welcome, Miss Heywood,' he says, 'it is a great pleasure to see you again and to welcome you to London. Shall we go in!'

Charlotte and Lord Somerset enter through a wide front door flanked on either side by white columns and walk into a grand foyer unlike anything Charlotte has seen in her life. She thinks back to Sanditon House and the wealth apparent but there is no comparing Sanditon House and this mansion. Lord Somerset walks Charlotte toward some large double doors flanked by two footmen explaining along the way that this house was designed by the Architect to the Prince Regent, John Nash. Yes, I have read of him, Charlotte thinks to herself, as she admires the beautiful Regency striped paper on the walls lined with portraits of handsome men and women, most on horseback. They continue on to the doors, which the footmen open with flourishes and bows, and they enter a grand salon flanked by tall windows that looks out onto a lawn seating area surrounded with budding and blooming red roses. Waiting inside is a elegantly dressed lady of aristocratic features whom Lord Somerset approaches with Charlotte in tow. He says, 'Your Grace, this is Miss Charlotte Heywood.' 'Somerset, Lady Susan, please,' she interjects. 'Yes, My Lady,' says Somerset with a smile. 'And Miss Heywood, this is Lady Susan, Duchess of Kent.' Charlotte curtsies as Susan looks at her intently then smiles and says, 'Welcome to my home, Miss Heywood. It is a great pleasure to see and meet you at long last. We shall retire to my garden and become better acquainted. Thank you, Somerset, for bringing Miss Heywood to me. We shall have a word later, but please excuse yourself for now.' Lord Somerset smiles and says, 'I shall see you a bit later, Miss Heywood, to ensure your safe return to Holborn and to give you a message to carry to Mr Sidney Parker.' He bows and goes out.

Lady Susan leads Charlotte through French doors out into the garden she had seen through the windows to a table set for two where a servant is waiting with tea service. The perfume from the roses is almost intoxicating, Charlotte thinks, and Susan is one of the most beautiful women I have ever seen. She is a rose but what am I, why am I here, a thorn among the roses and what will she tell me? What am I or my Papa to her that I should have privilege of a private meeting with such a personage? They sit and a servant pours for them then takes her departure. 'As I said, Miss Heywood,' begins Lady Susan, 'it is a pleasure to meet you. And, well, you have met

Somerset, whom you know, but perhaps you do not know that he is my cousin and that he is Lord Somerset, Earl of Tewkesbury?' 'Yes,' Charlotte replies, 'I did not know of his particulars, but we were acquainted when he came with Mr Sidney Parker several weeks back to attend the Sanditon Ball and then more recently, he came to me with some information to impart to Mr Sidney Parker a few weeks after the ball. He is a fine gentleman and excellent dancer whom I like very much.' 'Well,' says Lady Susan, 'I'm sure you are wondering what I wish to talk to you about and soon I shall get to it. But first, I feel I must satisfy any questions that you may have?' 'Well,' replies Charlotte, 'I am quite surprised that a daughter of a Country Gentleman should be provided an audience with a personage of your high position, My Lady. My Papa wrote to me before my coming to London that you should require me to call on you, but he said that he was not at liberty to tell me why. I should very much like to know the why of it, My Lady?' Lady Susan smiles gently and then says, 'First, Miss Heywood, Charlotte, I should very much like it if you would call me Susan.' 'Oh, I could not,' replies Charlotte. 'Yes, you must,' demands Lady Susan. Charlotte hesitates, thinking, what is it that I have a Papa who so clearly has a close acquaintance with this noble woman and yet we are but a family of country gentry. I cannot fathom it! Then she says, 'My Lady,... Susan, I shall do my best to meet your wishes in this regard but please forgive me if I should slip from time to time.'

Lady Susan smiles more broadly and then says, 'Charlotte, I cannot promise to satisfy all questions that you may have, but perhaps there are some that will allow us an understanding sufficient for the moment. Permit me to begin with these words. First, I have known your Father since childhood. He has been of immense service to me and to my family and I shall always be indebted to him and your Mother Jane as well.' Charlotte mulls that over for a minute and then asks, 'My Lady,... Susan, what service may I ask did my Father and Mother render that should gain such a debt?' 'Ah, my dear girl...', Charlotte, I should have known that one who has the intelligence and learning that has been reported to me should also have the brains to ask the question that goes to the heart of the matter. And you have asked the question which at this time I, like your Father, am not at liberty to answer.' Charlotte looks into Lady Susan's eyes and sees a yearning, for what she asks herself. She says, 'Then Susan, what can you tell me of the reasons that you should require my presence here today?' 'Well,' replies Susan, 'there is a matter which has come to my attention that I believe endangers your family and mine. I have learned of Mr Tom Parker's problems with his loans and what has been reported to me as mismanagement that could call unwanted attention to my family and to yours as well. I have been advised too that Mr Sidney Parker could also be entangled in money problems with the Sanditon Bathing Town which could lead to scandal and possibly bankruptcy for the Parker family.' 'But,' Charlotte interjects, 'even if that were true, I don't see how that is a problem for your Family or mine. I am only a guest of Tom and Mary Parker. I am acting as a sort of governess for the Parker children and I am helping Mr Tom Parker with this correspondence and bills, but no more than that.' 'Yes Charlotte,' replies Susan, 'but there is something else. I have learned of another entanglement that perhaps could lead to greater concerns.'

Charlotte sits for a few moments in silence looking at Lady Susan and puzzling over what that entanglement might be. Then Susan looks directly into her eyes and says, 'Charlotte, it is my understanding that you have developed some feelings of affection for Mr Sidney Parker. Is that true?' Charlotte tries to look back at Susan calmly, to hide her shock at the question, but discovers that she cannot and despite her best efforts to remain calm, feels to her horror that her face is growing warm. She says, 'Susan, Mr Sidney Parker is a member of the Parker family and I have become well acquainted with him in the short time I have known him and I like him but I believe that romantic attachments do not accurately describe our relationship.' 'Really,' responds Susan, 'this is not what I am hearing from Somerset who has told me that Mr Sidney Parker has your name on his lips very frequently, extolling your beauty, your courage and your grace on the dance floor. Somerset thinks Mr Sidney is quite smitten with you. In fact, Somerset believes he is in love with you.' 'What,' cries Charlotte, her head spinning, 'it cannot be. I do not believe it.' They sit in silence for a few minutes as Charlotte thinks over what she has just heard. She remembers Lord Somerset's words about Sidney's interest in her on the dance floor at the Sanditon Ball and again in the library, Mr Nisbet's comments about Sidney's interest in her, Mary's comments about Sidney coming to see her on the beach the consequence of which was that he saved her life and his attitude toward Mr Stringer's request to call on her. Can it be that Sidney has some small affection for me she wonders? Then Susan continues, 'That is why I asked Somerset to bring Tom Parker's money problems and the danger to Sidney Parker to your attention; so you could take them to him because I thought he would listen to you above all others.' 'And if there should be such a problem, why should it concern you, Susan,' asks Charlotte? 'Because,' she replies, 'if you become more than an acquaintance of Sidney Parker and he is ruined by his association with Tom Parker and his massive debt, your family and mine also could find themselves the subject of unwelcome attention. As I said, I owe a great debt to your Father and shall I say also that I have great concern for your future, neither of which I shall allow Tom Parker's incompetence to bring to ruin.'

As Charlotte sits trying to absorb what she has just heard, Susan rings for the footman and asks him to call Lord Somerset to them. In a few minutes, Somerset joins them and Susan says, 'Somerset, please accompany Charlotte back to the Parker residence. And Charlotte, please take my words to heart. But do not share details of our conversation here with any of them except with Mr Sidney Parker whom I wish for you to take into our confidence to the extent that he is aware of the threat to you of his putting his fortune at risk for his Brother, Tom.' 'But, My Lady,... Susan, I do not think that Mr Parker will take kindly to my meddling in his affairs. He undoubtedly will be angry and rightly so.' 'Well,' Susan replies, 'perhaps if he knows that his entanglement with his brother threatens you too, he will see it differently. I also shall ask Somerset to have a word with him to emphasize that Tom Parker's problems are not his alone but perhaps yours as well if it all goes wrong. And finally Charlotte, before you go, I have something for you.' She turns and picks up a small box which she hands to Charlotte. 'What is it,' asks Charlotte? 'Open it,' replies Susan. She does and discovers a beautifully painted jeweled mask that will cover her eyes and most of her face except for her mouth. 'It is beautiful,' Charlotte says. 'Yes,' responds Susan, 'this is a Venetian mask that I wish for you to wear to the Ball. It is how I shall easily recognize and find you there. I wish for you to be wearing it when you arrive at the Ball and to not remove it until you are safely away. Do you understand?' 'Yes, Susan,' replies Charlotte, 'but why?' 'I cannot tell you the why of it now, Charlotte, but someday I shall. Until then, please just trust that my reasons are what they are because it is best for you and do as I ask.' 'I shall,' affirms Charlotte.

Chapter 33

Friday - 22 May 1818 - London

It is the day of the Masked Ball. The previous day following that of Charlotte's call on the Duchess of Kent had been quiet. Minding Susan's words, Charlotte had been careful to keep her own counsel and despite Tom's curiosity, she had managed to avoid discussion of details from her meeting with the Duchess. And she had not yet had an opportunity to have a moment alone with Sidney to impart the words of warning that Susan had asked her to convey to him. Somerset had come in when he accompanied her back to the Parker London residence and he had had a quiet word with Sidney. But Sidney had as yet said nothing to her about his and Somerset's conversation although on occasions when they had seen each other since her return, she had noticed Sidney's eyes on her when they were together accompanied by a thoughtful expression. And she continues to puzzle over Susan's request or was it a demand that she wear the Venetian mask to the ball and not remove it while there.

The morning of the Ball is spent preparing for the event. Baths are drawn and gowns laid out for Charlotte, Georgiana and Mary. Charlotte has never been so pampered in her life. Her hair has been washed and then once dry, piled into an elaborate coiffure to be crowned later by plumes from some exotic bird. Both of the new gowns that Mrs Smith had made for her in Sanditon have been brought to London. She has a choice of a filmy white muslin or a sky blue silk both with high waisted elaborately trimmed bodices and shoulders, with décolletage necklines and decorated lower skirts ending just above the ankles. Charlotte tries both and has almost decided that the blue will do, but Mary asks her to parade both for Sidney. He professes that the first, the blue silk will do very well, but when he sees Charlotte in the diaphanous white muslin that flows like water around her body as she walks, his breath catches in his throat and he can scarcely breathe out his approval. Mary, who is closely watching Sidney as he views the beautiful vision he is have on his arm at the masked ball, can barely suppress a smile as she says, 'Charlotte, I think that while Sidney says the blue will do, the white is what your Knight whispers is right for you. Do you not, Sidney?' Sidney, who cannot take his eyes off of Charlotte, manages a barely perceptible nod. The choice is made.

Evening comes and preparations are made to go out to the carriage. Charlotte comes down and goes into the drawing room to join a richly gowned Georgiana in red and Mary in gold. Georgiana can barely contain her excitement wondering who will be at the Ball and how many dances she will have. Mary smiles at her and says, 'Georgiana, you should try to slow yourself, or you shall not last out the night.' Sidney and Tom come in and both compliment the ladies on their gowns. They are dressed elegantly in bespoke black tailcoats, black breeches over black stockings with white shirts and expertly tied white linen cravats. Charlotte wonders at her good fortune; to be escorted to a London Ball by the most handsome of men, a man whose beautiful eyes are now focused on her. He starts to walk over to her and just at that moment, Arthur bursts into the room followed by

Diana. 'Well,' says he, 'is this not a first; the Parker family is going to the famous Masked Ball and will we not also be the center of attention because we shall have the most beautiful and eligible young women in London or the world, Miss Heywood and Miss Lambe, in our party! Will you both please hold a place vacant on your dance cards for me,' Arthur concludes with a sweeping bow. 'Of course, we shall,' replies Charlotte; will be not, Georgiana?' Georgiana smiles at Arthur and nods. Tom then asks after sister Susan's health. Diana replies, 'Susan is doing poorly indeed and her husband Wilbur not much better as his consumption is giving him much trouble. Before we leave their house to return to Sanditon, we shall try to find them a physician who will be perhaps somewhat better than useless.' Tom responds, 'Diana, you must insist that they come to Sanditon where the sea air and sea bathing will cure them of all their ailments forthwith.' And with that, they all go out to waiting carriages.

The carriages bearing the Parker entourage arrive on Grosvenor Square to join a long line of elegant conveyances waiting to disgorge their masked occupants. All is excitement in the carriage shared by Charlotte, Georgiana, Sidney and Arthur whom it has been decided will be Georgiana's gallant for the evening. Tom, Mary and Diana have traveled in the second carriage. Their turn to dismount from their transport and enter the house finally arrives. Charlotte takes Sidney's arm and Georgiana Arthur's and they wait for Tom, Mary and Diana before all climb the few steps to enter the house. The grand foyer is full of people slowly winding their way toward the grand salon at the back of the house and the drawing room off of it both of which have been cleared of furniture except for chairs for the ladies to allow for mingling and dancing. The windows are open to provide for air to cool the crowd and the large French doors have been thrown open onto the garden where Charlotte had had tea with Susan. Many are dressed as are Charlotte, Georgiana and the Parkers, in traditional ball attire but a large number are dressed head to toe as royals, sailors, cunning folk, conjurers, chimney sweeps, jesters, ladies of the evening, too many to name, but all are masked.

As they make their way through the press of people talking, laughing and enjoying proffered drinks, a man dressed fancifully as a pirate approaches and welcomes them. Charlotte and Sidney recognize the voice of Lord Somerset. He says, 'Welcome to the Masked Ball. I trust that you will enjoy the evening. Susan at this moment is greeting a very special guest so she could not welcome you herself, but she will come to you later, perhaps with her special guest. We shall see.' He excuses himself with a please enjoy yourselves and goes on his way saying 'I must return to Esther.' Tom says, 'I shall start my rounds to bring attention to Sanditon. This is an opportunity not to be missed and it will be more difficult to accomplish once the dancing begins. Sidney, Arthur, I shall need your assistance with this endeavor as well.' Both nod in apparent agreement and then Tom disappears into the crowd leaving Mary behind. 'So this is to be my evening,' she says. 'Sidney, Arthur, please do not leave your ladies to charge around the house talking of nothing but Sanditon. This is a night to enjoy; a very special evening, the sight of which may never come our way again.'

After they all take a turn around the salon and drawing room, Charlotte suggests that they go out into the rose garden, except for Tom who is yet to reappear, as the heat from the press of people is growing unbearable. It is much cooler outside, and they amble around the garden admiring the costumes and enjoying the cool evening air. Inside they hear the musicians begin to tune their instruments and before long it is announced that the dancing will begin and the Duchess of Kent and guest will lead off the first dance. Sidney looks to Charlotte and asks, 'Miss Heywood, may I have the honor of being your partner for the first dance of the evening?'

Charlotte replies, 'Yes, Mr Parker, it will be my pleasure!' Georgiana who is standing nearby on Arthur's arm looks at them and says, 'For Heaven's sakes, Sidney and you too Charlotte, please call each other by your given names. How long are you going to maintain the pretense that you have not been introduced? You both practically live under the same roof, do you not!' As Charlotte and Sidney stand awkwardly looking at each other after Georgiana's outburst, Arthur laughs and says, 'Well said Georgiana. Indeed this poppycock formality between my brother and his beautiful companion has gone on far too long. If Sidney doesn't start to act like he is in love with Charlotte as I know he is, I shall step in and ask for her hand myself.' Sidney looks like a school boy on hearing those words thinks Charlotte, and here I am blushing like a young girl. Why is it that our desires can be seen so well through others' eyes but not through our own?

As Charlotte and Sidney find themselves wordless while Georgiana and Arthur look on, they hear the first dance being called. Together they walk toward the dance floor where a beautifully gowned lady and a man dressed as a medieval King in a most elegant costume of multicoloured silks with a jeweled dagger sheathed at his side walk to the center of the salon floor. Charlotte thinks to herself that it must be Susan because she is leading the ball off with the first dance and her mask is very like the one that Charlotte herself is wearing. But who she wonders can that elegantly dressed masked King of the Ball be? She has little time for further consideration as the music begins to play and Sidney offers his arm to move onto the dance floor. Charlotte accepts with a smile and she finds herself in Sidney's arms again for the first time since the Sanditon Ball...., no, the first time since she was crushed against his chest in those arms as he rescued her almost naked from the sea. The thought causes goosebumps to rise on her arms to be quickly followed by a blush when she looks up into those most beautiful eyes as they turn and step to the music. The dance ends all too soon as far as Charlotte is concerned. She feels that she would have been content to spend the entire evening in those arms under the eyes of the man to whom she says as they walk from the dance floor, 'Thank you, Sidney,' to which he replies, 'Thank you, Charlotte,' in a tone of voice that causes a delicious shiver to course through her body.

As they walk off of the dance floor, Tom comes to them with a Lady on his arm. He says, 'Sidney, look whom I have come across as I made my rounds. Charlotte, this is Mrs Maria Wickham and she is recently widowed. Sidney did you you know?' 'I did not know, my condolences, Mrs Wickham,' Sidney replies with a almost imperceptible frown that Charlotte notices. Then he turns to Charlotte and says, 'Charlotte, allow me to introduce you to Mrs Wickham.' 'Mrs Wickham,' Charlotte says with a curtsy, 'very pleased to meet you and I am very sorry to hear about the loss of your husband.' Mrs Wickham just looks at her then turns her attention to Sidney and says, 'Sidney, it has been so long and I have been so looking forward to seeing you.' Tom jumps in and says, 'Sidney, you shall surely want to dance with Maria. I know you will have much of interest to talk about. And I have taken the liberty of bringing our Sanditon Bathing Town to her attention as a possible investment opportunity.' Charlotte watches as Sidney casts a irritated glance at Tom then says to Maria, 'Perhaps you did not hear me, Mrs Wickham, when I introduced Miss Heywood who is my guest at the Ball tonight.' Now, Charlotte notices that it is Mrs Wickham's turn to show irritation but after a short hesitation as she searches Sidney's face, she nods her head slightly and says, 'Please forgive me, Miss Heywood, for my lack of civility, but I was so happy to see Sidney after so long that I quite forgot myself.' Charlotte smiles but stays silent and curtsies again while thinking back to Georgiana's description of Mrs Wickham as a witch and her teasing of Sidney in front of her husband the previous year. Sidney says, 'If you will pardon my absence for a time, Charlotte, I shall ask Mrs Wickham to dance.' He offers his arm to Mrs Wickham who gives Charlotte a calculating look before taking Sidney's arm and moving away with him onto the dance floor. As they do, Tom asks if Charlotte will accompany him to look for Mary and they move away though the crowd. Charlotte is wondering as she follows Tom if Mrs Wickham still is interested in Sidney because she seemed quite determined to ignore me as if I was a threat to her for Sidney's affection. Am I she asks herself, am I a threat to Mrs Wickham's designs on Sidney? If not, perhaps I should like to be.

At last, Tom spots Mary and Diana in the crowd and they go up to them. Mary says, 'There you are Charlotte and Tom, where have you been? And Charlotte what have you done with Sidney?' Charlotte replies, 'Tom brought Mrs Wickham to dance with Sidney.' 'She is here,' exclaims Mary! 'She should be in mourning. Her husband was buried not a month back. And Tom, why are you pushing Sidney and Maria together? You know that she broke his heart. She is heartless and I see no good for Sidney in reestablishing a connection between them.' 'Claptrap,' replies Tom, 'Maria is quite charming and she has a great fortune besides. She would be a great investor in Sanditon and if she and Sidney should marry, all the better.'

As Tom finishes speaking, Charlotte sees the costumed woman she thinks is Susan coming toward her with the man whom Charlotte saw her lead off the first dance with. They stop in front of Charlotte and indeed it is Susan who says, 'Miss Heywood, it is wonderful to see you.' 'Thank you, Your Grace,' she replies. 'Allow me to introduce Mr Tom Parker, his wife Mary and his sister Diana Parker.' Introductions made, Susan says, 'My friend here beside me would like to invite you to take to the dance floor with him, Miss Heywood. Please honor him with a dance.' The masked man who stands regally looking down at Charlotte does not say anything but extends his arm. This is odd thinks Charlotte but a smiling

Susan convinces her to accept. They move onto the dance floor as Sidney approaches with Arthur and Georgiana. Charlotte enjoys the dance thinking that she has never danced with anyone who dances so well with the possible exception of Sidney and wonders who could he be. The dance concludes and Charlotte is escorted back to her party. She sees that they all are watching her dance partner, wondering who is the beautifully dressed and masked man with the jeweled dagger at his side? 'Thank you for the dance, Miss Heywood,' the mysterious man says and then to Susan, 'perhaps it is time for me to take my leave' as he extends his arm to her. She takes it and touching Charlotte's hand, says, 'Remember my words, Miss Heywood,' then smiles as they move away gaining Charlotte more questioning looks from the the assembled party, especially from Sidney and Tom. Sidney offers his arm and leaning in close whispers, 'You are a wonder, Charlotte, who are you that you should be be welcome, no not only welcome, sought out by such personages so close to the crown itself? I am beginning to believe that I do not deserve to be in your company.'

Tom cannot contain his excitement at having had the opportunity to make the acquaintance of the Duchess of Kent herself. 'This could be very good for my Sanditon Bathing Town if the Duchess should become interested,' he says. 'But I wonder who her companion was? Charlotte did you gain that knowledge while you danced?' 'No, I did not,' returns Charlotte, 'he did not make me acquainted with his name.' 'But he surely is someone of great consequence to have the Duchess on his arm,' speculates Tom. 'Perhaps he was the Prince Regent himself,' he says with a chuckle, 'but now it is time for our party to make its way back to Holborn.'

As they move toward the front door to call for their carriages, Charlotte sees Mrs Wickham coming toward them. She stops expecting Mrs Wickham to go to Sidney to say goodbye but she walks by him as he looks away from her and continues toward the front door. Mrs Wickham falls in beside Charlotte, takes her arm in a painful grip and leaning in close, hisses, 'You shall not have him,' and then seeing Sidney turning back toward them, releases Charlotte's arm, pastes a smile on her face and says so Sidney can hear, 'It was a great pleasure to meet you, Miss Heywood and Sidney we shall see you again soon.' She takes her leave but Charlotte notices that she glances back and grimaces as Sidney offers her his arm which she takes. So, I have made an enemy, she thinks. Yes, perhaps I have and not one that I can easily defend myself against. If I have another opportunity to talk to Susan, I shall ask her advice.

Outside while waiting for their carriages, it begins to rain. There is nothing for it Charlotte thinks but Sidney removes his coat and uses it as a rain shelter for Charlotte. As she looks up to him gratefully, she notices out of the corner of her eye, a familiar face. Is it Sir Edward? Yes it is and he is standing close by another now familiar face, that of Mrs Maria Wickham as they both huddle faces averted inside a doorway to avoid the rain. They appear to be deep in conversation. What are they plotting Charlotte asks herself? Those are two acquaintances who give me pause because I do not believe that they are friends of mine. Her reverie concludes with the arrival of the carriages and rain that begins to bucket down which, despite the arrival of servants with umbrellas, forces a very unceremonious entry into the carriages. Charlotte finds herself squeezed into the bench opposite Georgiana and Mary with Sidney and Arthur, whose girth forces her almost into Sidney's lap to her mixed sense of mortification and a unfamiliar but not unpleasant feeling she struggles to define. Charlotte, she tells herself, be calm as she looks back at Mary and Georgiana smiling at her from the other bench.

The two carriages arrive in good time back at the Parker residence despite the heavy rain. Charlotte sees Tom and Diana emerge from their coach quickly having traveled in relative comfort with only two of them in the coach although they are soaked to the skin like Charlotte and her traveling companions. It proves more of a production to extract Charlotte's wet group of five. Arthur manages to get out through the door with a helpful shove from Sidney and then the footman hands out Mary and Georgiana. Charlotte is no hurry because she has enjoyed her journey crushed up against a broad chest that she remembers from her rescue from the sea. But this time is different, she notes, because she is aware of the heat and scent of the man next to her during the journey and she finds both to be quite intoxicating. And Sidney too seems to be slow in willing them to separate in the coach and as she looks up at him, he smiles at her and says, 'Thank you, Charlotte, for I believe you have helped me rediscover the joy of living that I had thought lost to me.' He rises, leaves the coach and then extends his hand to help Charlotte down. Yes, thinks Charlotte, this is the man of mystery, the one whose face I could not see in my dreams when I yet was young. But now I see that face, I feel in my heart that it is his, it is Sidney's.

Chapter 34

Saturday - 23 May 1818 - London

Charlotte opens her eyes to a new day, bright and clean after the rain. She throws open the window to her bed chamber and breathes in the freshly washed air. She turns and looks to her ball gown of the previous evening which she had hung up to dry before going to bed and it is almost dry and none the worse for getting wet. Her blue dance boots will take a while longer to dry she sees but will serve her well for many more balls. She smiles to herself as she looks at them and laughs at the thought that those blue dance boots are charmed for they have brought her to her mystery man, to Sidney. Then she blushes at the thought. I am getting my cart ahead of the horse. What would Papa and Mama say to my forwardness. And did Sidney mean anything more than politeness when he said the words last evening that I had helped him rediscover the joy of living. I shall see she thinks as a rumble in her stomach recalls the lateness of the morning hour and breakfast not yet eaten.

There is a knock at the door which Charlotte opens to find Georgiana. Georgiana comes into her bed chamber and says, 'I must see Charles before we leave back to Sanditon. Will you talk to Sidney with me to gain his approbation to allow Charles to call on me here while we are in London?' 'Yes, of course,' replies Charlotte. 'Let us go down to breakfast and if Sidney is there, we shall ask him straight away.' They go down to find Mary and Sidney at the dining table. Sidney rises, smiles and says, 'Good Morning, Charlotte, Good Morning, Georgiana, I hope you both slept well.' 'I did,' both return in chorus, to a broadening smile from Sidney and laughter from Mary. She says, 'So Sidney, you and Charlotte finally are on first name acquaintance. I am glad to hear it.' Georgiana laughs too and says, 'They both can thank Arthur and me for that. I insisted last night at the ball that they stop that Miss H and Mr P poppycock and Arthur threatened to ask for Charlotte's hand if Sidney did not drop the formality. That last threat of Arthur's seems to have worked if nothing else did.' At that, Charlotte finds herself unable to look at Sidney and when she finally does raise her eyes, she sees that Sidney seems to be looking anywhere and everywhere except at her as well. So she thinks, we are of the same mind then. She determines to change the subject and prays that the subject she chooses will silence Georgiana. It does.

'Sidney,' Charlotte says, 'Georgiana would like it very much if you would allow Charles to call on her here before we should return to Sanditon. I shall chaperone the visit of course and perhaps Mary too. I think it would be well if Mary should make Charles' acquaintance.' 'Yes,' replies Sidney, 'Charles may call on you, Georgiana. I know I was perhaps unreasonable in not allowing you to see him. He is a friend of long acquaintance I know, but you are my ward and your Father asked me to protect you on his death bed. Until you reach majority and even after, I shall always try to do that, to fulfill my obligation to him and to you.' 'Oh thank you, Sidney,' replies Georgiana with a huge smile on her face. 'I shall not disappoint you in any way. I know that you take your obligations to me and to my Father seriously and I will honor your and his trust always. Charlotte and Mary, thank you. May I send a message to Charles now to see if perhaps he can call on me this afternoon?' 'Certainly you may,' says Mary. 'It must be today I believe because Tom has made it known to me that he wishes to begin our return to Sanditon on the Monday and if so, we shall have only this afternoon for calls as our tomorrow will be taken with preparations to depart early on the appointed day. And this Mr Charles, does he have a surname that I may know?' 'Yes,' replies Charlotte, 'it is Porteus and he is a childhood friend of Georgiana's.' Following this exchange, Georgiana hastily scribbles a note, a servant is called and he is given instructions where to deliver the message and if he finds Mr Porteus at home to wait for his reply. It is done.

Sidney then looks at Charlotte and asks, 'Charlotte, may I have a word in private?' 'Yes, Sidney,' she replies and they excuse themselves and retire to the drawing room together. 'Charlotte, when Somerset brought you back here after your call on the Duchess of Kent, he told me that she had given you a warning concerning me; that you would tell me what it was in your own good time but if you didn't say anything, that I should come to you and insist that you tell me. So here am I. I beg you to tell me what it is that the Duchess warned you of?' 'Oh Mr Parker... Sidney,' responds Charlotte, 'she wanted me to know about Tom's loans, that you had pledged your fortune in support of those loans and she feels Tom's project will fail and take your fortune with it.' 'But why should that be your concern, or the Duchess' for that matter,' questions Sidney? Charlotte colours a bit, pauses for a little, then says, 'Sidney, Lady Susan believes that you and I... , that is I might have some affection for you...' Charlotte stops as she sees those beautiful eyes focused on her and thinks how forward are you to consider me now, Sidney? She continues, 'Lady Susan is concerned if that might be the situation of our relationship and her concerns about Tom's project should prove true, that it would bring her name and mine, my family's name, into the light of unwelcome attention.' 'But,' Sidney responds looking deeply into Charlotte's eyes, 'why would that be? What connection does your family have with the Duchess of Kent?' 'That I do not know,' returns Charlotte, 'and she would not tell me.' Sidney stands for a moment in silence looking at Charlotte with a combination of puzzlement and what else, she wonders, something, what?

Then Sidney says, 'Charlotte, as we were leaving the ball yesterday evening, I saw Maria, Mrs Wickham, come up to you and take your arm. What did she say? I heard her say it was a pleasure to meet you, but I saw her lack of civility when I first introduced you before Tom sent me to dance with her, so I feel that there was more said than what I saw between you and her. What is it?' Charlotte hesitates and again looks into those questioning eyes, those windows into the soul of this man whose nearness even now with the subject at hand disturbs her, then replies, 'She said, You shall not have him!' As Charlotte blushes at the implications evident in that statement, she watches Sidney's eyes change from a soft caressing look to one hard with fury as his face contorts into anger. 'She goes too far,' he growls quietly deep in his throat almost to himself, 'she almost destroyed me once with her trickery, she will not do it twice and she will not work her wiles on someone I... , on you, Charlotte.'

As Sidney fights to steady himself, Charlotte recalls seeing Mrs Wickham and Sir Edward huddled together in the dark in conversation as they left the ball. She considers whether to say anything about it to Sidney. Should I she asks herself. It probably is nothing but... . Before she can change her mind, she blurts out, 'Sidney, I saw Mrs Wickham and Sir Edward together as we left the ball last night. They were talking about something and I think they were trying to conceal themselves when they were together. Why should that be?' Sidney takes a deep breath and tries to

168

smile. He is not entirely successful, but his face takes on a thoughtful look. 'I don't know,' he says. 'As far as I know, Edward and Maria have nothing in common, but I will talk to Somerset and Nisbet and see what they know or what they can find out. Tom has always thought that Edward is his ally with regard to Lady Denham's investment in Sanditon and has cultivated him with the hope that as titular heir to Lady Denham's fortune, Edward will continue to support him and maintain her investment when Lady Denham passes. But perhaps that is a vain hope. Edward does not strike me as a man who has the interest or temperament to follow in Lady Denham's footsteps in anything. He will spend his days and money in London in frivolous pursuits if he inherits from his aunt and likely have nothing to do with his Sanditon estates except to collect his dividends from them.'

As they stand in silence, Charlotte mulls over what she has just heard from Sidney and she remembers again her Father's warning about people in Sanditon and the need to be careful. That warning is even more important to remember in London, she believes, among "The Ton", the well mannered London high society where avarice and danger may hide behind the welcoming smiles. She raises her eyes up to see Sidney looking at her with yet another expression new to her on his face and realizes how closely they have moved together while talking, so close that Charlotte can feel the heat of his body which for some reason sends a tremble through her. Sidney suddenly says, 'Charlotte, there is a another matter I would like to talk to you about. I wonder if I could ask you if you would consider allowing me to....'

Tom chooses that moment to bound into the drawing room. 'I have the most wonderful news,' he says, 'I have found my physician. I was today walking along Harley Street and my ankle that I injured in Willingden, Charlotte, that your expertise resolved, but today it was paining me, and I determined to look in on a physician. He happened to be a Dr Kniepp, Dr Gottfried Kniepp and as he examined my ankle, I mentioned my Sanditon Spa Town project and I found him to be quite enthusiastic about the benefits of sea bathing. He has great experience and training and has worked in Germany before coming to London in several spa towns. He will come to Sanditon the week soon after our return and we shall explore our future together in the furtherance of enterprise and good health. And I have told him of Susan's and Wilbur's ailments and he will call on them before coming to Sanditon that our poor sister and her husband also may benefit from his expertise. So I can say that our London visit has been a wonderful success for the future of my Sanditon Sea Bathing Town. I have my physician who will give my town even greater legitimacy as the place for the Beau Monde to come on the south coast to improve their health, and I believe I shall have a new and important investor in the person of Mrs Wickham to whom I have extended an invitation to visit and stay without cost in one of our new apartments.'

'What,' shouts Sidney! 'That will be a major expense, Tom. You will have to provide furnishings and servants. How do you plan to pay for that?' 'Do not concern yourself, Sidney,' Tom replies looking insulted. 'We shall work it out and the cost will matter little in relation to the major investment that I expect from Mrs Wickham.' 'Tom, you are a fool,' explodes Sidney. 'You will get nothing from her except the back of her hand. She is using you for what purpose I cannot guess but she is using you as she did me all those years ago. She cannot be trusted. Why can you not understand that? And never again push me to do anything with her, including dance. Maria is in my past and there she shall remain. Do you understand me?' Tom sputters, 'I don't understand you, Sidney. Here you have a chance to marry a fortune and ensure the success of my, our Sanditon Town. Why would you not take it and make all of our futures secure? Charlotte,' he continues, 'don't you

170

agree?' Charlotte looks between Sidney and Tom and asks herself, what am I to say to that? Then, 'Tom, I think it is Sidney's decision about whom he marries. His determinations are his to make,' glancing as she says it at Sidney who appears to be listening closely to her words.

The conversation is interrupted by Mary's entry into the drawing room. 'What is keeping you,' she asks looking at each of them in turn; Tom looking flustered, Sidney angry and Charlotte looking back at Mary and asking herself what is Mary to think of me in a muddle between these two men. But Mary just smiles and says, 'Charlotte Dear, I am in need of your company. Our servant who carried Georgiana's message to Mr Porteus came back with more than an answer; he came with Mr Porteus himself who insisted on coming immediately in answer to Georgiana's summons. He is in the hall and I would like to bring him here to talk a while with Georgiana, you and me.' Tom speaks up, 'Mary, please bring him in. Sidney and I will retire to the parlor to finish our conversation.' 'No,' responds Sidney, 'our conversation is finished, Tom. I wish to be a part of Georgiana's meeting with Mr Porteus.' Tom gives Sidney an angry look and leaves the room. Mary looks questioningly at Sidney and then goes out and in a few moments returns with Mr Porteus and Georgiana. Georgiana looks very happy thinks Charlotte while Charles looks a bit apprehensive especially when he sees Sidney. But Sidney surprises him by saying, 'Welcome Charles , it is a pleasure to see you again. Mary, allow me to introduce you to Mr Charles Porteus if Georgiana perhaps did not. He was but a child of eleven years when I arrived in Antigua all those years back and a playmate of Georgiana's.' Mary smiles welcomingly, invites all to sit and calls for tea.

Charlotte is enjoying the close feeling of family as the group takes their tea. She listens as Georgiana relates to Mary some of what she had told her during their first walk together several weeks back about her life and family in Antigua, and about the roles Charles and Sidney played in it there. Charlotte observes that Sidney is watching Georgiana, who is glowing with happiness, very closely during her telling of her life. I believe he is seeing the world a little differently she thinks. Then Georgiana says, 'Sidney, I would like your permission for Charles to call on me from time to time in Sanditon. I so enjoy his company and he is my connection to my lost home in Antigua.' Sidney looks to Charlotte and then Mary and says, 'I shall allow that, Georgiana, if Charlotte and Mary agree to serve as chaperones during your visits.' Mary replies, 'Of course, Sidney!' Charlotte nods her head in agreement. 'And Charles,' Sidney continues, 'I know you are engaged in trade as I am. I wonder if I could convince you to join my trading company as a partner to help me run my London office? I believe that I shall be spending more of my time in Sanditon going forward...' pausing to look at Charlotte as he speaks those words, 'and I will need someone to stand in for me during my absences.' Charles' face lights up at hearing that and he says, 'Yes Sidney, it would be my great honor to join your company.' Georgiana is delighted and says, 'Oh Sidney, that is wonderful. We shall be a family again. I like family so much better than guardian and ward. Thank you.'

Chapter 35

Charlotte awakens well rested on the day of departure to Sanditon. The previous day had gone quickly with church in the morning and then departure preparations in the afternoon. She and Sidney had not had an opportunity to continue the conversation Sidney had begun when they were interrupted by Tom. But Charlotte had allowed her imagination to run about where Sidney had intended to go with those words as he stood close to her and said, 'I wonder if you would consider allowing me to...' Oh Tom, she thinks, you are a man of dreams and I so enjoy them but sometimes you trample on mine. Well, perhaps Sidney will say his words again in whole without interruption. I can only hope the words end the way I would like for them to. We shall see and now to close my trunk, go down to breakfast to see what the day shall bring.

All are at the breakfast table as Charlotte enters the dining room. Tom is explaining that it has been agreed that Arthur and Diana will remain in London another week to facilitate a call on Sister Susan and her husband Wilbur by Doctor Kniepp. They then will travel back to Sanditon bringing

Dr Kniepp with them to discuss further the possibility of his taking a role as physician in Sanditon, at least during the prime summer months. Sidney asks, 'Will this require you paying him, Tom?' 'No,' responds Tom, 'Dr Kniepp will receive his compensation from his patients. But I have offered him space in one of our buildings at no cost to entice him further to come to Sanditon.' Charlotte expects Sidney to explode again at Tom on hearing that, but Sidney just shakes his head and remains silent for a moment, then says, 'I shall have to go to my work place now to acquaint Charles, who agreed to meet me at my place of business, with my expectations of him as my partner and to introduce him to my foreman and a few of my suppliers in London so that he may immediately be in support of my business. But I shall return by the noon hour to begin our journey back to Sanditon. Charlotte, would you like to accompany me?' 'Oh, yes,' replies Charlotte, 'I should very much like to see your place of business and have a word with Charles before our departure back to Sanditon.' At that, Georgiana speaks up and says, 'I am complete in my preparations to return to Sanditon and I should like to accompany you and say goodbye to Charles, if I may.' Charlotte notices an expression of perhaps disappointment flit across Sidney's face but he says, 'Of course you may, Georgiana,' to Georgiana's delight. Hmmm, thinks Charlotte, well perhaps Sidney and I will not finish that conversation yet again today, but when the time is right we shall.

Charlotte is impressed at the scale and scope of Sidney's business located in a large warehouse in the busy West India Docks area in the Port of London along the Thames. Although Sidney tells Charlotte that he is engaged in the cotton trade as well which comes in mostly through Liverpool, his warehouse in London is dedicated to the wine trade. Indeed his warehouse is stocked floor to ceiling with barrels of wines from France and Spain, Marsala from Sicily and Port from Portugal. After meeting with Charles and making him acquainted with his warehouse foreman and two suppliers, Sidney and Charles agree that he will return to London within a fortnight and bring Charles fully into the fold as a partner and a manager of the enterprise. Leaving Georgiana and Charles alone for a few minutes to say goodbye, Sidney takes Charlotte for a short stroll though the warehouse then when out of earshot of Georgiana and Charles, he stops and says, 'Charlotte, I was unable to finish my words to you Saturday last because Tom interrupted me, but now I beg the opportunity to finish them with your approbation.' 'Yes Sidney,' Charlotte replies, 'please do.' 'Charlotte, I wonder if you might one day consider me as someone who is more than a friend, someone that you might someday consider even as your husband? I have never met anyone like you. You show me the world through fresh eyes, with openness rather than suspicion, with love rather than fear. I am a better man when I am with you, because of you.' 'Sidney,' Charlotte replies, 'you never have been far from my thoughts since I met you in the gale as I walked with Esther back from Sanditon House. I enjoy being with you, I look forward to seeing you at every opportunity so yes, you are more than a friend to me and have been almost from the first moment I met you.' As Charlotte finishes her words, she watches Sidney's face change from serious to joyous. He moves closer, takes her hands in his and raising them, brushes her fingers with his lips. With Sidney's words fresh in her mind and her fingers still tingling from the touch of his lips, Charlotte accompanies Sidney back to gather Georgiana for their return to Holborn. She watches as Georgiana says goodbye and Charles promises to come to Sanditon as soon as he can. Then they board the carriage for the return trip to Holborn.

On arrival, all is in readiness for the departure to Sanditon and they set off. They have an uneventful trip in fine weather to Tunbridge Wells where they are to spend the night, arriving late in the evening. As the Parker entourage goes into the Inn, Charlotte recognizes the proprietor, Mr Catchpole, whom she remembers from her visit to London with Anne and her Papa six years earlier. He recognizes her as well and says, 'Miss Heywood, it has been many years since I saw you with Stephen, your Father. You indeed have lived up to the promise I saw back then to become a beautiful young woman of whom I am sure Mr Heywood is very proud. He spoke of you when he was here just two days back on his way home to Willingden from London.' 'What,' exclaims a surprised Charlotte! 'My Father was here, on his way back from London..., two days ago?' 'Yes,'

175

replies Mr Catchpole, 'he was.' Charlotte continues up to her chamber with Georgiana with whom she is to share a bed for the night. As she settles into her room, she puzzles over the news that her Papa was in London and had not let her know nor indeed as far as she knew, had tried to see her while there. He knew when I was to be in London and yet he did not say or let me know. Why would he not? As her eyes close, she thinks I should so like to sit with my Papa and ask him again about the mystery of Heywood and Kent. I shall write to him at my earliest opportunity.

Chapter 36

The next morning sees an early departure from Tunbridge Wells as Tom is anxious to get back to Sanditon before dark. It is a fine day and the coach makes very good time arriving to a warm afternoon and the scents of the sea which to Charlotte feels like home. She, Mary and Georgiana have shared a bench opposite Tom and Sidney and engaged in off and on conversation amongst themselves about the masked ball and other events and happenings during their London visit. She finds herself looking back at Sidney who seems to never remove his eyes from her, at least so it seems to Charlotte because every time she raises her eyes to his, he seems to be looking directly into hers. It is a happy arrival as the Parker children are pleased to see their Mother and Father after their absence and Charlotte in particular finds the three all competing simultaneously for her attention. She laughs as she enjoys the play with them and notices that Sidney is standing off to the side watching her exchanges with the children with a gentle smile on his face. It is good to be home, she thinks, yes, it is good to be with those you love.

Evening comes. It has been a long two days of travel from London and Charlotte is more than ready to enjoy the comfort of her bed. As she prepares herself for the night, Charlotte thinks to herself of all she has learned from her London travel. I have met the beautiful and mysterious Great Lady of Kent who for some reason has an interest in me, what reason I cannot fathom, and her even more mysterious companion who wished a dance with me but would not divulge his name, nor would Lady Susan. And what of the mask, which Lady Susan demanded, yes it was a demand, that I not remove at the ball? Am I so plain that I should cause embarrassment to her? And if so, why should she care? What am I to her? I am but a country girl, the daughter of a farmer and of the gentry yes, but I am far from the court and those of import to the Crown. And my Father, my humble and quiet Papa, who for some reason has a bond with her that neither he nor Lady Susan will explain, but it is there. And I am at the center of it. Why I do not know but I think I must discover it. My life will not be mine until I know, I shall again write to try for an answer.

Trafalgar House Sanditon

Tuesday 26 May 1818

Dear Papa

Please forgive my dereliction in writing back to you. Somehow the days have flown by and it has been more than two weeks since I received your last post. We have just returned to Sanditon this day in good time and it is very pleasing to me I must say to be back at the shore and away from London which I found to be dirty and confining.

But now I must ask you to reveal to me the mystery of our family's connection to the Duchess of Kent, Susan as she would have me call her. I called on her in response to her demand that you told me would be forthcoming. She is a beautiful lady of high standing in the court of the Prince Regent but I cannot for the life of me determine why she should have an interest in me and she would not reveal it. But more than that, there is a mystery here about why she should, as she told me when we met, be indebted to you and why my affairs are of such great interest to her. I cannot grasp a reason and like with you, she was opaque in providing an answer. And she required of me to be masked at the ball. Yes, it was a masked ball but she asked, no demanded of me, that my mask should not be removed at the ball. I ask that you reveal the heart of this mystery to me for it vexes me greatly.

Now, Papa, I have yet another question. When we passed through Tunbridge Wells on our journey back to Sanditon a day ago, Mr Catchpole brought to my attention that you had just come through from London two days before me on the way back to Willingden. May I ask why you did not let me know that you were to be in London at the same time as I? I should very much have liked to talk to you, to see you, and yet, there was no announcement of your presence. Perhaps there was a note revealing your stay in London and it went astray. If so, I should very much like to know that you attempted it or if not, please advise me as to why you did not wish to make me aware of your presence.

Please forgive, Papa, my being so demanding of you. Know that if it is not within your power to answer my questions, I shall find a way to be content not knowing them from you even if I shall continue to look for those answers asked by myself and to hope that someday soon you will be able to give me the answers I desire.

In closing, I hope Mama and everyone is well and ask that you convey my greetings to them. And if there has been progress made toward determining when Anne might come to Sanditon, I should like to know it as I believe she will find Sanditon as charming and worthy a place to call home as I have.

I am,

Your loving daughter,

Charlotte

Chapter 37

Wednesday - 27 May 1818 - Sanditon

It has been a busy Wednesday as Charlotte and the Parker family have settled themselves back into the routine of Trafalgar House and Georgiana has returned to Mrs Griffiths' care. At breakfast, Tom has resolved to call on Lady Denham and bring her up to date on his progress although he confesses at the table that he really has nothing to report. 'Will you not come with me, Sidney,' he asks? 'I shall,' Sidney replies, 'but I cannot this morning as I have another obligation to fulfill.' 'And what is that,' asks Tom? Sidney does not respond and as they sit in silence, Robert Stringer is announced and he and Tom retire to the drawing room together. After a few minutes, Tom emerges looking upset followed by Robert who wishes them all good day and leaves. Tom says, 'I don't understand what is happening, but Mr Stringer reports that my suppliers are refusing to send building materials. I shall have to send letters to them to see why they will not honor their contracts and do it today. Sidney will you accompany me to see Lady Denham in the afternoon,' he asks? 'I fear that this news will reach her before I can find an answer but I must prepare her for the news if she has not heard it already.' 'I shall,' replies Sidney, 'but first I must call on Georgiana.' Charlotte watches as Tom sighs deeply with relief on hearing Sidney's words. Yes, she thinks to herself, one is the sail at the mercy of the wind and the other the anchor, holding the Parker Sanditon ship from the rocks.

As Charlotte sits musing the drama of the Parker brothers, Sidney says, 'Charlotte, will you accompany me to call on Georgiana? I wish to make sure that she is well and settled at Mrs Griffiths' house. Thanks to you, she is someone whom I can treat again as a sister rather than as a ward. I wish to reassure her that I shall remain a friend and brother while at the same time, she has you as her confidant that she may turn to when she needs sisterly advice and counsel.' 'Yes, of course,' replies Charlotte. 'I shall be ready as soon as I can retrieve my bonnet and cape.' Sidney and Charlotte go out onto the street a few minutes later promising Mary to return before morning tea. Sidney offers his arm and Charlotte takes it wondering what will the gossip be as she is unchaperoned and on the arm of Mr Sidney Parker. I shall not mind the gossip, she thinks, Sidney and I are almost family, almost like brother and sister. Sidney breaks the silence and asks, 'Charlotte, shall we take a detour from our call on Georgiana? I should very much like to take a turn on the cliff to enjoy the sea air.' Charlotte looks up to the handsome, smiling face of the man beside her and says, 'I should enjoy that very much, Sidney!' They continue on past Mrs Griffiths' and then take the lane off the promenade that leads up to the cliff walk. It is a beautiful morning with a soft breeze that smells of the sea and wild flowers. Charlotte is enjoying the feel of the breeze as it swirls her unbound curls below her bonnet. She looks up at Sidney who is keeping his thoughts to himself as he walks quietly along side her. He is looking at me as if he is willing me to say something, but what shall I say, Charlotte asks herself? I am more than content to be as I am on this delightful day on the arm of the most handsome man with the most beautiful eyes in all of the Empire.

Suddenly Sidney stops and turns to her. He drops to one knee and extends his hand. Unsure of what to do, Charlotte takes his proffered hand. 'Charlotte,' Sidney says, 'I know that I have been less than the man I should have been from our first meeting. I have been lacking in proper civility at times and I know that you deserve better than me. But I have loved you since I carried you in my arms from the sea thinking that you were lost to me. I could not bear it then, the thought of living in a world with you not in it and I cannot bear it now. Seeing you take a breath and open your eyes on the beach was the happiest moment of my life. I have tried to become a better man since I have known you and I shall always endeavor to be my best self with you. I love you, Charlotte, and I want to spend the rest of my life with you at my side. Can you love me, Charlotte, will you have me, will you marry me?'

Charlotte stands stunned at the words thinking this cannot be. This is something from my dreams. I must be asleep and soon I shall awake and go about my day as this glorious dream fades from my mind. But willing herself to wake does not change anything about the vision of the man on one knee before her looking up into her eyes and waiting for an answer. She takes a deep tremulous breath and then says, 'Yes Sidney, I think I have loved you since the first moment I saw you on that cliff top road in that howling gale, wet to the skin and offering to take me to warmth and safety of Trafalgar House. Yes Sidney, you are the man in my heart, the man who is my champion. Yes, Sidney, I love you with all of my heart and I shall marry you.' At that, Sidney jumps up with a huge smile on his face and asks, 'Charlotte, may I kiss you?' 'Yes you may,' replies Charlotte. Sidney takes her in his arms and lowers his face toward hers. She lifts her face to his and looks into his eyes before closing hers as their lips meet for the first time. Oh this is bliss, she thinks. This is the delight of man and woman, a closeness and joy unlimited with a man who is to be my husband, with whom I shall have my children, with whom I shall grow old but never regret a minute of my life with him. I know it, I feel it. He is the one, the man of mystery of whom I dreamed as a young girl who is mystery no more. He was not just a childish dream. He is here. He is mine and I am his.

Charlotte is walking on clouds as she and Sidney descend from the cliff tops back down onto the promenade. They stop at Mrs Griffiths' to call on Georgiana for a few minutes. Georgiana immediate speaks up and says, 'Charlotte, you are all aglow. What has happened?' She looks at Sidney and then back to Charlotte, and says, 'He has asked for your hand, has he not?' Charlotte cannot stop a blush and gains a laugh from Georgiana. 'Well then Sidney,' Georgiana continues, 'so you have decided to settle down. I hope you know that you are marrying above your station. Charlotte is a jewel, a prize for any man and I hope you deserve her.' 'Stop it, Georgiana,' replies Charlotte as Sidney stands tongue tied. 'Oh if you only knew,' laughs Georgiana, 'the man who thought he could manage my love life now shall have to manage his own. You shall no doubt have your work cut out for you, Charlotte,' then looking at Sidney concludes, 'but perhaps he is worth it.'

After leaving Georgiana, Charlotte and Sidney continue on to Trafalgar House. They go in to find Mary and Tom in the drawing room. Tom is holding a letter. Seeing Sidney, he says, 'I have received this letter from Mrs Wickham. She would like to take advantage of my offer to come to Sanditon and invest in my town. I must make all haste to find the furnishings and servants so she shall have a good opinion of Sanditon. She says that she is almost at the point of making a decision. We must have all in readiness when she comes.' 'Tom,' Sidney replies, 'you shall have to take furnishings from Trafalgar House and servants too during her visit. You do not have time nor money to procure new furnishings nor do you have the money to hire servants who could meet her expectations.' 'And Sidney,' Tom continues as he appears to not have heard Sidney's words, 'Maria has demanded that you be her escort and guide during her visit. I'm sure that you will find that agreeable.' 'Tom,' Sidney growls, 'do you not remember what I said after the ball just days ago, that I shall have nothing to do with Maria Wickham?' 'But you must, Sidney,' responds Tom, 'She demands it! She has it in her power to ruin me with her influence with the London Banks. Surely you can see that good relations with her are in all of our interests. She loves you still, she told me so at the Ball. She would accept your hand in marriage if you would but offer it. Why would you not, she is beautiful and she is rich?'

'Tom..., Mary,' responds Sidney, 'I have an announcement to make. I have asked for Charlotte's hand and she has accepted.' 'Oh Sidney, Charlotte,' cries Mary, 'congratulations. I am so happy for you both.' 'Thank you Mary,' responds Charlotte. 'Sidney surprised me on the cliff tops just an hour ago. I am so happy.' Tom just stands and looks between Sidney and Charlotte. He clearly is unhappy observes Charlotte. Sidney has thrown his plans to land a big investor for his bathing town into the dustbin. Finally he says grudgingly, 'Congratulations, Charlotte,' but says nothing to Sidney. Then, 'We must call on Lady Denham, Sidney. You promised to accompany me when we talked this morning.' 'I remember, Tom,' responds Sidney, 'let us go now!' Charlotte says, 'I would like to accompany you if I may, Sidney, I should like to call on Clara while you and Tom talk to Lady Denham.' 'Of course, Charlotte,' replies Sidney.

Tom, Sidney and Charlotte arrive in good time at Sanditon House. They announce their intentions and are admitted. Clara emerges from the drawing room and says to Tom, 'Lady Denham, is very angry, Mr Parker. She has been advised that your suppliers have stopped deliveries for your building project for nonpayment by your banks.' 'What,' bleats Tom, 'who is spreading such scurrilous lies?' 'They are not lies,' says Sir Edward as he emerges from the drawing room with a smirk on his face, 'it is the honest truth. Come in to Lady Denham. She is waiting for you.' And he continues, 'Ah Miss Heywood, you are looking uncommonly well today, I must say. To what do we owe the pleasure of your call?' 'Pay him no mind, Charlotte,' says Clara. 'Edward is up to no good and is feeling uncommonly proud of himself for it,' earning herself a scowl from Sir Edward in return. Hawkins then comes from the drawing room and announces Lady Denham is waiting to receive them. Tom and Sidney go in with Sir Edward and the doors are closed.

Clara gestures to Charlotte to follow her into a small sitting room just off of the drawing room. She says, 'I believe Tom is in serious trouble with Lady Denham... Agatha. I don't know what happened nor what Edward is up to but since he came back from London last week, he has had Agatha in a state telling her that her investment in Sanditon Town is at serious risk. She is furious and worried. I don't know the truth of it, but I think that Agatha believes Edward because she is considering withdrawing her investment from the town.' 'That would bankrupt Tom,' replies Charlotte, 'and perhaps Sidney too. She surely would learn the truth of the matter before taking such a serious step because she undoubtedly would not be able to recover her entire investment. It is tied up in the new houses, apartments and buildings.' 'Well, all I know,' responds Clara, 'is that she is considering it.' She continues, 'Charlotte, there is another matter that I should like you to know. I am on the point of leaving Agatha and returning

186

to London. Francis has made his intentions known concerning plans for his future and mine. Perhaps it will include marriage at some point but for now he has offered me a position in his London residence as house-keeper. We enjoy each other's company and my employment there will make our relationship easier. Also, Agatha has made it known to me that my role in her house will not continue much longer. I don't know what her plans are to replace me nor even if she has any, but with Francis' offer and that knowledge in hand, I think it prudent to go now.' 'Have you told Lady Denham, Clara,' asks Charlotte? 'Yes,' she replies. 'Well, I shall miss you, Clara,' responds Charlotte. 'I have valued your friendship and advice.' 'I shall miss you too, Charlotte, but perhaps I shall see you in London as well,' says Clara. 'Perhaps you will, Clara,' replies Charlotte. 'I prefer Sanditon to London but surely I shall visit London more often in the future and I have some news that I would ask you to keep to yourself for now.' She takes a deep, steadying breath and then says, 'Sidney asked for my hand this morning and I accepted.' 'That is wonderful news, Charlotte, if you love him..., do you,' asks Clara? 'Yes,' says Charlotte with a smile. 'I love him very much. Of course, he has not yet asked my Father, but I know he will not say no. I am of age and Papa has always had the confidence in me to allow me to know my own mind and make my decisions accordingly.'

They hear the door to the drawing room open and go out to see Tom and Sidney with Edward and Lady Denham emerging from it. Charlotte notes that Tom has a worried look on his face. Sidney's face is inscrutable, but Edward still has a supercilious smirk on his face while Lady Denham just seems angry. She looks over as Charlotte and Clara emerge from the sitting room and says, 'What have you two been plotting in there?' And then, 'Miss Heywood, I would like a word in private with you. Come in and sit with me for a moment!' 'Yes, My Lady,' replies Charlotte and follows her into the drawing room as Sidney whispers, 'I shall wait for you, Charlotte.'

After the doors close behind them and they are seated, Lady Denham says, 'Miss Heywood, I know you are close to Mary Parker; indeed she is a fine woman. But her husband, Tom Parker, is going to be bankrupted and probably his whole family because of his lack of attention to spending and may I say it, his blindness to anything except his grand overwrought vision for his Sanditon Town. I have been a great supporter, his largest investor, but it appears that he has managed to squander my money and that of many others due to his incompetence. It seems that his largest loan is being bought or soon will be by another investor who I am informed will call it in. That will bankrupt him and no doubt put him into debtor's prison. But that is not the reason I asked you to come in. I have a proposition that I wish to put to you. Clara has made it known to me that she has a romantic involvement that will take her back to London. I will therefore be in need of a companion to replace her sometime in the coming summer. I would like to offer her position to you. I have been impressed by how quick and smart you are and your ability to stand your ground when it is called for. You are nobody's fool. You are like me or at least you remind me of myself when I was a young woman. So, what do you say, Miss Heywood?' Charlotte hesitates a moment then says, 'My Lady, I am honored that you would ask me, but I cannot accept your offer at this time.' 'Why not,' demands Lady Denham? 'Your situation will be much improved over that which you have at Trafalgar House, especially if Tom Parker is bankrupted by coming events. And surely the gossip I have heard about a romantic involvement with Sidney Parker has no foundation?' 'Well, yes,' says Charlotte, 'Mr Parker has this day asked for my hand.' 'Has your Father approved of it,' Lady Denham asks? 'No,' Charlotte responds, 'Mr Parker has not yet had the opportunity to put the question to him.' 'Then he surely will not approve, especially if Tom Parker is bankrupted and takes Sidney Parker with him to debtor's prison as is very likely to happen. Think on it,

Miss Heywood, I shall leave my offer to you open as long as Clara remains in my house, but I shall need to have someone in her position by the time she goes. Now, if you will take yourself out, I must have my morning rest.'

Charlotte goes out to find Sidney waiting for her in the foyer and they begin their walk back to Trafalgar House. Sidney says, 'Charlotte, Tom has managed to put his Sanditon Town project into serious trouble if what Sir Edward said to Tom and me in the presence of Lady Denham is true. He said there is an investor who has bought Tom's largest loan, not one that I pledged my assets to because I could not. I don't know how or why the loan was bought, but apparently the bank wanted to get the loan off of their books and sold it at a discount to the face value because they do not have faith that Tom will be successful. But Edward seemed quite delighted to be in a position to convey the news, which he already had to Lady Denham before Tom and I arrived. She is upset as you probably know.' 'Yes,' Charlotte replies, 'Clara told me. What are you going to do?' 'I don't know,' returns Sidney, 'my own fortune is tied up with other of Tom's loans and if that unknown investor calls the largest loan and Lady Denham demands her investment back, Tom and I both shall be bankrupted because the rest of the loans probably will be called as well if we cannot keep up the payments and I don't see how we can.' Charlotte suddenly remembers Edward's and Maria's covert conversation at the masked ball and says, 'Sidney, you don't suppose Mrs Wickham is involved in this, do you? Remember, I told you that I saw her and Sir Edward talking together as we left the ball and trying to stay hidden.' Sidney knits his brow and takes on a thoughtful look. 'I can't imagine how or why. What possible interest would Maria have in buying Tom's loan?' 'Well,' replies Charlotte, 'she is coming to Sanditon next week, is she not, at Tom's invitation? Perhaps she is interested in investing in Sanditon Bathing Town, or perhaps she just is interested in seeing you again, Sidney!' 'I told Maria that I had no interest in reestablishing any sort of relationship with her, Charlotte,' responds Sidney. 'But,' returns Charlotte, 'she may very well have an interest in reestablishing a relationship with you, Sidney. She does not strike me as someone who takes no for an answer if she has her mind set on something.' As they approach Trafalgar House, Charlotte resolves to write this night to Susan. Perhaps she will know something.

Trafalgar House Sanditon

27 May 1818

Dear Susan:

I am in receipt of some unfortunate news with regard to Mr Tom Parker's Sanditon Sea Bathing Town Project. It seems that Tom's largest loan has been bought by an investor in London, this news from Sir Edward Denham, whom I may say seems delighted by it. He has used this information to stir up Lady Denham to the point that she is considering withdrawing her investment even if it might involve significant loss to her. This is a major worry to Tom and Sidney as well so I wonder if I might impose on you to see what you may find out about that London investor and if the intention to call the loan may be true.

Please forgive my demand on you and thank you for any information you may provide.

I remain,

Your friend

Charlotte

Chapter 38

Tuesday - 2 June 1818 - Sanditon

A week has flown by. Mary has directed an effort to furnish the apartment to be occupied by Mrs Wickham from the best of the furnishings from Trafalgar House. And she also has put her trusted footman, Morgan, her cook Mrs Morgan, and a her own maid into the apartment to care for Tom's guest and hoped for investor. All is in readiness for Mrs Wickham's visit and Tom is euphoric about his prospects of gaining her as an investor who can make his dreams for Sanditon Town come true. Charlotte has enjoyed Sidney's company and attention too as they have taken long walks along the beach and on the cliff tops and talked about their future together. But they both share a sense of dread about Mrs Wickham's visit and looming loan problems that cast a shadow over their happiness. Charlotte has told Sidney about Lady Denham's offer for her to become her companion and Sidney has urged her to consider it, given the uncertain circumstances of the Parker finances. Charlotte also has hoped for a response to her letter to Susan before Mrs Wickham's arrival, but the post has not brought a reply.

Charlotte and Sidney arrive back from their walk in time to take morning tea. They go in to the drawing room and are surprised to find Lord Somerset sitting with Mary. He rises at their entry and Sidney says, 'Somerset, I had not expected to see you here until the high summer ball.' Somerset smiles and says, 'I had not expected to be here either until then but Lady Susan has sent me to have a word with Charlotte. And, I did not need much convincing because it gives me a chance to see Esther.' Mary speaks up and says, 'If you will pardon me, I must go by the apartment being readied for Mrs Wickham to see that all is in order.' She goes out leaving Charlotte with Somerset and Sidney. Somerset's face takes on a serious cast as he turns to them. He says, 'Charlotte, Susan was very concerned when she received your post because it confirmed some rumors that had been circulating about some troubles with the banks. Many are overextended with non performing loans and the bank holding Tom's largest loan is one of the banks in serious trouble and in danger of failing. The bank has been trying to raise capital and looking for investors to take their riskiest loans off of their books. A certain investor has stepped into buy Tom's loan at a large discount to face value.' He stops and looks at Sidney. 'Who is it,' asks Sidney? 'Maria Wickham,' replies Somerset. 'And she will be here tomorrow at Tom's expense,' says Sidney with a rueful smile. 'How wonderful! And now she will own Tom, own me.'

Chapter 39

Wednesday - 3 June 1818 - Sanditon

The day dawns with a promise of storm as lighting flashes from over the horizon out at sea accompanied by low rumbles of thunder. I hope it holds off for the day, thinks Charlotte. I should not wish to see the discomfort of rain added to a day sure to be fraught with enough drama from Mrs Wickham's visit. She goes down to find Tom, Mary and Sidney discussing the coming visit of Mrs Wickham who is expected to arrive from Eastbourne at the noon hour. Tom says stridently, 'Sidney, you must meet and welcome Maria with Mary and me at the apartment. She will expect to see you there as I have already made clear to you. Why do you have to make a simple meeting so difficult?' 'I have already told you the why of it, Tom, and yet you refuse to listen.' 'Yes,' says Tom, 'but now Maria truly holds my fate and the fate of Sanditon Town in her hands as the holder of my largest loan as you related Lord Somerset's news to me. It can only help our situation if you can meet her and be her escort for the duration of the visit as she has demanded. Can you not do this for me, for us all including yourself whose fortune is at risk as well? It will cost you nothing except a little of your time.' Sidney turns to Charlotte and says, 'Charlotte, you know what my objections are to having anything to do with Mrs Wickham. What do you say to Tom's plan?' Charlotte thinks a moment then offers, 'Sidney, I see no way forward except for you to do as Tom asks. Perhaps you can use your time with Mrs Wickham to make her understand that you no longer have feelings for her but you do appreciate that she may have feelings for you even if you no longer reciprocate them. Then she can move on with her life and you with yours.' Tom smiles and says, 'Charlotte, that is a splendid idea. What would we do without you! I am sure that strategy will reap benefits for us all. What say you, Sidney?' 'I still don't like it, Tom,' replies Sidney, 'but with Charlotte's approbation, I shall do as you ask.'

'Shall we go to the apartment,' asks Mary? 'It is approaching the noon hour and Maria will no doubt be arriving any minute. We should not be late in greeting her.' The party of four go out from Trafalgar House and walk the short distance to the apartment on the promenade looking out over the beach and sea. Morgan is standing outside the door with Mrs Morgan and the maid and he reports that all is in place for the coming visit. They only have a few minutes to wait before a carriage pulls into view and continues to a stop in front of the apartment. The footman jumps down and opens the carriage door. Out steps Sir Edward with a haughty look on his face followed by a smiling Mrs Wickham whom he hands down from the carriage. 'Oh Sidney,' she gushes with a brilliant smile, 'it is so good of you to meet me. And Tom, Mary good to see you again as well.' She ignores Charlotte who thinks to herself, so this is how it is to be. I am the unwelcome outlier in this party. Perhaps I should excuse myself to avoid further discomfort. 'Sidney,' she says, 'perhaps I should let you, Mary and Tom get Mrs Wickham settled and I shall return to Trafalgar House.' Sidney shoots a angry look at Mrs Wickham, then speaks up and says, 'No, Charlotte, I should wish for you to stay if you are willing,' staring at Mrs Wickham as she glares back at him. Oh Sidney, you are my champion thinks Charlotte but this is a fight perhaps best not to escalate. 'I shall return to Trafalgar House,' Charlotte says. 'And I shall accompany you Charlotte,' responds Mary. 'Tom, Sidney and the servants are quite sufficient to get Mrs Wickham properly settled and there is no need for either you, Charlotte, or me to do anything more here. Mrs Wickham and Sir Edward are here on business and need to discuss matters before them without distraction.'

Charlotte and Mary walk slowly back toward Trafalgar House after leaving the apartment. Mary says, 'Charlotte, I wonder if Sidney will tell Mrs Wickham that he is engaged to you?' 'I don't know,' replies Charlotte, 'but if he does, I hope he says it in a way that is sympathetic to her love for him. She is not someone to trifle with and I fear that she could be a formidable enemy.'

They arrive at Trafalgar House to see Esther at the door. They go in and Mary asks if she would like to join them for tea. Esther accepts and they sit in the parlor. She is animated and can barely contain herself; she sits and then stands again. Suddenly she blurts out, 'Charlotte, Mary, I have wonderful news. Lord Somerset has asked me for my hand, and I have accepted.' Charlotte jumps up and hugs Esther. Mary says, 'Congratulations, Esther. Does Lady Denham know?' 'Yes, she does,' replies Esther. 'Somerset asked me at Sanditon House and then we told her. She is very happy for me. I am a worry off of her mind she told me.' 'How wonderful,' cries Charlotte. 'Have you decided when the wedding shall be?' 'No we have not,' replies Esther, 'but Somerset is on his way back to London now and I expect that we shall be married shortly after the high summer ball here in Sanditon.' 'Will you live in Sanditon then,' asks Charlotte, 'or perhaps London?' 'I am not sure,' Esther replies. 'Somerset has a London home in Mayfair and his Tewksbury estate and I am sure we will share our time between them. But

Somerset has spoken of purchasing an apartment or home here in Sanditon on the sea as well. He enjoys the sea air as do I, especially in the summer months. I believe that your enthusiasm, Charlotte, for Sanditon has rubbed off on him and he quite values Sidney's company as well and Sidney has made it known to him that Sanditon has become ever more a place he wishes to call home, especially over the last few months. So I expect after marriage that at least part of our year will be spent here.'

'I am so happy for you, Esther,' says Charlotte, 'and I have some news as well. I am to be wed to Sidney.' Esther hugs Charlotte and laughingly says, 'I was wondering how long Sidney could resist your charms, Charlotte. Congratulations. Perhaps we shall see a double wedding. The Reverend Mr Hankins will have his work cut out for him but I am sure he will be up to the task.' Esther continues, 'Now if I could but settle my brother Edward. I fear he is untethered to reality. He is concerned for his future. He is not in high favor of Aunt Agatha because of his drinking and womanizing and perhaps he believes that she will not leave him her fortune when the time comes. He has been making frequent trips to London and I believe he is deliberately trying to turn Aunt Agatha against the Sanditon Town project. I think he is plotting something, but I know not what. Tom should be cautious around Edward, Mary, and not reveal too much of his business to him in my opinion. And Charlotte, please be careful around Edward, he is I believe obsessed with you.' 'I shall,' replies Charlotte. 'Well,' Esther concludes, 'I must be on my way,' and she goes out after goodbyes are said all around with promises made to call again soon.

Charlotte sits quietly with Mary after Esther's departure thinking about what Esther had said about Sir Edward and his plotting. So, I think Esther's instincts are right. Edward is plotting and he is plotting with Mrs Wickham to somehow harm the future of Sanditon Town but why? And she recalls Mary's earlier warning about Sir Edward to never let him get you alone. She asks, 'Mary, why did you warn me about not letting Sir Edward get me alone with him?' 'Well,' replies Mary, 'his reputation around young women is not the best. I don't know anything specific about him, but there are enough rumors about misbehavior that I worry there is truth to them.'

As Charlotte mulls that over, she hears the sound of voices outside the door. It opens, Sidney and Tom come in. Tom says, 'Mrs Wickham seemed pleased with her accommodations and I am sure that she already is seeing the value of her investment in the quality of the workmanship and the potential of Sanditon as the summer destination of choice for the London Beau Monde. And she was very appreciative of your presence to welcome her to our beautiful shore, was she not, Sidney?' 'Oh yes,' responds Sidney, 'she treated me like she owned me and Tom, did you not see the smirking Edward and her glances to him as you extolled your vision of Sanditon to her? In my opinion, she is not here as an interested investor, she is here for something more and I don't believe it is your good that she has in mind.' 'Balderdash,' blusters Tom, 'surely she can see the potential of Sanditon and of the great return likely on her investment. And you Sidney, you could have been more solicitous of her. She asked for a private moment with you and you refused her. If you would but accede to her requests, I am sure that all will be well.' 'Tom, Maria has no interest in Sanditon as an investment. Her "investment" will be used as a cudgel to get what she wants. That is the woman she is,' exclaims Sidney! 'She is not your friend nor mine.' Mary speaks up, 'So what now, do you know how long she plans to be here and what obligation does she now, being the holder of your largest loan, impose on you, on us, Tom?' 'Well,' replies Tom, 'tomorrow she wishes to see the state of completion of our construction and she wishes to know if I have resources enough to complete construction. I am sure that she will be pleased.' 'But Tom,' asks Sidney, 'do you have the wherewithal to complete the construction without the need of further funds?' 'Perhaps not,' says Tom laughing nervously, 'but I am sure funds will be forthcoming when they are needed.' 'And,' asks Sidney, 'where will they be forthcoming from? Are you not now again behind in paying your suppliers and perhaps your workers as well? I have put the bulk of my fortune at risk to back the other two loans you have and that says nothing about the outcome if Lady Denham should decide to withdraw her investment as she threatened to do just last week.' 'Do not concern yourself further, Sidney,' Tom huffs impatiently, 'it will work itself out. Perhaps other investors will be forthcoming now that Maria has taken a ownership interest in my Sanditon Town. And I shall enquire of Arthur if he might consider an investment.'

Tom continues, 'But to speak of Arthur and other more immediate matters, he and Diana will be arriving tomorrow with Dr Kniepp whose presence will add luster to Maria's perspective on Sanditon I am sure. And I shall have to spend the bulk of my day with him to discuss his needs and consider where he might house his practice. I shall expect you Sidney to address any needs or questions that Maria may have.' Charlotte looks at Sidney and sees him exchange glances with Mary on hearing Tom's comments and demands and wonders to herself how a man like Tom who has such a wonderful vision can also be so blind to his own difficulties and the concerns he creates for those around him. This is obsession perhaps that excludes all except the goal but the means of attaining that goal are something that escapes him. He may be a visionary and a dreamer but he is no businessman. And did he not hear Sidney's wish to avoid Mrs Wickham? Here Tom is again pushing them together when he should know that is last thing Sidney wants.

Chapter 40

Thursday - 4 June 1818 - Sanditon

The morning dawns and Charlotte awakens to memory of yesterday's conversations centered on Mrs Maria Wickham. She feels that events are building to a confrontation of some kind between Sidney, Tom, Mrs Wickham and Sir Edward. Tom's obsession is driving the Parker family toward disaster, she believes, and she wishes that there was something she could do. She goes down to find Mary alone. 'Where are Tom and Sidney,' she asks? 'They have gone out,' Mary replies. 'Tom has gone to the hotel. It turns out that Arthur and Diana came home last night with Dr Kniepp. Dr Kniepp was lodged in the hotel and as soon as Tom received Arthur's note this morning, he determined to call on Dr Kniepp. Sidney has gone out as well, I think to see to the needs of Maria although he was in a terrible mood because he did not wish to go. He did request that I ask if you could be so kind as to join him at the apartment after you had had your breakfast. I believe he does not wish to spend any time more than necessary in Maria's company, especially not alone.' 'I shall go immediately,' cries Charlotte. 'I should walk with you,' says Mary, 'but I cannot just now.' Charlotte relies,

'It is but a very short way, Mary, and I will be fine to walk by myself.' She readies herself and goes out.

As she walks toward the apartment through a construction area deserted of workers or people, she suddenly finds herself in the grasp of someone who has come up behind her. A hand is clasped over her mouth and she is dragged into a nearby alley. Struggling to free herself, she bites down hard on the hand over her mouth eliciting a shout of pain from the owner of the hand and a release from the hands holding her. She turns to see Sir Edward holding his injured hand. Before she can do or say anything, Edward says, 'I only wanted to talk to you Charlotte, there was no need to injure me.' 'To put your hands on me and drag me into an alley is no way to talk to me, Sir Edward,' Charlotte responds as she strives to hide the storm raging in her while putting her disturbed bonnet and clothing back in place. 'And please do not call me Charlotte. I have no wish to know you better.' 'But you must see that I have affection for you, Miss Heywood. I have several times tried to make that known to you but you have ignored my advances on every occasion,' Edward replies. 'I am engaged to Sidney Parker, Sir Edward,' responds Charlotte. 'I have no interest in you and I know that your intentions are not honorable because your aunt told me that you must marry a fortune and I do not have one as you know.' 'Oh don't you, Miss Heywood, that is not the story I have heard,' smirks Edward, 'and in any case, you shall never marry Sidney Parker. Maria Wickham has designs on him and he will be unable to resist her, shall I say, charms.' 'Sir Edward, I shall not stand here with you in the shadows,' replies Charlotte. 'If you wish to talk further to me, let us do it as we walk to Mrs Wickham's apartment.' 'Very well,' replies Edward, 'let us continue.' As they begin walking, Edward tries to take Charlotte's arm but she shakes him off. He snarls, 'Soon you shall do as I wish and Sidney Parker will have no say in it.' They arrive at the door and Morgan opens it. He looks at Charlotte and Sir

Edward and asks, 'Are you alright, Miss?' 'Yes Mr Morgan,' she replies, 'is Mr Sidney Parker here?' 'Yes, he is, Miss Heywood,' Morgan responds, 'he is with Mrs Wickham in the drawing room.'

Mrs Wickham and Sidney look up at Charlotte's and Edward's entry. Sidney rises and comes to Charlotte. 'Are you alright,' he asks? Behind him, Maria laughs and says, 'So you were successful in intercepting this little chit, Edward! I hope you were able to further sully her no doubt already soiled reputation.' Sidney wheels around and looks at Maria with disgust. He says, 'Be careful, Mrs Wickham you are talking to my betrothed.' "You shall never marry her, Sidney, I shall not allow it. I own you,' she replies. As Sidney stands trembling with rage, he glances to Edward who is nursing his hand. He sees the bite mark and asks, 'Charlotte, did he put his hands on you?' Edward does not give Charlotte a chance to answer before sneering, 'I did and she was quite amenable to it. The bite was just love play.' Sidney looks at the state of Charlotte's clothing then steps toward Edward, his face and lips pale and tight with fury. 'I shall have satisfaction, Edward. And if you ever touch Miss Heywood again, I will kill you.' Charlotte sees the fear in Edward's eyes as he steps back from Sidney's raised fists. She reaches for Sidney's arm and says, 'Please don't Sidney, he is not worth it.' Sidney looks down at her pleading face and his face softens. Then Maria speaks up again and says, 'If you do not marry me Sidney, I will destroy you and your family.' 'I have pledged Miss Heywood my troth, Mrs Wickham, and even if I would break it, I cannot,' replies Sidney. 'That is no matter Sidney,' says Mrs Wickham. 'Charlotte will release you from your commitment, won't you Charlotte,' she says with a mirthless smile. Charlotte looks to Sidney then back to Mrs Wickham and says, 'I would release him if he should ask me because I love him, Mrs Wickham, as I am sure from your tactics that you do not. Sidney is not someone to be possessed or owned just as you would not wish that to be your condition. He is someone to share with in an equality and in a partnership as man and wife.' At those words, Sidney smiles at Charlotte and says, 'Let us go out from here, Charlotte, and return to Trafalgar House,' to which they hear back from Maria a parting, 'which shall be mine soon enough along with all the rest of this miserable fishing village.'

As Charlotte and Sidney walk back toward Trafalgar House, Sidney asks, 'Did Edward hurt you Charlotte? I should have beaten him to within an inch of his life. How dare he put his hands on you. I cannot bear the thought of it, that he would manhandle you, my Dearest Charlotte!' 'I am alright Sidney,' Charlotte replies. 'In his heart, Edward Denham is a coward and I am sure he will never touch me again. I saw his face when you threatened him. But what are we to do about the loan now owing to Mrs Wickham? She is sure to try to ruin Tom and through him, you.' 'Charlotte,' Sidney asks, 'shall we walk a little longer, perhaps on the cliff top? There is a matter that I wish to discuss with you and you alone before we return to Trafalgar House.' 'Yes, Sidney,' Charlotte replies.

They continue in silence for several minutes as Sidney appears to be deep in thought. Finally he stops, turns to her and says, 'My beautiful, my dearest Charlotte, I have been all morning thinking about this conundrum of money and obsession and I know now that this is my fault...,' seeing Charlotte start to object, he continues, 'yes it is. I enabled Tom to spend above his means. I should have been watching over him, taken a larger role. I am his Brother and it was my obligation as his Brother and as a member of the Parker family to do my best to help him manage his finances as he should have. But I did not and now Tom and I, indeed all of the Parker family, may pay the price. But I cannot allow you to pay it, pay for Tom's and my missteps. And today as I listened to the corruption and conspiracy that is Maria and Edward, I realized the magnitude of my mistake. And, my sweet Charlotte, I cannot, I will not make you a part of paying for it. Charlotte, I cannot marry you! The scandal of Tom's bankruptcy and mine sure to follow will engulf you too. I shall not allow it.'

Charlotte stands in shock thinking how can it be, can it be true that the man I found, the man of my dreams, the man I love, the man who loves me, may be lost to me because of another man's obsession? Charlotte replies in a quavering voice, 'Sidney, I understand, but there is still a chance that all will be well.' 'Perhaps,' replies Sidney, 'but not if Maria can help it. I must return to London forthwith to see if I can find other sources of financing. And Charlotte, I did not tell you this before but I saw Somerset again after he came to Trafalgar House to talk to you on Tuesday, and I told him of our intended marriage. He told me, no he demanded of me, that this disastrous Sanditon Bathing Town project be resolved before I marry you. He said Lady Susan knows of our affection for each other but our marriage is something that she will not accept unless Tom's… our financial difficulties can be resolved. I do not understand what her role in our marriage might be, and Somerset could not or would not elaborate on the why of it, but he said that I should not underestimate her power. But that is no matter anyway because as I have said, I cannot and shall not make you a part of our Sanditon financing quagmire.'

The day turns to afternoon and tea time. Sidney and Charlotte join Mary while Tom still has not made an appearance. But as they sit down to tea, Tom comes in accompanied by a man of indeterminate age whom he introduces to be Doctor Kniepp. As he and Sidney exchange courtesies, Charlotte observes that he appears to be a kindly man as he turns from Sidney and greets her and Mary with a sweeping bow and says, 'This must be Fräu Parker of whom I have heard so much,' and then turns his twinkling blue eyes on Charlotte. 'Fräulein,' he says, 'you are a vision indeed.

And I presume that you are the Miss Heywood with whom I am more than pleased to make an acquaintance. Mr Tom Parker has apprised me of your skills at attending to sprains, wounds and such, and I am in awe of what I have heard about you. I hope I can look to you for assistance when needed here in Sanditon. I shall have to share my time between London and here as my patients, those who Herr Parker has assured me will be here in great numbers during the summer, will likely return to London for the most part for the rest of the year. But there will also be times in the summer when I may not be here and if I could depend on you for some of those unavoidable absences, it would be very well indeed for my practice.' Sidney speaks up and asks, 'so you will keep your clinic on Harley Street then?' 'Oh yes, Herr Parker. But this situation will suit me very well because many of my London patients need spa treatments which I am well trained to provide and I believe that Sanditon will be a perfect compliment to my London practice.' 'Yes,' says Tom, 'I told you, Sidney, of the value of a physician here in Sanditon and Dr Kniepp with his wealthy patients in London will be well positioned to provide the care they need in our bathing town where the sea and the air will restore their spirits as well as their bodies. We have just come from Lady Denham's and she was quite enthusiastic about having such a fine physician as Dr Kniepp in our town, was she not, Dr Kniepp?' 'Well,' he responds with a laugh, 'I am not sure I should use the word enthusiastic but she will perhaps see more value in me as time passes. But now I must return to my hotel and rest because tomorrow I shall return to London. So for now, I bid you all Good Day,' and goes out with Tom.

So, thinks Charlotte, Tom has his physician and perhaps his dream is closer to realization but for Mrs Wickham. She looks up from her thoughts and sees that Sidney is watching her. He smiles and says, 'So Charlotte you are to become a surgeon in Dr Kniepp's sea bathing infirmary as well as Tom's coadjutor for his Sanditon Sea Bathing Town and Lady Denham's companion. If we could but solve the conundrum of money, all would be well, except that I should never see you because you shall be always employed to other persons' demands except for my own.' 'I shall always have time for you, Sidney, to the exclusion of all else,' replies Charlotte to smiles from Sidney and Mary.

Chapter 41

Friday - 5 June 1818 - Sanditon

Charlotte awakens to sounds of birds enjoying themselves under the eves in the bright and warm June morning following her restless night filled with dreams that included Sidney and Mrs Wickham. Sidney is to leave for London this morning and Charlotte hurries down to breakfast to find Tom and Mary. Looking around with disappointment plain in her voice, she asks 'Oh, where is Sidney? Has he gone already?' 'No he has not, and would not without a proper goodbye,' comes a voice from behind her that raises those now familiar goosebumps and she turns to see Sidney looking down at her with a smile. Charlotte blushes and wonders what Mary and Tom think of her as Sidney takes her hand and leads her from the dining room into the drawing room where he takes both of her hands in his and pulls her close. 'I must be on my way to London and Mrs Wickham where I can only hope to reach an accommodation with her on this loan and I must see Charles to bring him fully into my business as I promised him I should. We shall see what the cost of Maria's infatuation with me may be but whatever it will be, I shall be willing to pay it if the end result is that the banns can be read so that you can become my wife.' 'Please do not be gone too long, Sidney, I shall miss you, how much you cannot know,' replies Charlotte. 'I shall return as soon as I can,' Sidney says with a smile, 'you may be sure of it,' as he brings his lips to her hands.

In the afternoon, Charlotte determines to call on Georgiana. She walks the few steps from Trafalgar House to Mrs Griffiths' where she goes in to discover Arthur and Diana also are there. As she enters, Charlotte overhears Arthur regaling Georgiana with a report that they shall soon have a physician in residence in Sanditon which he and Diana quite look forward to. Georgiana jumps up with a welcoming smile as Charlotte comes in. 'Charlotte,' she says, 'have you heard the news that we are to have our own physician here in Sanditon?' 'Yes,' Charlotte replies, 'I met the man, Dr Gottfried Kniepp, and he seems quite enthusiastic to begin his practice here.' 'Oh yes,' responds Diana, 'Arthur and I thought he worked miracles with our Sister Susan and husband Wilbur with his consumption, before we returned to Sanditon with him. And Arthur and I with all of our ailments will benefit greatly from his presence here. He was trained in the great spa towns of Baden Baden and Wiesbaden you know and he will bring those skills here to us and I am sure that Arthur and I will benefit greatly, will we not Arthur.' 'Yes, indeed,' he responds, 'we both shall be blessed with great health soon with Dr Kniepp's help.'

'But to you, Charlotte, what news do you have for us,' Arthur asks with a smile? 'I am lately apprised that my threat at the masked ball to ask for your hand has created an urgency in Sidney that led him to ask for your hand before I could. Is that true?' Charlotte blushes and says with a laugh, 'Yes it is true,' to smiles and congratulations from Diana and Arthur, 'but we shall have to wait a while for Sidney to resolve a matter of debt with Tom's Sanditon Bathing Town Project.' 'Yes, we know of it,' responds

Arthur. 'I have offered my small fortune as has Diana in the furtherance of that goal. If Sidney accepts, perhaps it will go in some small way toward resolving the most important matter at hand, your marriage.' 'And a sum of my fortune as well, I have offered Sidney, as a wedding gift to Charlotte,' says Georgiana. 'Of course he will not accept it, but in less than two years I shall attain my majority and then I may put my money where I wish and I wish it to go to ensuring the happiness of the woman who made Sidney a brother to me again, and that woman is you, Charlotte.' 'I could not take it,' responds Charlotte. 'Well, perhaps you shall not need it,' says Georgiana, 'but it will be yours anyway.' What wonderful friends and family I have found here, thinks Charlotte. How lucky was it that a carriage overturning in Willingden should have brought me thus to such happiness. She says her goodbyes, promises to see Georgiana again soon and in good spirits walks in the company of Arthur and Diana back to Trafalgar House where they say their goodbyes and continue on their way.

Charlotte goes in to have a letter placed in her hands by Morgan who says it was delivered at the door while she was out. It is in a feminine hand with which she is unfamiliar. She takes it and goes into the drawing room to read. Opening it, she glances quickly to the bottom where she sees with a shock the name; Maria Wickham.

4 June 1818

Sanditon

Miss Heywood:

I know that the intercourse in our two meetings including today's have not been pleasant, neither for you nor for me I can assure you. But you must understand that Sidney was my love long before he ever met you. I did love him and do love him still despite your opinion to the contrary and you must know that my marriage to Mr Wickham was not my choice, but my family's. I have dreamed of the day that I should be reunited with Sidney and I shall be reunited with him despite his passing affection for you.

You must realize that Tom Parker and perhaps Sidney too will go to debtor's prison if they are not saved from Tom Parker's extravagance. I am the one who can save them, save Sidney from the ignominy of bankruptcy and debtor's prison. I shall be returning to London tomorrow where I shall hope to meet with Sidney at the earliest opportunity and make it clear to him that you are an impediment to his and to my happiness. He will live in wealth and comfort as will Tom Parker and the rest of the Parker family if you will but step away. You told me that you should if Sidney would but ask you. I don't believe, because he is the gentleman that he is, that he will ask you to do that so I ask you on his behalf to renounce your engagement and free him to marry me. It is to be your decision but know that, if you truly love Sidney, it is the right thing to do to secure his future.

Maria Wickham

Charlotte sits back with her mind in turmoil. How, she wonders, does Mrs Wickham see herself as capable of love. Is love to her something she thinks can be bought? I cannot bear the thought. Oh I wish you were here, Sidney, that I could talk to you, to let you know again that you must do what is best for you and for your family. As she looks up to a sound, she sees Mary through a sheen of tears. Mary cries, 'Charlotte what is the matter?' Charlotte in her anguish cannot speak and wordlessly hands the letter to Mary who reads through it quickly. Mary finishes reading, spreads her arms wide and Charlotte goes into them. She says, 'Charlotte, I did not know the financial situation was so bad, but I am sure of one thing and that is Sidney will come back to you. I know he loves you dearly, Charlotte.' 'But what if he cannot,' cries Charlotte, 'what if he must marry Mrs Wickham? I cannot bear to think of it. And if he must, I shall have to go and never see him again nor any of you, Mary. What shall I do? I cannot be the means by which Mrs Wickham destroys Sidney, destroys you all.' After sitting with Mary a little longer, Charlotte wishes her good night and retires to her bed chamber. Once there, she looks around the room that has been hers for more than two months in a place that she has come to think of as home. Perhaps, she feels, it was not to be, my dreams are not to be realized and I must go to save Sidney, Mary and the Parker family. She resolves to write to Sidney.

Sanditon

5 June 1818

My Dearest Sidney:

I am missing you greatly and I wish you could be here with me so that I could talk to you instead of writing. But perhaps on paper, I can put my thoughts more clearly to your benefit and mine and perhaps if you were in my presence, I should not have the courage to do what I feel I must.

Today I received a post from Mrs Wickham making it very clear that she holds your fate, your very life in her hands and Mary's and Tom's as well. She professes to love you and perhaps in her own way she does. But, she told me in her letter that your rescue from the debt weighing on you and the Parker family rests on my releasing you from your obligation to me. I hereby do that so that you may be free to take whatever steps, including marriage to Mrs Wickham, that you must to resolve the debt that hangs over Sanditon and you.

Having made this decision, I feel it is best that I leave Sanditon and return to Willingden. I pray a miracle will happen that yet will allow us to be together, Sidney, because I love you with all of my heart. But I cannot be the one who would be the reason that the Sanditon dream is destroyed, who would be the cause of your destruction, who would put you in debtor's prison. So I shall go.

I shall always be your,

Charlotte

⸱ ——— ⸱

After completing the letter, Charlotte retires to her bed thinking about the conundrum and pain of having a dream come true and then finding that it is lost to you. I found the man of my dreams, my man of mystery and now I have lost him. She cries herself to sleep.

Chapter 42

Charlotte awakens after a restless and almost sleepless night. She rises to a blue sky day that on any other would inspire her to take a walk on the beach to enjoy the sea air and the sounds of the sea washing onto the shore. But today is a day of her doom she feels; her resolution to depart Sanditon and return to Willingden, leaving behind all that she has learned to love over the last two months and especially to leave with her heart broken is a matter that weighs heavily on her as she dresses. She goes down with her letter to Sidney in her hand. Her plan is to post it before she loses her resolution to do so and she sees Morgan. 'Oh Mr Morgan,' she says, 'you have returned from Mrs Wickham's apartment.' 'Yes, Miss,' he replies, 'she left yesterday to return to London. And may I say, that I am very happy to be back at Trafalgar House. I don't wish to speak ill of Mrs Wickham, but she is the most unkind person I have ever had the occasion to be of service to. She was most demanding and unthankful, especially of the Missus. Nothing I nor the Missus nor the maid did was good enough for her. And if you will forgive me for speaking ill of her, she was most indelicate with her affections toward Sir Edward. And he was most scandalous in his actions toward her and I must say that she did nothing to discourage it.' 'Do you think them to be romantically involved,' asks Charlotte? 'I don't know,' he replies, 'but if I may say, Sir Edward is no gentleman despite his airs and Mrs Wickham..., well I do not wish to speak ill of her or any woman, but...!'

I must think on this, Charlotte muses to herself. Mrs Wickham professes to love Sidney, but she does not seem to balk at encouraging Sir Edward if what Mr Morgan observed is accurate. But how can I relate this to Sidney without his thinking badly of me. I cannot but trust that he will see her for what she is. I believe he already does, but it does not change anything about my need to allow Sidney to make the best decision for himself and his family and so I must post my letter and say nothing of Mr Morgan's observations. To that end, she asks Morgan if he will convey her letter to the post inn. He takes the post from her then asks, 'Are you alright, Miss Heywood? I fear that you are not happy, for what reason, I know not.' 'Thank you, Mr Morgan, you have always been most kind to me. I would ask you if you could help me bring down my trunk as well and perhaps wheel it down to the post inn along with my letter.' 'You are not leaving us, Miss Heywood, tell me you are not,' he responds. 'I am afraid I must,' replies Charlotte. 'I shall return to Willingden on the afternoon coach.' 'But you will come back to Sanditon, Miss Heywood,' he asks? 'That I do not know,' she says as Mary enters the room.

As Morgan goes out with Charlotte's letter in hand to retrieve her trunk, Mary cries, 'You are not planning to leave us?' 'I am afraid I must, Mary,' replies Charlotte. 'You read Mrs Wickham's letter and I shall not be an impediment to saving Sidney and your family from the work house. I have written to Sidney to inform him of my decision and Mr Morgan is on his way to posting it as we speak.' 'I shall not hear of it,' replies Mary, 'you cannot leave us. You have been the means of restoring Sidney and Tom has grown to depend on you although he would not acknowledge it, and the children and I have grown to love you as family. How shall we live without you? I can tell you now that Sidney cannot.' 'I am sorry, Mary,' responds Charlotte, 'but I have made my decision. I shall not have time to say goodbye to everyone as I should but I must call on Georgiana before I go.' Charlotte hugs Mary tightly and then goes out to the short walk to Mrs Griffiths'.

Charlotte goes in to find Mrs Griffiths in a state. 'Oh Miss Heywood', she cries, 'I'm so glad you came. I don't know what to do. Georgiana is very ill and has a high fever. The nearest doctor I know of is in Eastbourne and I am afraid for her life.' Charlotte runs up to Georgiana's bed chamber to find her in her bed with her eyes closed. 'Georgiana,' she cries, 'wake up,' shaking her gently at the same time. But Georgiana does not respond. Charlotte calls to Mrs Griffiths, 'Please fetch me some water and cloths. We must bring her temperature down.' In a few minutes, Mrs Griffiths appears with the requirements. Charlotte thanks her and then says, 'Perhaps this is a influenza contagion and if it is, it will be better if you and the Beaufort sisters stay away from Georgiana until we see how the disease progresses.' 'But Miss Heywood, are you not also in danger if it is so?' 'Yes, perhaps,' Charlotte replies, 'but someone must care for her. It shall be me. Please go to Mary Parker and ask her to send Morgan to retrieve my trunk from the post inn.' 'You were leaving today,' responds Mrs Griffiths! 'I was,' replies Charlotte, 'but now I must remain a little longer in Sanditon.' Mrs Griffiths goes out to do Charlotte's biding. After a short time as Charlotte stands next to Georgiana placing a water cooled cloth on her forehead, there is a knock at the door. It opens and Mary is there. Staying outside the room, she says, 'Charlotte, Morgan was successful in retrieving your trunk from the post inn, but not your letter to Sidney.' 'That is as it should be,' replies Charlotte.

'I shall delay my journey for a day or so only to care for Georgiana, and then I shall go. There is no need to engage Sidney's attention in this as he no doubt will be occupied trying to resolve the threat to Sanditon Town.' 'Well, I shall leave you then,' responds Mary, 'and perhaps see you in the evening before you retire.' Returns Charlotte, 'I shall remain here to be near Georgiana until I see some improvement but I will endeavor to come to Trafalgar House when I can get Mrs Griffiths to watch over Georgiana, probably sometime this evening or tomorrow morning.' 'Very well,' says Mary as she retires from the doorway.

Charlotte spends a long afternoon and evening by Georgiana's side frequently changing the cooling cloths. As the evening grows late, Georgiana opens her eyes and says, 'Charlotte, what are you doing here?' 'You are awake, Georgiana, how do you feel,' Charlotte asks? 'Much better, Charlotte. Yesterday my head hurt me badly though I tried not to show it when you, Arthur and Diana called and then this morning, I felt very ill but now, I do not feel badly at all. I should like to rise from my bed.' 'It is late Georgiana,' replies Charlotte, 'and perhaps it is best that you rest through the night and then tomorrow we shall see.' 'As you wish Doctor Charlotte,' says Georgiana with a smile. 'But back to my question, what are you doing here?'

As she offers Georgiana a sip of water, Charlotte replies, 'Georgiana, I had come this morning to say goodbye because I am leaving Sanditon to return to Willingden.' 'No, you cannot Charlotte,' says Georgiana. 'Why will you do that?' 'I cannot be an impediment to the resolution of Tom's debt,' responds Charlotte. 'Mrs Wickham has demanded that I give up my engagement to Sidney as a condition to her goodwill toward the future of Sanditon. I have acceded to her demand to release him and informed Sidney of it by post which went on the London coach this morning.'

'Charlotte, you cannot mean it,' cries Georgiana! 'Sidney will never have anything to do with that witch, Maria.' 'I must and I have, Georgiana,' says Charlotte. 'I shall not put my happiness in the way of saving Sanditon.' 'Your happiness..., what of Sidney's happiness,' cries Georgiana? 'Have you thought about him, Charlotte? He adores you. Do you wish him to again become that lost, that jaded, angry man I knew, that you met when you first came? He will become that again if you abandon him to Mrs Wickham. Is saving Sanditon worth Sidney's life? That will be the outcome if you give him to Maria Wickham. He will ignore his health and drink himself to death. I know it!' As she has talked, Georgiana has gradually raised herself from her bed and the volume of her voice along with it.

Charlotte sinks down onto the bed asking herself, is that what have I done? Is Georgiana right? But what else could I do? She looks up at Georgiana and says, 'You are right Georgiana. I acted in haste. But it is done. I have written it and Sidney is released from his proposal. If he is successful in resolving the matter of Tom Parker's Sanditon debt without having to marry Mrs Wickham, perhaps he will ask me again.' 'Oh, Sidney will ask again,' replies Georgiana, 'I have no doubt that he will be on horseback on his way back to you five minutes after he opens your letter. And remember, you shall have a dowry of twenty-five thousand pounds from me when I reach majority. You can count on it.' Charlotte smiles at Georgiana and says, 'Georgiana, you are wise beyond your nineteen years, but I cannot take your money.' 'Yes, you can and you shall Charlotte,' replies Georgiana. 'I am what you allowed me to be thanks to your power over Sidney. I have no wish to have the old Sidney return. I love you Charlotte. You are the sister I never had and I shall not allow Maria Wickham nor Tom Parker to take you away from me nor Sidney either.'

With Georgiana's recovery seemingly well in hand, Charlotte determines to return to Trafalgar House even though it is late in the evening. She feels that what ever Georgiana's illness was, it has passed. She asks Mrs Griffiths to check on Georgiana from time to time in the night and to send a servant to fetch her if Georgiana should show any signs of a relapse. Then she promises to come in the morning to check on her. Mrs Griffiths refuses to allow her to walk the few steps back to Trafalgar House by herself in the dark and despite Charlotte's protests, sends a servant to accompany her to the door. As she walks, Charlotte thinks over what Georgiana has told her. She asks herself what would have happened if Georgiana's illness had not stopped her from her precipitous decision to leave Sanditon. "Out of the mouths of babes and sucklings" she thinks, smiling to herself. I needed to hear some wise words and I heard them from my delightful Georgiana. She has given me the strength to face what will come. She looks up from her thoughts and sees that she is in front of the Trafalgar House door. She thanks the servant for accompanying her and goes in. As she is removing her bonnet and cape, Mary emerges from the parlor. 'You have waited up for me Mary', says Charlotte surprised, 'you should not have done.' 'Of course I should have done,' replies Mary, 'you are family. Please come in and sit with me a while. And let us have a glass of Madeira as well.' 'Thank you, Mary, says Charlotte gratefully with a smile, 'I should like that very much.' They sit and Mary pours the drinks.

Mary says, 'You know, Charlotte, Sidney would never have forgiven me if I had allowed you to leave as you intended. I cannot but think that Georgiana's illness was a miracle. I know that Sidney will be heartbroken to receive your letter, but let us think a bit about how your letter may lead him back to you. He will no doubt be on his way back to Sanditon as soon as he reads your letter, but perhaps it will be best if you are not here when he arrives. You know that the heart grows more fond in absence and perhaps if you have indeed gone to Willingden, it will make the point to him that he needs to have made. He is conflicted now with Tom's debt problems and his love for you. But I know that he is at his best when he is with you. He needs your support and love if he is to make the best decisions for all of us. I have seen it. You are the rock in Sidney's life. Everything will be right if he knows that you are with him, that you love him and support him. So if you should not be here when he returns, then he will see and understand that nothing matters if you are not by his side. He will know it and that is what matters to you, to all of us. You will give Sidney the strength to fight and save us all if having you as his wife is at the end of it. Give him that, Charlotte, and we all shall all win in the end.' 'But is that not unfair to Sidney, to play with his affections in such a way,' asks Charlotte? 'Perhaps it is, Charlotte,' replies Mary with a gentle smile, 'but my dear girl, Sidney must see what a hole there is in his life without you in it, we all must and your absence will make us know it.' 'Well then Mary, I shall take your wise words to heart and if Georgiana is well in the morning, I shall ask poor Mr Morgan to again cart my trunk to the post inn and take my departure to Willingden.' She stands, goes to Mary who also rises and embraces her. 'I shall miss you, Mary!' 'And I you, Charlotte, but your absence will be a short one. I am certain of that,' replies Mary.

'Oh yes, Mary, I almost forgot,' announces Charlotte as she prepares to go to her bed, 'I should tell you that Lady Denham has requested that I come to her as her companion in place of Clara Brereton who will move back to London. I am now of the opinion that I should accept that position in her house. Sidney is aware of it and has encouraged me to take it. So, perhaps after a few weeks in Willingden, I shall be back and in the service of Lady Denham.' 'Well,' replies Mary, 'I should prefer that you would be here, but perhaps a position at Sanditon House is a better situation for you.'

Chapter 43

Sunday - 7 June 1818 - Sanditon/Willingden

Morning comes for Charlotte who awakes well rested in comparison to the previous morning. As she stretches in her bed, she thinks, what a difference a day makes. Yes, Mary is right. It was a miracle, Georgiana's brief illness, because it kept me from a precipitous departure. It gave me time to think and to take advice from Georgiana and Mary that I would not have had if I had gone yesterday as I had determined to do. Now perhaps I can see a pathway to happiness and a life with Sidney. And I shall write a brief note now for delivery to Lady Denham this morning before my departure to let her know of my continuing interest in her companion position. After completing her note, she goes down to join Mary and Tom in the breakfast room.

Tom jumps up and says, 'Charlotte, Mary has told me of your plans to leave us. I am so sorry but perhaps it is for the best. Sidney will marry Maria as he has always wanted to do and all will be well. But if you should ever like to come for a visit after Sidney's wedding, we shall welcome you, will we not Mary!' 'Tom,' cries Mary raising her voice, 'no it is not for the best. I am ashamed that you would even think that let alone say it. Sidney is in love with Charlotte as you know very well because he asked for her hand. Do not spout claptrap! I want Charlotte to stay and even if she has determined to leave us for a while, she will return to us. She is a part of our family as far as I am concerned and you shall do well to remember it.' 'But,' sputters Tom, 'I only meant…!' 'I know what you meant, Tom,' interrupts Mary angrily, 'and I shall hear no more of it.' Tom sits down red faced. After a few moments of silence, Charlotte says, 'I shall ask, Mary, if Mr Morgan can barrow my trunk again to the post inn and also, handing her the note addressed to Lady Denham, if he might also deliver this. It tells her of my interest in becoming her companion this summer. And then, after I call on Georgiana, I shall wait for the coach to Willingden.' Mary accepts the note and says, 'Yes, I shall ensure that Morgan takes care of your trunk and this note and I shall join you on your stop at Mrs Griffiths' to see Georgiana.' 'Thank you Mary,' replies Charlotte, 'and Tom I shall wish you well and hope that fortune shines on you in saving Sanditon from your creditors; Goodbye.' Tom looks to Mary quickly then acknowledges her goodbye with a nod.

All is well at Mrs Griffiths' boarding house. Mrs Griffiths is happy at the quick recovery of Georgiana and that she had not had an illness to share with her, Victoria and Rose. Georgiana is very chipper and greets Charlotte and Mary with a enthusiastic Good Morning. Charlotte says, 'It is wonderful to see you well, Georgiana. I could not have left Sanditon knowing that you are not in the best of health. Sidney would have not forgiven me if I had done so.' Georgiana laughs and says, 'Oh Charlotte, Sidney would forgive you anything. But still you are going,' she ends with a look of disappointment. 'Yes, I must,' responds Charlotte, 'but fear not, I shall return. You and Mary have convinced me of the right of it and I know that Sanditon is my home. So, I shall visit my Willingden family for a few weeks and then try to return in time for the High Summer Ball.' 'Then,' replies Georgiana, 'I shall be able to bear it. But what shall I say to Sidney? He will no doubt be distraught after he reads your letter and I would expect to see him back here within the week as soon as he does.' 'You may tell him that I shall be back, and that I expect to accept Lady's Denham's offer to become her companion later in the summer.' 'I shall,' replies Georgiana, 'and please do come back to us as soon as you can.' Mary speaks up and reminds, 'Charlotte, do not forget that the High Summer Ball, the last of the season, will be held here on 26th June. You must be here for it.' With that, goodbyes are said all around and Charlotte and Mary walk to the post inn to find Morgan standing protectively over Charlotte's trunk. 'Goodbye Miss Heywood,' he says. 'I hope to see you very soon again in Sanditon and rest assured that I shall convey your note to Lady Denham forthwith.' 'Thank you, Mr Morgan,' replies Charlotte, 'and goodbye for now.'

Charlotte boards the waiting coach as her trunk is being loaded and waves goodbye to Mary and Morgan as the coach starts off. Well, you shall have several hours to think now, Charlotte, she says to herself. Perhaps I shall puzzle out a solution to the conundrum of the how and why of love and life. And I shall have the occasion now to at long last read the book, "Pride and Prejudice" by Miss Jane Austen that Anne sent with me when I left Willingden for Sanditon forever ago, although it is just more than two months. How can it be that time passes so quickly and yet at the same time so much can happen? Yes, life is a puzzle and a whirl. But now to the book.

It seems but minutes but the four hour traverse to Willingden is over as is a good part of the book and the coach jolts to a stop in front of the Willingden post inn. Charlotte gets down and waits as her trunk is offloaded and carried into the post. The Proprietor, Mr Allen, welcomes her back with, 'Miss Heywood, I was not expecting to see you back this summer. One of your brothers, George I believe it was, told me that they were not expecting your return to Willingden until the Fall.' 'Well, I determined to come for a visit, Mr Allen,' replies Charlotte, 'and here am I.' 'It is wonderful to see you, Miss Heywood,' he says, 'and the local lads have missed your presence, I assure you,' he continues with a smile. 'Shall I have the curricle harnessed up for you? Then you can take your trunk as well.' 'No thank you Mr Allen,' replies Charlotte, 'I fancy a walk and one of the boys, Thomas or George, will come with the cart and fetch it later.'

She goes out and begins to walk the lane back to the Heywood estate. I can see now through new eyes, she thinks as she walks and enjoys the familiar sights and smells of the countryside. I should so like to bring Sidney to see my home and to introduce him as my husband to be. I wonder what would be the reaction to the knowledge that he has asked for my hand even if I now cannot say anything about it since I have released him? Is Georgiana right, will he come back and ask for my hand a second time? Oh I hope he will be able.

Before she knows it, Charlotte is at the head of the lane leading to the house. As she walks down it to approach the house, she sees Annabella, Henry and Sarah playing and they see her at the same time. They run toward her shouting her name and surround her holding onto her skirts. Charlotte hears, 'What is all of this commotion about?' then sees her Mama emerge from the house. 'Charlotte you are home. We did not expect you. Why did you not write and let us know of your coming?' 'I shall explain, Mama,' responds Charlotte and goes into the house surrounded by a joyful gaggle of brothers and sisters. 'Where is Papa,' she asks? 'He is in the fields with some of the boys,' Mama replies. 'When they come, we shall celebrate your return and then we shall hear your story later after the young ones are abed.' Charlotte hears a gasp and turns to see Anne behind her. 'Oh

Charlotte,' she cries, 'it is so good to see you. I have missed you so. Will you be with us long?' 'That I yet do not know, returns Charlotte, 'we shall see.' 'Well then Charlotte,' asks Mama, 'where is your trunk?' 'It is with Mr Allen at the post inn,' she replies. Mama calls to the boys, 'George, go fetch Charlotte's trunk and then we shall sit down to supper when Papa, Benjamin and Thomas come in from the fields. And yes, she says to a excited Henry, you may go with George to retrieve Charlotte's trunk. Charlotte, we shall put you back with Anne and perhaps you will wish to shake off some of the road dust.' 'Yes, Mama,' smiles Charlotte, 'that will be well, and I have a packet of hard boiled lemon and peppermint sweets in my trunk that I am sure will be popular with all,' to screams of delight from the younger ones.

Evening comes to Willingden. It a family reunion full of happiness and celebration. All are surprised and joyful at Charlotte's unannounced arrival. Each of her brothers and sisters wants a report on her life in Sanditon and each has their own story to tell. Charlotte weaves a tale of the excitement and beauty of Sanditon Town, the beach, the sea and how wonderful the people all are that she has met there. Evening turns into night and her siblings one by one go off to bed until only her Mama, Papa and Anne are sitting with her. Papa says, 'Charlotte your Mama and I are so pleased you are home but we are a bit surprised that you arrived so suddenly with no letter letting us know!' Charlotte looks into the caring eyes of her parents and suddenly the tears well. Her Mother rises and comes to put an arm around her. 'What has happened Charlotte,' Papa asks? 'Are you in trouble?' 'No, Papa,' Charlotte replies! 'Then what is it', he asks, 'what has happened?'

Charlotte struggles to regain her composure as she dries her eyes then replies, 'It is a matter related to money, Papa. Mr Tom Parker has proven to be a not very good financial manager of his Sanditon project that he told us about when he was here and there is a certain person who has bought one of his loans and is threatening to call it in which could put Mr Parker in debtor's prison. His brother, Sidney Parker, is in London now trying to find a way to forestall that. I don't know if he will be successful. I hope he is. His own fortune is at risk because he has backed some of his brothers's loans from his own capital.' 'But why should that cause you ill Charlotte,' asks Papa, 'why should that send you back to us with no notice? What are the Parker family's finances to you?'

Charlotte avoids the questioning eyes while she wonders how she should answer that question. Then looking back up to her Mama's and Papa's questioning faces, and with a quick glance at Anne, takes a deep breath and blurts out, 'because Mr Sidney Parker asked for my hand!' 'What,' cries Mama, 'you are betrothed?' 'No,' responds Charlotte, 'I posted a letter to Sidney before I left Sanditon freeing him from his obligation to me.' 'But why should you do that, do you not love him,' asks Mama? 'I love him very much, Mama, Papa, but the certain person I mentioned, the owner of that loan, demanded it as a condition to saving Tom Parker from debtor's prison. She wishes to marry Sidney and if he does marry her, she will put her fortune into his hands to save Sanditon Bathing Town.' 'Who is this personage,' asks Papa? 'She is Mrs Maria Wickham,' replies Charlotte. 'Yes, I know of her,' responds Papa. 'I saw the obituary for Mr Wickham in the the London Morning Post not much more than a month back if I remember rightly. But what is her connection to Mr Sidney Parker?' 'She and Sidney were in love and hoped to marry more than ten years ago,' replies Charlotte, 'but then she married Mr Wickham for his wealth. Now with his passing, she wants Sidney to return to her and she is using her wealth to try to regain him. I determined that I could not be an imped-iment to Sidney's decisions to do what he must to save the Parker family from bankruptcy and ruin.'

'Well my Sweet Charlotte,' replies Papa, 'I wonder if Mr Parker deserves you? Is there any man out there who deserves you? And should I give him your hand? I must meet him. But now to bed. Tomorrow is a another day of harvest and it must come in. As the good book says, "*While the earth remaineth, seedtime and harvest, and cold and heat, and summer and winter, and day and night shall not cease.*" It will be a full day and I must have my rest. We shall talk more of this but Mama and I are very happy you have come home safe to us.'

Chapter 44

Charlotte awakens and for a minute wonders where she is. She rolls over to stretch as she has become accustomed to do and her hand smacks into a face from which comes a yelp of pain. Anne says, 'Thank you for that Charlotte. You do know that you are sharing a bed and it seemed to me last night that you were rather selfish of the covers and quilt and I found myself almost on the floor at times.' 'I'm sorry Anne,' replies Charlotte. 'I have become accustomed to sleeping alone in Sanditon where I had my own bed chamber which had a bed fit for a Queen.' 'Well, Your Highness,' laughs Anne, 'now you are a commoner again so please keep to your side of the bed henceforth.' Charlotte laughs and says, 'Anne, you shall not have to suffer my presence very long because I shall return to Sanditon after perhaps a fortnight here. But I wonder if you would like to go with me. I have been offered a position as companion to the great Lady of Sanditon, Lady Denham. Perhaps you remember me mentioning her in one of my letters?' 'Yes, I remember,' replies Anne, 'but I believe you wrote that she is rather formidable and not at all polite. I should fear to be in her presence.' 'Well,

I have changed my opinion of her since my early first impressions, Anne,' responds Charlotte. 'She is of strong opinion and often speaks her mind which can be intimidating, but she thinks the same of me. I do believe that I should be quite happy in her employ. And if you should like to accompany me, I am sure Lady Denham shall have room for you to join me in her grand house. Papa told me that he and Mama had talked to you about my request that you join me in Sanditon in a letter of a month ago.' 'Yes,' replies Anne, 'Papa and Mama have talked to me about that and I should love to come with you. I believe they said end June or early July would be a good time for me to go for a few months and we are almost there.' 'Yes,' responds Charlotte, 'it will be when I am ready go back to Sanditon in a fortnight and in time for us to attend the High Summer Ball, the ball of The Season in Sanditon. It is to be held in Sanditon House, Lady Denham's grand pile, and I know that you shall find it a wonderful experience, one that I myself yet have not had at that house, but do indeed look forward to.'

Charlotte and Anne go out to the kitchen and join with Mama and 18 year old sister Elizabeth, who is Mama's right hand in the kitchen, and the younger siblings. 'Good Morning, Charlotte,' says Mama, 'I trust you slept well.' 'I did, I believe, although Anne tells me she did not because of me rolling about. But where are Papa and the boys?' 'They are already in the fields with the men bringing in the turnips and cabbages. It looks to be a good harvest this year in contrast to the past few,' replies Mama. Perhaps you and Anne can take the food Cook, Lizzy and I are preparing to the fields for the men a little later.' 'Of course Mama,' responds Charlotte with a smile, 'we shall be happy to do it.' She notices Elizabeth who looks up at the mention of her nickname, Lizzy, smiles and thinks to herself, I now see the beauty of the family who will break many hearts no doubt. My time away from Willingden has opened my eyes to many things that I could not see before I went to Sanditon. The morning flies by as Charlotte enjoys talking with Lizzy about their mutual love of dancing and with their underfoot younger sisters and brothers led by 12 year old Harriet who thinks of herself as little Mama to her younger siblings, Annabella 11, Henry 9, Sarah 7, Ellen 5 and little John 3. Oh my, thinks Charlotte, shall this be me? Shall I have children in such numbers? And Sidney..., she blushes at the thought of Sidney as Papa and herself as Mama! Charlotte, do not think such thoughts. You yet do not know what the future holds, even if Sidney shall ever be yours. Quiet yourself.

Her thoughts are interrupted when Mama calls to her and announces that the food is ready to be delivered to the fields. Charlotte and Anne go out heavily burdened with large baskets of cold meat, bread, cheese and cool cider from the root cellar to wash it down. They arrive to find their Papa, brothers Benjamin, Thomas and George along with a dozen other men hard at work digging turnips and throwing them into piles. They stop as they see Charlotte and Anne arrive and come over to gather under the shade of a spreading oak to eat their lunch. 'Well,' says Papa, 'you are settling back into farm life, I see Charlotte.' 'Yes, Papa, I am. But Papa, I want you to know that I shall return to Sanditon as Lady Denham's companion in a fortnight. I have but to write and accept the employment, and I should like Anne to come with me. It will almost be July.' 'Yes, Mama and I have discussed that and Anne may accompany you,' says Papa. 'Then I shall write to Lady Denham this night to have ready for tomorrow's post,' replies Charlotte. 'Thank you, Papa.'

Evening comes quickly, as there is always so much to do on a farm and the time flies as a consequence of it, thinks Charlotte. I had forgotten that work never stops even on a Sunday at harvest time, unlike Sanditon where it is a day to attend church and then enjoy what the day brings in conversation and walks on the promenade, cliff tops or beach. She sits down to write.

Willingden

Monday 8 June 1818

Dear Lady Denham

Please forgive my dereliction that I did not call to say goodbye before I left Sanditon this Sunday last. My departure was rather precipitous but it was necessary that I do as I did, the why of it I can share with you at a later date if you wish. However, I want you to know that I have used my visit with my family in Willingden to sort a few matters that relate to your offer of employment as your companion. I should like to accept your offer if it still is open to me. I should also like to bring my sister, Anne of 20 years, who would very much like to accompany me if that would be something that you would consider favorably? If you should approve this plan, Anne and I shall try our best to arrive sometime around the Summer Solstice if that should be agreeable to you.

I shall look forward to your response, My Lady.

With most high regard,

Charlotte Heywood

Chapter 45

A week has come and gone since Charlotte's arrival back in Willingden. She has enjoyed getting back into the routine of life on the farm despite her worries about her future with Sidney. The summer days are long and the work never ends, but it is satisfying and she has enjoyed getting reacquainted with her siblings. They all have grown, particularly the young ones, how quick they grow and change she thinks with wonder. Also her return to Willingden has not gone unnoticed by several of the eligible young men of past acquaintance, two of whom already have called to see if perhaps Charlotte might consider a chaperoned walk with them. They have gone away disappointed as Charlotte has refused to give them any hope of her interest in them now or in the future. But she has been looking forward to Lady Denham's response to her letter about her interest in becoming her companion. She has secretly been disappointed as well that she has not had any correspondence from Sanditon nor from Sidney. But she consoles herself that very little time has passed and perhaps posts are on the way.

Charlotte decides to walk into the village. She will call at the post inn to see if perhaps there is mail for her. She asks if anyone would like to accompany her. Anne and George volunteer their services as walking companions and they set off. It is warm and dusty along the road and they scuff their feet through it enjoying the scent of the dust and ripening hay behind the hedgerows. The mile passes very quickly and soon they find themselves in the village in front of the post inn. Going in, Mr Allen greets them with 'Good Day to you, Miss Heywoods and Master George. How may I be of service?' 'We are just calling for the post,' replies Charlotte. 'Is there anything for us today?' 'Yes, there is,' he answers. 'Let's see, yes, a letter for Mr Heywood, the London Morning Post, and more, two letters addressed to you, Miss.' Charlotte thanks Mr Allen and quickly looks at the letters for her, sees that one has Lady Denham's Sanditon House crest and the other Mary's initials M.P. and Sanditon. She feels a sharp pang of disappointment that there is nothing from Sidney. Well, she asks herself, why should there be? He has barely had time to receive my letter, and I have in it severed my life from his. He must do what he must to save Tom, Mary and himself and he has no obligation to involve me in his decision making.

As they walk back out of the post inn, a man detaches himself from the side of the building and walks toward her and her companions. 'Miss Heywood,' he says with a smile, 'may I have a word?' 'I don't know you, Sir,' she replies. 'May I know the purpose of your approach?' 'I should like a private word,' he responds as his smile twists into more of a unpleasant grin. 'No Sir, you shall not have a private word,' replies Charlotte. 'I repeat that I do not know you and if you have good cause to talk with me, it will have to be in the presence of my Father.' 'Then,' he replies, 'let me just say that you should stay away from Sidney Parker on pain of scandal if you do not. Consider this a friendly warning.' 'Who has sent you, Sir,' Charlotte demands? 'You have been warned,' he smirks as he walks away.

'Why would that man say what he said,' asks Anne as George looks on? 'I did not like that man,' states George. 'Papa would have sent him packing!' They continue on their way back to the homestead as Charlotte mulls over the strange encounter. She thinks, yes, this has the feel of Mrs Wickham. At least I would not put it past her to try to frighten me away from Sidney, but what can she fear now; surely Sidney has told her that I have released him from his bond to me. As she finishes the thought, she glances at the letter addressed to her Papa. The handwriting is familiar but it has no crest on the seal nor other identifying marks. Where have I seen this handwriting before, she asks herself? Then it strikes her, it is Lady Susan's hand. Dare I ask Papa about this letter? This mystery of Heywood and Kent must be solved. She resolves to ask as she, Anne and George arrive back at the house.

Charlotte goes out into the garden alone and sits with her letters in her hand. She looks at both hesitating to open them as she thinks about what news, good and bad, they might contain. Will there be news of Sidney is foremost in her mind. She determines to open the Sanditon House letter first. She reads:

Sanditon House

12 June 1818

My Dear Miss Heywood

I take pen in hand to tell you that I was very pleased to receive your post of 8th June explaining a bit more about your precipitous departure from Sanditon although I should have wished for you to advise me of that by calling rather than by note before your departure. However, I have heard rumors of the reason for it and I forgive you your lapse in civility on this occasion.

With regard to your proposal to accept my previous offer and come back to Sanditon to serve as my companion, Clara remains in Sanditon for a few weeks longer but she informs me that July will see the back of her and I believe it will be well for you to be with us while Clara yet remains in residence. She can help prepare you for my expectations of you as my companion and spare me some of the effort. So I shall look forward to your arrival in the near future. I shall have appropriate quarters prepared for you in the main house, not far from my bed chamber, and yes, your sister Anne may accompany you. She shall have a bed chamber next to yours.

Finally I should wish you to know that Mr Tom Parker has called on me to inform with great enthusiasm that he believes he soon will have a new investor in the person of Mrs Maria Wickham. I shall believe it when I see it because Mr Tom Parker's acquaintance with the truth is often proved to be tenuous. We shall see.

I shall look forward to your earliest arrival,

Lady Agatha Denham

Charlotte sits back and mulls over her future. So Anne and I are to be welcomed to Sanditon House. I am sure Anne will be pleased but will I be? I fear that I shall find myself torn, to be in familiar surroundings but with oh so different standing. Will Lady Denham find my independence of opinion so worthy of her approbation then when I am in her employ? And how will it be when I shall see Sidney again as it is inevitable that I shall? Well, Charlotte, she says to herself, those are bridges to cross when you come to them. Now to read what Mary has wrote;

Trafalgar House

13 June 1818

Dearest Charlotte

By the time you receive this, you will have been gone from us for more than a week, and I can tell you that you are sorely missed by the children, by Tom and by me. Tom is helpless without you with his bills and correspondence and he needs the encouragement and support of your enthusiasm for his town that I cannot give him as he struggles with the culmination of all of his missteps in trying to realize his dream. The children want to know where their Auntie Charlotte is and Uncle Sidney too and why they cannot play with them? We all are lost without you.

I have not heard from Sidney since his departure to London a few days before you left for Willingden. However, there has been news just this day from a unexpected source, Mr Nisbet, which worries me greatly. You know from your experience that Mr Nisbet would not seem to be a man to concern himself unnecessarily with the welfare of others. However, he called on me today; he is in Sanditon and it seems he is courting Miss Brereton; but back to his news. He professes to be greatly concerned with Sidney's drinking and his health and a confession Sidney made to him while in his cups concerning you, My Dear. I do not wish to to cause you more pain than you know already but I must tell you that Sidney confessed his love for you to Mr Nisbet. Mr Nisbet said that he believes Sidney will never marry Mrs Wickham but if he does, it will be the destruction of him. Our Sidney, your Sidney has given you his heart and it always will be yours.

Please forgive me, Charlotte, for sharing this with you but I know you love Sidney and you should know as much as I know about the man we both love. I am unsure what to do about this. Tom is of no help. Despite everything, he still believes that Sidney is in love with Maria. He cannot see because he does not wish to see.

So Dear Charlotte, I close by saying that I pray that you are well and that there will be brighter days ahead for us all.

Yours with affection,

Mary

———◦◦◦———

Charlotte raises eyes which have clouded with tears from Mary's letter and looks at the beauty of the garden around her. Oh, Sidney, she thinks, would that I could be by your side or better still that you could be here by my side. Please do not destroy yourself with drink. And I fear that your search for alternatives to marriage to Mrs Wickham is not going well, this I take from Mary's letter. Someone must save you, and me, from that fate. But who, Lady Susan, will it be you? I must get word of this to her.

Evening comes and after a supper featuring delicious roast rabbit, new garden vegetables and greens of the season with freshly baked bread and a desert, strawberry tart with snow cream, the young ones cluster around Charlotte in the parlor and beg her for another adventure story. Charlotte has been a popular story teller over the last week because she has had so many unheard stories to tell. She resolves to tell them about how a handsome young prince saved a beautiful young princess from drowning after the princess had saved a child from a raging sea but could not escape the water to save herself. As she tells the tale, she notices that Mama and Papa are listening closely as well. She wraps up the story with a happy ending to the satisfaction of the wide eyed children around her then shoos them off to bed. She starts to go with them to tuck them into their beds, but Mama calls her back. 'Charlotte,' she says, 'Anne can tuck the children in but that story you just told has a ring of truth about it. Did it really happen... and was that young princess you?'

Charlotte thinks a moment about how well her Mama can see through her and wonders if all Mothers are so acute in their observations then says, 'Yes, Mama, it was I who almost drowned not long after I had arrived in Sanditon.' 'And was that handsome young prince of the story who saved you Mr Sidney Parker,' continues Mama? Now, Charlotte feels a blush beginning to warm her face as she sees Mama and Papa are watching her closely. She takes a deep breath and then says, 'Yes Mama, it was. Young Henry Parker was pulled into the water by the force of the waves and I ran in and caught him and pushed him toward the shore where he could clamber out but my clothing was so heavy from the water that I could not escape it myself. Sidney was nearby and he pulled me from the water just as I thought to give myself up to the sea. Yes, he saved my life.' 'Oh, Charlotte, my Darling,' cries Mama, 'we could have lost you then and not known it for days or even weeks. I must thank Mr Parker...,' 'And so we shall; perhaps Mr Parker does deserve you after all,' Papa concludes with a smile at Charlotte's obvious discomfort.

Charlotte starts to rise to escape knowing smiles and the exchanges of looks between her Mama and Papa but suddenly decides to take advantage of the moment to ask about the mystery of Lady Susan and today's letter from her. 'Papa,' she says, 'there is a story I should very much like for you to tell me. I wish to know about the Duchess of Kent, and her family's connection with ours. I saw a letter to you today that I brought from the post inn. It was in Lady Susan's hand, but it was lacking her seal; only closed with simple wax. I think of my meeting in London before her masked ball when she summoned me as you wrote she would, and the mystery of our connection I asked of her which she also would not divulge and then at the masked ball when she had me dance with a royally dressed masked man who would not give me his name. I cannot understand it. Then I wrote to her after my return to Sanditon asking if she could find out anything about Tom Parker's loan that had been bought. She did not write back but she sent her cousin, Lord Somerset, the Earl of Tewkesbury, to Sanditon to answer my question. What connection can you have with a Duchess, Papa, that would gain me such treatment? Please tell me.'

She watches as Mama and Papa exchange looks then both turn serious faces to her. 'Our sweet and oh so smart girl, no not girl, our most beautiful young lady,' replies Papa, 'you ask the question again that is not ours to answer, that we are bound by oath not to answer. You must keep those words to yourself, even telling that there is an oath is too much. Please forgive and forget my slip of the tongue. Just know that you will know when the time is right for you to know. I beg you to not ask that question of anyone ever again. It is Lady Susan's secret alone to share with you or not and none other. Just know that it is not us, our family, who have that connection you asked about with Lady Susan, it is you alone and leave it at that.'

'Yes, Papa,' replies Charlotte as she looks into the grave and unsmiling faces of Mama and Papa. 'I shall take your words to heart. But there is one other matter to bring to your attention. There was a strange man in Willingden today who approached me when I went to the post inn with Anne and George, and as we left the inn, he asked for a private word with me. I refused him and demanded that he should come to you first if he wished to have a word with me. He then went on his way saying that I should stay away from Sidney Parker on pain of suffering scandal if I did not. I think he must be a lackey of Mrs Wickham but what scandal he warns of I cannot guess.' She watches as her Mama and Papa again exchange glances then, Papa says, 'You must be cautious, Charlotte. There are many with connections in London like Mrs Wickham who may try to tarnish the reputations of those who stand in their way. Threats of scandal are the ways of The Ton and the Court so take that threat seriously and be careful but do not worry yourself to much about it while you are here in Willingden. But now I must be off to bed.'

Chapter 46

Charlotte comes into the kitchen the next morning still thinking of the conversation with Mama and Papa of the night before - so many questions and still so few answers. Papa said I am the connection to Lady Susan, not the Heywood family but I am never to speak of it. And he and Mama have taken an oath to say nothing of it. She is startled out of her reverie by the sound of a unfamiliar voice in the dining room. She goes in to find a well dressed young man in stylish riding clothes standing near her father whom she expected to already be in the fields at this time of the morning but he is not. They both look up at her entry. The young man bows and says, 'Miss Heywood, it is a pleasure.' Charlotte looks questioningly to her Father who nods, then curtseys and says, 'I have not had the pleasure of your acquaintance, Sir.' Papa smiles and says, 'Charlotte, this is Philip Stanley. He is Lord Somerset's Brother. I was advised of Lady Susan's travel to Brighton in that letter you brought to me yesterday, Charlotte, and Philip is here to take us to her.' 'She is here, Lady Susan is here, in Willingden,' asks Charlotte? 'No, she is not here but she is at an estate not too far from here and she wishes to speak with you, with us today,' replies Papa. 'It is a matter of the utmost urgency.' 'Yes, Papa, I shall be ready shortly,' agrees Charlotte. 'How shall we go?' 'On horseback,' responds Papa, 'it will be faster and Philip has brought us horses to speed our journey.' Charlotte goes back to her bed chamber and dresses to ride.

After Charlotte returns to the kitchen where Mama has bundled some breakfast to eat as they travel, all go out into the courtyard where the horses wait. Oh what wonderful creatures of great breeding, thinks Charlotte as she sees the horses. I'm sure they are of racing stock. Philip points to a beautiful chestnut mare as her horse. She asks, 'What is her name, Mr Stanley?' 'Her name is Lady, Miss Heywood,' he replies. Charlotte speaks her name, introduces herself to Lady and then Philip helps her mount. As he does, Mr Heywood comes out of the house and looks with a proud smile at Charlotte sitting her horse. 'Is she not a vision, Mr Stanley,' he asks? 'Indeed she is, Sir,' he replies to Charlotte's embarrassment. She archly offers back, 'Surely Papa, you refer to Lady, my horse,' to amused laughs from both Philip and Papa. The two men mount up and the party sets off at a canter. As they travel, Mr Stanley admiringly observes Charlotte's handling of Lady and says, 'You sit a horse very well indeed, Miss Heywood. Lady is very spirited and can be a handful for anyone less than expert on her back. She knows who is a Master or Mistress and who is not. She seems very pleased to have you on her back. My compliments on how well you handle her.' 'Thank you, Sir,' replies Charlotte. 'She is a beautiful creature and I think it possible that I may never let her go.' 'To that, I cannot answer, Miss Heywood,' responds Philip. 'You shall have to make your appeal to her owner.' 'Whose is she,' Charlotte asks? 'She is from the stables of the Duchess,' he replies. 'She sits a horse very well as you do and is a frequent rider when she is at one of her country estates.' Ah yes Charlotte, she muses to herself, here you are yet again on your way to a rendezvous with Lady

Susan this time in the company of Papa and a brother of Somerset. Am I on this occasion to discover the Heywood connection, my connection with Lady Susan? We shall see.

They ride in the direction of Brighton with Philip leading the way. Charlotte is enjoying the beautiful day and admiring the countryside as she rides beside Papa who keeps his own counsel and seems lost in thought. She wonders what he is thinking about but refrains from asking because she thinks it best to leave her questions for the coming call on Lady Susan wherever she is. She has enjoyed nibbling on the food from Mama's breakfast bundle as she has ridden along aided by Lady's smooth gait. The speed of the fine horses has allowed rapid progress and soon they find themselves approaching a rather grand country house surrounded by open fields where horses seem to predominate. Charlotte coaxes a little more speed out of Lady to come up beside Philip. 'Is this Lady Susan's estate,' she asks? 'Yes,' he replies, 'it is one of them. It is called Warwick Court. Lady Susan prefers to stay a bit inland rather than on the shore when she comes down to Brighton in the summer so she always stays here where she can enjoy riding and her horses. We are about five miles from the sea here.' They continue up to the house and then on around to the stables at the rear. As they pull up, Charlotte glimpses Lady Susan in beautiful riding costume standing next to a black horse with a white blaze on his forehead. Lady Susan looks up and smiles as she recognizes Charlotte and company. Philip quickly dismounts and assists Charlotte down from her mount. Then she and Papa walk over to where Lady Susan is standing as she greets them. 'Welcome, Charlotte, Stephen, it is wonderful to see you.' Charlotte curtseys and Papa bows, then Lady Susan says, 'I want you to meet my horse, Prince Regent. He is the love of my life. He has sired many of the superb offspring you will see around here and is unmatched of any horse I have ever come across.' Prince Regent on hearing his name nickers

245

and lowers his head to be scratched behind the ears. Susan laughs and then says, 'How was your journey?' 'It is a beautiful day for a ride,' answers Papa, 'and we made very good time. We easily should be able to make it back to Willingden by nightfall as it is only about three hours.' 'Well,' responds Lady Susan, 'we shall see. Perhaps it will be best to stay the night if you are willing, or if you are not, perhaps Charlotte can stay the night and I can return her by coach tomorrow.' 'As you wish, My Lady,' responds Papa, 'but the turnip and cabbage harvest is in full swing and I believe, if you can spare me, I shall return this night.' 'Very well Stephen,' replies Lady Susan, 'as you wish. Charlotte if you will stay, I shall send you by carriage tomorrow and you shall be accompanied by one of my ladies in waiting for your comfort and security.' 'I shall be happy to stay, Susan,' agrees Charlotte, 'if Papa is amenable?' 'Yes, you are your own woman,' says Papa looking to Charlotte, 'and if you are amenable to it, I am as well.' 'Very good,' replies Lady Susan, 'we are agreed. Perhaps we should go in and have tea and then we can talk further in confidence.'

Lady Susan leads the way into the house where after a little time, with the assistance of a maid, Charlotte has removed some of the detritus of road travel, and then she is shown into the drawing room where she finds Lady Susan and Papa deep in discussion with their heads close together. They look up as Charlotte enters and Lady Susan invites her to sit then calls for tea. The tea is served and once the servant has left the room, Susan looks at Charlotte for a moment then says, 'Charlotte, there is a matter of which you must be made aware. I know you have asked before when we met in London before the masked ball and Stephen has told me that you have asked him as well. You are a beautiful young woman now, no longer a child, and we believe,' looking at Papa as she says, 'it is time for some of the puzzle you have asked about to be revealed to you. It is a secret, one that has been held closely for all of your life to now and it is one that must be kept for as long as we and you shall live. It can never be told, not to anyone, ever. Should the secret be told, it should cause untold trouble to you, to me, to the Regency itself. There are only a few who know, not a handful more including your Mother than we three here at this moment. And it must remain that way forever. Do you understand?'

Charlotte looks into Susan's searching, beautiful eyes and then into her Papa's. She says, 'There is one who must know if I am to know. That is the man who will become my husband if a way can be found. I shall keep nothing from him, from Sidney Parker, if I should become his wife. If you can accept that proviso, then you can trust me with your secret forever. If you cannot, please do not reveal it to me.' Susan smiles gently at her and then turning to Papa says, 'Stephen, I shall be forever grateful for your and Jane's raising of this beautiful, smart, brave and strong young woman. She is without match in the realm either man or woman and would do a King proud to have at his side. Mr Sidney Parker is a man truly blessed to have captured her heart. I should hope he knows it.'

Lady Susan continues. 'Charlotte, first you should know who I am. I am the daughter of the Duke and Duchess of Kent. They have both passed as I'm sure you know. I had one brother, the Marquess, who died without a heir on the quarterdeck of Vice-Admiral Collingwood's ship of the line, Royal Sovereign, at the Battle of Trafalgar. I received my title upon my brother's death because, and it is rare and I know not the reason for it, but letters patent for the Kent dukedom allow that a woman can gain the title if there are no lawfully begotten male heirs, so in truth I am a Duke rather than a Duchess,' she says with a laugh, 'but I prefer to be known as Lady Susan. Be that as it may, here am I and with the fortune and estates that came with it. But that is not the secret and I can see in your face that you know it is not. There is more and to expose the secret, I must dig back further into the previous century. Are you ready to hear it?' Charlotte looks at Susan and then Papa, thinking how serious they both look and is there something of sadness that I see in Papa's face? 'Yes,' she replies, 'I am ready to hear it if you wish me to know it.'

Lady Susan continues, 'This secret has to do with the Prince Regent. It is why I called you to me when you came to London before my masked ball. It is a matter of the utmost seriousness and it relates to a marriage..., and a child.' She pauses as if to question herself whether or not she should continue, thinks Charlotte. What could a country gentry family, my family, possibly have to do with the Prince Regent, the future King and Lady Susan? Lady Susan looks around the room then says, 'I shall not continue my story now. It is possible that there are too many ears here. I should like to ride to a place that I know far from any listeners except you, Charlotte, and your Papa if you are amenable?' Charlotte glances around at the closed doors and even tightly shut windows on this warm day and wonders at such a secret that perhaps even the privacy of Lady Susan's drawing room is not sufficient then looks at Papa and says, 'Yes, Susan, I am amenable to a ride if my Papa also is.' Charlotte watches as her Papa smiles fondly at her and then says, 'Let us go then.'

They go out to the stables where Lady Susan orders their horses be saddled and after a few minutes, the horses; Lady, Prince Regent and Papa's mount are led out. 'What do you think of your mount, Lady, Charlotte,' Lady Susan asks? 'Oh, she is beautiful and I love her,' Charlotte replies, 'I shall miss her.' 'You shall not,' replies Lady Susan with a smile, 'she is yours.' 'What,' says Charlotte in a stunned tone, 'you are teasing me, Susan. And in any case, I cannot accept. She surely is worth a fortune. I am not worthy of nor deserving of such a gift.' 'You are, Dear Girl,' responds Lady Susan. Charlotte looks from Lady Susan to her Papa standing near by and asks, 'Papa, surely this we cannot accept? Lady Susan's generosity is beyond all bounds, but we must decline.' Papa looks back at her and says, 'This is not a decision for me to make, Charlotte. Let us ride for a bit and you can think on it.' A groom assists Lady Susan in mounting while Papa assists Charlotte then he mounts his horse and they set off with Susan leading the way. Charlotte rides along side of her Papa for a while keeping her silence as she mulls over the day's events to this point. She is feeling that she is living some kind of dream, can this all be real, that I am on my way to a secret meeting place with the Duchess of Kent, that I have been gifted a horse worth a fortune by that same personage who insists that I call her Susan? I am lost as to finding an explanation for it. Turning to her Papa who is riding close beside her, she whispers, 'Papa, am I to fear what I am to hear when we reach our destination with Lady Susan?' He looks back at her with a gentle, soft, and is it she thinks a little sad expression in his gaze then says, 'Dearest Charlotte, you are not to fear it, but I must tell you that what you are to hear as I know it will come as a shock and perhaps cause you pain. But you must trust that it will be the truth and that you deserve to know it. You must know it for your own security.'

As they travel to Lady Susan's meeting place, Charlotte's party is embraced by a early afternoon sky of royal blue and and bright sun accompanied by a light breeze giving the varying green shades of fields of grains and grasses a rippling texture reminding Charlotte of waves in the sea. They continue what proves to be short ride from the stables along a cart track through the fields and then up into a copse of huge oak trees that stand on a promontory from which Charlotte sees as they reach the top, a view of the sea sparkling in the distance. Lady Susan pulls Prince Regent to a stop and waits for Papa to dismount and assist her down which he does before turning to help Charlotte down from Lady's back. Lady Susan walks over to two benches set at an angle to each other facing in the direction of the sea and invites Charlotte to sit with her as Papa lowers himself down onto the neighboring bench. 'Well, Charlotte,' she says, 'here we shall not be disturbed nor shall we be overheard. I shall tell you my story and you shall have the opportunity to ask what you wish after you have heard it. I caution that perhaps you will not find what you hear to your liking but it will be the truth and I believe that now is the time for you to know it for it is your story too. Are you ready?' Charlotte takes a deep breath, glances at her Papa who smiles his reassurance then says, 'Yes!'

'Once upon a time,' begins Lady Susan with a smile, 'there was a young girl of sixteen years who found herself in love with a man of much male beauty and charm. He was older than she in years, but young in heart and after a time, he too found himself returning her professions of love. He called her his Princess. They talked much of love and marriage and thought their dream should become real. And for a time it seemed that it should. For two years they talked of it and at last just a few months after her 18th birthday, he asked for her hand. It was joy for her, a dream come true. But this man, he was not just any man. He was a Prince, her Prince, but more than her Prince alone. That man, her love, was His Highness, the Prince of Wales. And he could not marry without the consent of his Father, the King. He did not have that consent, but he thought that he could gain it. After all, this girl was the daughter of a Duke, a Duke of high regard and status and wealth in the realm. But no, his entreaties to the King, his Father, were rebuffed. No, you shall not he was told. You must marry another who would make the throne stronger through ties with our allies on the continent. The Prince deigned not to hear what he was told. No, it would not be, he would not give up the girl, the women that he loved. So he took the next step that he could. He found a good man, a young man of the church that he knew, who knowing it was a crime, yet put his future at risk to join together two who loved each other and he married them on 1st April 1795.

He was well paid of course, and he left the church shortly thereafter to parts unknown to take up a new life in the former colonies of the Americas. But the marriage was done and in secret and for a short time, all was happiness and joy. And the young woman soon found that she was with child. Then came a summons from the King. The Prince was told that a bride had been found, a woman of high birth and a Princess in her own right. This will be a marriage that will strengthen the crown against our enemies, the French and Spanish, and help restore the prestige that was lost with the American colonies. And when you are King, he was told, you will rule the world. It is your destiny. But protested the Prince, I am married already. What…, you are not, thundered the King! But I am replied the Prince. I will not hear it shouted the King. You did not gain my consent. The marriage shall be annulled forthwith. The Prince appealed and yet appealed again that he loved his wife, that he could not give her up but the King was unmoved. You may have her as your mistress, the King replied, but you shall marry the Princess. It was done. The marriage was broken and the Prince married as he was ordered. But what of the woman with child and now with no husband. She must be hidden away and she was until after the birth of the child. Then she could take her place at court again. But what of the child? The child could not and could never be acknowledged by the Prince, nor by the Mother. If he should, he may lose his place in line of succession to the crown. Yes, the child is his and was conceived in marriage. The child is legitimate in the eyes of God and the Mother Church but not under English civil law because the marriage was not sanctioned by the King and as a consequence, it can never be acknowledged. And if she, the Mother, should acknowledge the fact, it would be made a story of scandal and per-haps prevent that child from inheriting what is due it when the time comes.'

Lady Susan stops. Charlotte, who is sitting quietly, looks back at her asking herself, is that it, is that the secret, a child born of true love but

251

whom circumstances made an outlier, someone though no fault of his?/ her? own became a secret, a scandal that could destroy a King? And who is this child? Is that child me...? If not, why am I being told of it? Charlotte looks over to her Father who appears to be lost in his own thoughts. She looks back at Lady Susan who seems to be holding her breath and whose hands are clasped so tightly together that her knuckles are white.

Charlotte takes a deep breath then asks in a voice that despite her best efforts has a slight quaver in it, 'Susan, was the child a boy or a girl and when was he or she born?' Lady Susan raises eyes that threaten tears to Charlotte's. She says simply, 'The child was a girl and she was born on 18th February 1796.' Charlotte gazes into Susan's eyes and then looks to her Papa who sits slumped as if in pain on the other bench. 'So I am the secret,' quietly responds Charlotte! 'Yes you are, my Darling,' says Lady Susan almost in a whisper. 'You are my daughter and that of the Prince Regent who one day will be King and you are named after your grand-mother, Queen Charlotte, who is one of the handful privy to your secret, our secret, and who supported the Prince's marriage to me.' 'And what of my Papa and my Mama, my brothers and sisters,' Charlotte asks? 'I am not Charlotte Heywood, then? 'Yes, you shall always be Charlotte Heywood,' responds Susan. 'Jane and Stephen are your Mother and Father. They raised you and gave you the love I could not that made you into the beautiful, smart and brave young woman that you are while I by necessity watched from afar. But I always loved you and always shall love you as my own till the end of my days.'

Charlotte sits quietly on the bench thinking of what she has just heard. How can it be that I am not who I thought I was. I was so sure of my place in the world and now I am not. I am part of a family that I love but I am not of it. Lady Susan is my Mother and the Prince Regent is my Father, neither of whom I can ever acknowledge nor they me. But here is love. Papa, Stephen Heywood, would not be here if he did not love me, care for me and neither would Susan, my birth Mother. So, have courage, Charlotte, you shall need more than you ever thought and still you must find a way to resolve the problem of debt and thereby the future of Sanditon and your own future with Sidney, if it is to be. She looks up from her thoughts and gazes out over the countryside to the sea, now a part of her as Sanditon also is then turns to Lady Susan.

'Susan..., I am not sure I can continue to call you that, now that I know you are my..., my Mother but Mama cannot be since we can never be that outside of this meeting and Mama I have in Willingden...' Lady Susan raises her head and smiles. 'You are very wise for one so young and you may continue to call me Susan, Charlotte. Perhaps it will help if you begin to consider me more like a older sister. That way we can be family in our own minds but without making public acknowledgement or raising suspicions that we are more than good acquaintances.' Charlotte manages a smile and says, 'Yes Susan, that will work very well in my mind. I shall see you as my older sister.' 'Then that is what we shall be Charlotte; Sisters, loving Sisters in our minds and good acquaintances for others to know. Well then with that decided, have you any more questions for me now,' Lady Susan concludes? 'Yes, replies Charlotte, 'that royally dressed masked man who would not tell me his name that I danced with at the ball; was he the Prince Regent?' 'Oh, you clever girl,' laughs Lady Susan. 'Yes, he was!' 'Did he know I am his daughter when he danced with me,' Charlotte asks? 'Yes, he did,' Lady Susan responds, 'but he can never be in your presence again, nor you in his, it is too dangerous, but he could not pass on the opportunity to dance with you, his daughter, the issue of our love for one another which always shall be but can never be known.'

Charlotte shakes her head which is swimming with thought and looks over at her Father..., Papa, you will always be that to me. 'Susan, Papa, I do wish to know how I became a part of the Heywood family.' Papa smiles and nods toward Lady Susan. Susan smiles back and then says, 'Your Papa and his forebears have long been associated with my family. Before Stephen returned to Willingden where the Heywood family had ancestral lands, he was to become the House Steward for the Duke of Kent as was his father and his father's father before him. He and Jane were just starting their young family; at the time of your birth only one child had been born, your Brother Benjamin who was the age of one; and it was determined in consultation with my Father, the Duke, that Stephen and Jane should move to Willingden and reestablish the Heywood presence at the farm which had been in the hands of a tenant for many years. That is what they did, arriving in Willingden with young Benjamin and a baby Charlotte in the summer of 1796. Those travels to London "to receive his dividends" which you are so well aware of Charlotte and I must say caused your Papa so much discomfort that was reported to me because of your demands to accompany him in later years,' she says with a smile, 'those travels were to report to me on you, my dearest love. I suppose we must still continue those so as to not raise suspicions though now that you know, perhaps they are not necessary since I am your acquaintance and friend.'

Lady Susan's comment prompts a thought in Charlotte's mind. 'Susan,' she says, 'there may be suspicions of wealth in my future. Sir Edward intimated as much when he was pushing unwanted attentions on me before I left Sanditon. I do not know whence such rumors might come, but he is in league with Mrs Wickham, I think, so I believe you..., we must be careful to not stoke any such rumors.' 'Yes Charlotte,' she replies, 'we shall be. But now, I believe we must be going back if Stephen, your Papa, is to make a homeward journey today in good time.' Papa helps Charlotte and Lady Susan mount then gains his own seat for the ride back to the stables. On arrival, he is given a fresh horse and sustenance for the homeward journey. He comes to Charlotte before mounting, embraces her and says, 'I shall see you tomorrow evening, Charlotte.' 'Have a safe journey home, Papa,' Charlotte replies. Then he mounts his horse, waves to her and urges his horse into a trot out of the courtyard. Charlotte watches her Papa until he is out of sight then turns and goes into the house where Susan awaits.

Chapter 47

Wednesday - 17 June 1818 - Morning - Warwick Court

Morning comes at Warwick Court and Charlotte awakens well rested. She had enjoyed a fine supper and good conversation with Susan and Philip Stanley the previous evening finding him charming and very like his older brother, Lord Somerset. She also had taken the opportunity to study Susan during supper and found her affection for her growing by the moment. My Mother, she thinks, yes Mama Jane is my mother as well. I am blessed with two wonderful Mothers who love and care for me. I cannot quite encompass it yet, but I shall. She goes down to the dining room to find Susan alone. Susan looks up with a smile at her entry and asks, 'Did you sleep well, Charlotte?' 'Oh yes, Susan, thank you. I slept very soundly and I feel guilt about it. I fear that I have done nothing to advance a rescue of Tom Parker's Sanditon Spa Town debt problem and Sidney too remains at risk of bankruptcy and ruin.'

'Oh but you have Charlotte,' replies Susan. 'I have been working at that since I received your letter of 27th May about the matter. And now that we have had our talk of yesterday and you understand the delicacy of the matter for you and me, we shall take steps to solve the difficulty. I have many ways to influence outcomes to the good for people who are deserving of it. Perhaps Tom Parker does not deserve it, but you do.' 'I know Mr Tom Parker is a not very good manager of money,' replies Charlotte, 'but his Sanditon project should and can be a success I hope and believe. But I fear for Sidney. He sees himself in a hopeless quandary and he may think his only way out to resolve the debt is marriage to Mrs Wickham. What if he has already done so, engaged himself to Mrs Wickham? I freed him from his obligation to me so he could do that if he must to save Tom and himself, but I have been warned that she would destroy him; he would destroy himself if he should find himself trapped in a marriage with her and I should share in the blame if so because I released him into her grasp.' 'Oh my dear Girl,' replies Susan, rising to come over to where Charlotte is seated and taking her hands, 'you would take the woe of the world on your shoulders. I shall not allow it.'

Lady Susan continues, 'There will be rescue, but when it is to be, change must come to Sanditon Town and that change will see determinations on the expenditure of investment funds in hands that are not Tom Parker's. You and perhaps Sidney shall be entrusted with that obligation going forward.' Charlotte looks at Susan with new hope in her eyes and heart. 'Oh Susan, if there is anything you can do to save Sanditon, to save Tom Parker and Sidney Parker from ruin, I shall be forever grateful.' 'It shall be done, Charlotte,' responds Susan. 'It will cost a pretty penny of your birthright, but it shall be done as I said with the proviso that the decisions on how the funds shall be spent rest in your hands rather than Tom Parker's. And perhaps the risk can be shared rather than taking all from my hands because I have many friends at court who are looking for places for their capital outside the banks which they now fear are in danger of collapse as many are since the defeat of Napoleon at Waterloo. This is the reason Mr Parker's bank sold his loan to Mrs Wickham. They need capital and Mr Tom Parker's sinking reputation made his loan a foregone determination to be rid of. Mr Parker has by necessity perhaps depended on the banks for loans but those loans are too much at the whim of bankers to be sure of accomplishing what needs to be done in Sanditon and of course now we know another danger of them besides bankruptcy and debtors prison, and that is they can be sold to someone who wishes to revenge themself upon another party.'

Chapter 48

Charlotte will return to Willingden on Lady's back. Lady Susan has insisted that Lady is Charlotte's and that she will hear no more protestations about it. With the matter settled, at least to Lady Susan's satisfaction, Charlotte refuses Susan's offer of a phaeton to return to Willingden and opts instead to ride Lady. Susan is adamant that she will not ride unaccompanied so Philip Stanley's services as a companion for Charlotte's return travel to Willingden are offered and accepted. After a uneventful journey, they arrive in the late afternoon and as they turn into the courtyard at Heywood House, Charlotte notices a unfamiliar horse tethered at the post and wonders who is calling. Philip helps her down and she invites him to come in for refreshment before beginning his return journey to Warwick Court. She pats Lady's neck and is nuzzled in return. Philip laughs and says, 'Lady Susan choose well for you, Charlotte. Lady is your horse, of that there is no doubt.' Charlotte smiles in response and replies, 'Yes, she has taken to me quite well as I have to her. Shall we go in?' At that moment, Annabella comes out, sees Charlotte, then welcomes her back with a smile and a hug and then says, 'Charlotte, we did not know you were here. There is a visitor for you, and he is from Sanditon.' Charlotte takes a deep breath and asks herself can it be, is it Sidney? She takes another breath to compose herself and then asks, 'Who is it?' Annabella replies, 'I heard his name but

261

I do not remember it. But he is here in the drawing room with Papa, Mama and Anne.'

Charlotte goes in, removes her hat and cape stopping by the hall mirror to check her face and the state of her riding habit before continuing on in to the drawing room followed by Philip. As she enters, she sees Papa, Mama, Anne and with surprise accompanied by a pang of disappointment, Mr Stringer. She finds a smile to welcome him and moves toward them as they look to her. 'Mr Stringer,' Charlotte says with a welcoming smile, 'to what do we owe the pleasure of your call at Heywood House?' Then she notices the unsmiling looks exchanged as Mr Stringer replies simply without returning a smile, 'Miss Heywood, it is a pleasure to see you again. But I am afraid that I am here on a unhappy mission.' Charlotte wonders, with a sinking heart, what can bring Mr Stringer which can be so serious that he comes all the way to Willingden with such a heavy heart as she looks at him questioningly. He continues, 'I shall not sugar coat it. Mr Parker is seriously ill and may be at death's door. Dr Kniepp has been sent for and I was asked to ride to Willingden to fetch you.' 'What,' exclaims Charlotte, 'Tom Parker is ill and may die? How can that be? He was so healthy always in my experience. What can be the matter? And poor Mary, I must go to comfort her.' She sees another exchange of looks and then all faces turn to her.

'No,' responds Mr Stringer, 'it is not Mr Tom Parker who is ill.' Charlotte takes a breath and holds it while thinking to herself, if not Tom then Arthur who always is full of complaints of his health and perhaps to those we should have paid more attention. I cannot bear to hear it..., but I must. Releasing her breath, she breaks the silence and asks, 'Then who is it?' Robert Stringer looks at her sympathetically then says, 'It is Mr Sidney Parker who is ill!' Charlotte's heart stops at those words. She feels her legs begin to give way as a wave of darkness sweeps over her and she reaches to a nearby chair back to steady herself. No, she screams in her mind, not Sidney, not him, not the man with the beautiful eyes, not the man who saved me from the sea, not the man in whose arms I am most secure, not my champion, not my love. I could not have heard it right. It cannot be. She does not realize that she has spoken those last words, 'it cannot be' aloud, until Mr Stringer says, 'I am sorry, Miss Heywood, but it is!'

Mama comes over and puts her arms around her as they move to a settee together. They sit quietly for a few moments as Charlotte feels the comfort of Mama's arms, then she summons her courage and asks, 'What has happened Mr Stringer?' 'I do not know the particulars of it,' he replies, 'only that Mr Parker arrived back in Sanditon early this morning and came to Trafalgar House where he collapsed. But I am to take you there forthwith if you are willing and able.' Charlotte raises her head and says, 'Of course, I am ready to ride now.' She looks at Philip and then says, 'Mr Stringer, Mr Stanley, please pardon my incivility.' She introduces the two men and they exchange civilities then the subject turns to transportation. Papa says, 'Charlotte, if you go on horse back, you will not be able to take your trunk. And remember that Anne was to accompany you back to Sanditon. Perhaps you should take the curricle so that your trunk and Anne can travel with you.' 'That will be very well,' replies Charlotte, 'but Papa, I have Lady, my horse, whom you will remember from Warwick Court yesterday and I wish to take her with me.' She turns to Philip and asks, 'Will you return to Warwick Court and let Lady Susan know of Sidney's illness and my need to immediately return to Sanditon?' 'Yes Miss Heywood,' he agrees, 'and please accept my sympathy and hope for a quick recovery by Mr Parker. I shall go directly to Lady Susan and deliver your message.' 'Thank you, Philip,' she replies. Mrs Heywood speaks up and says, 'Mr Stanley, allow me to have food and drink prepared for you to sustain you on your homeward journey.' 'Thank you,' he replies and they go out. Mr Stringer then says, 'I will be pleased to drive the curricle with Miss Anne to carry her trunk and Miss Charlotte's as well. I can tether my horse at the rear.' 'That will be very agreeable I am sure,' says Mr Heywood, 'but I shall require the curricle and horses back here at the earliest opportunity. I shall send Mr Elkins, my groom, to accompany you for added security and to bring the rig and horses back.' It is agreed.

'Anne,' asks Charlotte, 'is your trunk already packed?' 'It almost is,' she responds. 'I shall go now and complete the packing if Mama can help me.' 'Yes, Dear,' replies Mrs Heywood who has come back from ensuring that Mr Stanley has been provided food and drink for his travel back to Warwick Court. They go out leaving Charlotte with Papa and Stringer. She says, 'Thank you, Mr Stringer. You cannot know what it means to me that you would come all this way. I know you are very busy with the work.' 'No, I was not,' he replies, 'the work has stopped. There have been no deliveries of supplies and there is great anger among the men because they have not been paid.' 'Well,' says Charlotte, 'we shall soon remedy that. I cannot at this time provide you with the particulars, but rest assured that you and your work-men shall be paid and we shall see Sanditon Town completed.' 'That is very good news indeed,' Stringer replies as Papa looks on in surprise. Charlotte then says, 'Mr Stringer, if will pardon us for a few minutes, I need to have a few words with my Papa.' He goes out. Charlotte turns to her Father and says, 'Papa, Lady Susan has promised to provide the funding to repay Tom Parker's loans and put Sanditon Town back on firm footing. She will try raise interest among her friends in investing as well and she thinks she will have some success because many of her wealthy acquaintances and friends are very wary of keeping their funds in banks at the moment because of the likelihood of bank failures. Her only condition is that Tom Parker can have no access to the funds. They will be in my hands.'

'So' Papa replies, 'you and Lady Susan have reached an accommodation. Mama will be so pleased as I am. But have we lost you?' 'No, Papa, you will never lose me. I shall always be a Heywood,' Charlotte returns as she goes into his arms, 'but now I must make haste.' She runs to Anne's room and finds Mama and Anne closing her trunk. She quickly throws her gowns, other garments and shoes into her own trunk and then continues on out into the courtyard where she finds Papa and Stringer with the curricle and Elkins who will ride with them to bring the rig back to Willingden. Charlotte asks Elkins to go and fetch the trunks to the rig. She can barely contain herself at the slow pace of the travel preparations because all she wants to do is throw herself onto Lady's back and ride as fast as she can to Trafalgar House. But at last all is ready. Stringer and Anne are in the curricle with the trunks and Elkins is on Stringer's horse. Charlotte quickly hugs Mama and Papa and promises to send a report on Sidney with Elkins when he returns with the curricle the next day. Then Papa helps her mount Lady and with a wave, she sets off followed by the curricle out of the courtyard.

They are fortunate to have a full moon for their travels since it is already dusk when they set off. Charlotte looks at the ghostly moon lighted landscape around her and it brings to mind a stanza by Lord Byron.

When we two parted. In silence and tears,

Half broken-hearted. To sever for years,

Pale grew thy cheek and cold, Colder thy kiss;

Truly that hour foretold. Sorrow to this.

Oh my dearest Sidney, runs through her head again and again. I shall not be able to bear it if you should leave me this night and I am not there; that I should never see your eyes on me again, never feel your touch again. That those beautiful eyes of yours should be forever closed to me will leave me but a dream of what could have been. What will be my life without your arms to go to when I need? Were you on your way back to me? Why was I not there to receive you when you came; perhaps even now if I was with you there is something I could do. I could at least hold your hand that you would know I am close. What will it matter now that Sanditon is saved if you are not there; Meaningless to me, It all shall be. She lowers her head onto Lady's neck drawing what comfort she can from the closeness. But the pace is so slow with the heavily loaded curricle. Charlotte considers if she should give Lady her head. She could have me in Sanditon in short order if I but dare, but I cannot abandon Anne. Oh what shall I do? She rides back to come along side the rig. Trying to keep her mind from Sidney, she looks at Stringer and Anne in the curricle and thinks to herself what a pair they make. I believe I can see cause perhaps for a certain young man I see here to be returning to Willingden to ask Papa a question if Anne should prove amenable to it. Still more than an hour we must travel this road. Charlotte's mind wonders back to Sidney. Is he living still? Surely I must feel it if he is no longer in this world. Stop it Charlotte, she says to herself. You must have faith that all will be well. But what if it is not comes the unwelcome next thought?

She drops back to Elkins who is riding in silence behind the curricle. 'Mr Elkins,' she says, 'Thank you so much for accompanying us to Sanditon.' 'It is my pleasure and duty,' he responds. 'And how is the Missus,' asks Charlotte? 'She very well indeed, Miss, I shall always be grateful for the many kindnesses Mr Heywood and Mrs Heywood have shown us. You know that I was in Willingden on the estate when they brought Mr Benjamin and you there. I remember that much effort was required to make Heywood house the comfortable place that it is now because over the years it had fallen into a state of great disrepair. My Missus, Martha, was entrusted with helping your Mother with your and young Benjamin's care while Mr Heywood settled his affairs I know not where, but it required several long absences from Willingden on his part.' 'I did not know that, Mr Elkins,' responds Charlotte, thinking that there are many things I did not know until I left Willingden.

Chapter 49

Charlotte suddenly realizes that her musing over Anne and Mr Stringer and her conversation with Mr Elkins has passed the time very well for she can hear the sound of the sea carried on the breeze and knows that Sanditon is near. In another half hour, they are descending into Sanditon and soon they find themselves in front of Trafalgar House which, in contrast to other houses that are dark, is blazing light from the windows though it is near the midnight hour. Charlotte jumps down from Lady, not waiting for help, hands her reins to Elkins, then goes to Anne whom Robert Stringer is handing down from the curricle. She takes Anne by the hand, then runs to the door and without ringing, lets Anne and herself in.

The first person she sees is Morgan who on hearing the door open comes into the hall. He stops with a look of surprise on his face, then says, 'Miss Heywood, Mrs Parker was so hoping you would arrive tonight. Let me fetch her for you.' 'Where is Mr Sidney Parker,' Charlotte asks? Morgan turns back toward her, looks down to avoid her eyes and says, 'He is upstairs, Miss, in your old bed chamber. I am sorry to tell you that there has been no improvement in his condition.' 'I must see him,' responds Charlotte and starts toward the stairs with Anne in tow. But just then Mary comes out of the drawing room and says, 'Charlotte, I thought I heard your voice. Please come into the drawing room,' turning as she says it and Charlotte follows with Anne. She finds Tom sitting on the settee looking forlorn. He looks up as Charlotte comes in and says, 'Charlotte, I am glad you are back but I fear that Sidney is lost to us. What will become of us all without Sidney?' 'Tom,' Mary cries, 'please do not speak that way. There is yet hope. Charlotte has returned and her presence gives me hope and when Sidney knows that she is here, he will fight ever harder to live.' 'Where is the Doctor,' queries Charlotte, 'is he with Sidney?' 'No,' Mary responds, 'Doctor Kniepp has not yet arrived. Miss Lambe and The Reverend Hankins are with him.' 'Oh I must go to Sidney at once,' cries Charlotte. Mary says, 'I caution you, Charlotte, that it will pain you greatly to see him.' 'It matters not, I must be with him,' says she. 'But Mary, this is my sister Anne who has accompanied me from Willingden. And Mr Stringer and Mr Elkins, my Father's groom, are outside with the rig and horses that need to be stabled. Can you manage that and also find a place for Mr Elkins to lay his head for what remains of the night? 'Of course,' replies Mary turning to Morgan who is standing at the drawing room door and listening. He nods and says, 'Do not concern yourself, Miss Heywood, I will take those worries off your mind,' and then goes out. 'Thank you, Mr Morgan,' Charlotte calls after him as she runs to the stairs leading to the bed chamber which was hers and now Sidney's.

Charlotte opens the closed door of her bed chamber and goes in. Georgiana is standing by the bed with a cloth and basin of water and the Reverend Hankins is reading aloud from his bible. They both look up at Charlotte's entry. 'Charlotte,' cries Georgiana, 'I am so glad that you are here. I don't know what to do nor how to comfort Sidney. He has been calling for you. He is so hot, he is burning up like with the cholera and all I can do is try to cool him and help him drink a little water. And he took some brandy. But nothing helps. He seems to be in great pain but he is getting weaker I think. He no longer is moving very much and seems not to hear well anymore. Reverend Hankins has tried to calm him, and perhaps he has but...,' looking beseechingly to Charlotte, 'please help him.'

Charlotte goes over to the bed and looks down. She sees a man whom she almost does not recognize. He is pale but blotchy with fever and the pain of his illness has twisted his features almost to make him a stranger. She reaches down and takes one of his hands in hers then sits on the edge of the bed. As she does, he opens his eyes and Charlotte feels that her heart will break as she sees the suffering in those beautiful eyes now clouded with pain looking up into hers. 'Charlotte,' he says in a almost inaudible whisper, 'you are here. You did not abandon me...' He tries to raise himself and cannot but his features relax and the hint of a contented smile crosses his lips as he slumps back and closes his eyes. 'Is he...,' asks Georgiana fearfully? Charlotte leans in close with her heart feeling as if it is caught in a vice and places her ear to his chest. 'He is breathes still,' she says as she lets out the breath she had been holding.

Charlotte hears a commotion on the stairs and Dr Kniepp enters the room. 'Mein Gott, Fräulein Heywood, I came as fast as I could. Let me examine Mr Parker. Please clear the room, except you, Miss Heywood. I must examine Mr Parker to see if I can discover his illness.' He begins to examine Sidney. He asks, 'Fräulein, do you know anything about the source of Mr Parker's illness, were there any complaints he made?' 'I don't know,' replies Charlotte, 'I was not here. But I heard that he collapsed. Mary may know because she received him.' 'Go and fetch her here at once,' commands Dr Kniepp. Charlotte goes out and down to the drawing room, finds Mary there with Anne, Georgiana and Reverend Hankins and says,

'Mary, Dr Kniepp needs to ask you about Sidney's illness. Pray come with me.' 'Of course,' replies Mary and follows Charlotte back up the stairs. 'Mrs Parker,' asks Dr Kniepp, 'did Mr Sidney have any complaint when he came here?' 'No,' answers Mary, 'but he was very pale and sweating profusely despite the cool of the morning. Oh and he was holding his side.' 'Where,' demands Dr Kniepp, 'show me!' 'Here,' says Mary pointing to right side of Sidney's stomach. 'Thank you, Mrs Parker,' Dr Kniepp says. 'You may go now, but Miss Heywood, please stay. I shall require your assistance.' Mary goes out and Dr Kniepp asks Charlotte to help him remove Sidney's shirt and breeches. Then he begins his examination. He gently presses on Sidney's lower abdomen and Charlotte sees Sidney's body recoil from his touch! 'What is it Dr. Kniepp,' she asks?

He looks at Charlotte with sympathy and says 'the muscles are very tense in an area which gives me cause to believe that he has perityphilitis (appendicitis). I will need to operate immediately, but I must warn you, Liebchen, that if the offending appendage has burst and perhaps even if it has not, he will die.' 'But Doctor, do you have what you need to carry out this surgery,' asks Charlotte? 'No, I do not,' Dr Kniepp replies. 'I must be honest with you, Fräulein. This surgery is seldom successful even with the best of surgical tools and never so if the appendage has burst. But Mr Parker will surely die before he can be moved to a operating theater so I have no choice but to do my best with what I have. Is Mr Parker a close friend of yours, Fräulein? I must ask because he very well may die while I carry out the cutting. If that is something that you cannot bear, then I will ask you to leave the room while I do the work.' Tears spring to Charlotte's eyes at the words which she notes that the good doctor sees. She replies, 'Mr Parker and I were to be wed and I hope we still shall be. I shall pray never to lose him, but it would be immeasurably worse if I should go and the surgery was unsuccessful because you needed assistance I could have provided. I shall stay and you may depend upon my constancy come what may.' 'Sehr gut,' the good doctor replies, 'then we must begin posthaste. I shall need plenty of hot water and some clean linens and please ask some-one to bring my saddle bags up. There are instruments and medicals that I shall require.' 'Yes, Doctor, I shall manage that,' replies Charlotte, then she goes down, finds Morgan, asks him to fetch the Doctor's bags and contin-ues to the drawing room.

Dr Kniepp follows Charlotte down and joins with Mary, Tom, Georgiana and Mr Hankins. Charlotte listens as he reports. 'I will do my very best to save Mr. Parker, but I fear the worst. Would that I could have arrived earlier but...,' he cuts his comment short and then says, 'I will need clean linens and plenty of hot water. Mr Parker must have surgery on his vitals. I have a new sleeping potion with me that may help. Miss Heywood will assist me.' Mary asks, 'Charlotte, are you sure you wish to assist Dr Kniepp? I worry that it will cause you great distress, and if Sidney should...,' Charlotte interrupts. 'No, Mary I must assist Dr Kniepp. I should never forgive myself if Sidney should die and I was not there with him; did not do all I could to save him.' Mary nods with understanding and then goes out to the kitchen. In short order, hot water is ready and a armful of fresh linens are delivered by Morgan into Charlotte's arms. Dr Kniepp looks him over and says, 'This man is strong and we may need his assistance to lift or turn Mr Parker before and during the procedure if he is willing.' Morgan replies, 'I shall be glad to be of assistance however I am needed, and I know Miss Heywood will be of great help in the surgery. She sewed a wound on my head better than any apothecary or surgeon in my experience.' 'Then let us make haste to go up and begin,' asserts Dr Kniepp. 'Though it already may be too late, we can but try our best.'

Georgiana touches Charlotte's arm as she follows Dr Kniepp out and asks, 'What can I do, Charlotte?' Charlotte looks into Georgiana's eyes and says, 'Try to rest a little, Georgiana. I will need you to help me watch over Sidney as he recovers,' then smiles and hugs her close for a moment. 'And what of your sister,' asks Georgiana looking to Anne who is sitting in a chair behind which now stands Robert Stringer who has slipped in unannounced. 'She may share my bed at Mrs Griffiths' tonight if she is willing.' 'Oh thank you, Georgiana, I know Anne is tired and that will be a great help.' 'Anne,' Charlotte asks, 'will that arrangement meet with your approbation?' Anne nods and smiles her appreciation. 'Mr Hankins,' Charlotte continues, 'pray can you walk Georgiana and Anne to Mrs Griffiths'?' 'Of course,' he replies, 'and I shall return in the light of day to see how Mr Parker is doing.' 'Thank you Mr Hankins and thank you too Mr Stringer,' says Charlotte gratefully.

Charlotte then returns to Sidney's bedside where, with Morgan's assistance, they lift and place clean linens under him. Dr Kniepp washes the area on Sidney's abdomen where he will cut and mixes a solution which he liberally applies to the area. Then he takes a corked bottle from his bag and says, 'Fräulein, pour some of this liquid onto this cloth and hold it over Mr Parker's mouth and nose. He may be unconscious and not feel the cutting, but this medicant will ensure that he is asleep so he does not feel it. But be careful to keep it from your face because it will make you dizzy or even unconscious yourself if you breathe it in.' Charlotte does as instructed then after a few minutes, watches as Dr Kniepp cuts into the man she loves. Oh Sidney she thinks, I pray that you cannot feel the knife; I pray that you know that I am here with you. Please do not leave me. Dr Kniepp suddenly exclaims, 'The appendage has not yet burst and that is good news indeed.' Charlotte watches as he ties the swollen, blackened tissue off and cuts it away. He closes the wound and says, 'Now we must wait, Fräulein! Why don't you rest?' Charlotte replies, 'No, I shall not leave him!' 'Then,' replies Dr Kniepp, 'I suggest that you get some rest here. Perhaps a pallet can be prepared on the floor next to the bed. I shall ask Mrs Parker and then I myself will return to the hotel for a few hours rest. I shall leave you a bottle of laudanum to give Mr Parker for the pain if he should awaken before I return. I wish you good night.' 'Thank you, Doctor,' responds Charlotte. 'I shall be forever grateful for your efforts to save Sidney.' He bows, goes out and Charlotte stands looking at a sleeping Sidney for a few minutes. She mulls over in her mind how uncertain life is and how what is most important at one moment is of the least concern in the next. Then Mary comes into the room followed by a maid with some bed clothes in her arms and says, 'Dr Kniepp has asked that a pallet be prepared for you here on the floor and it shall be done. You must rest, Charlotte. You will be of no help to Sidney if you should become ill yourself because you do not take proper care of your own health.' The pallet is prepared, good nights exchanged then Mary and the maid leave Charlotte alone with Sidney. I cannot rest. I must watch him thinks Charlotte as she lies down on the pallet, I cannot... as her eyes close.

Chapter 50

Thursday - 18 June 1818 - Morning - Sanditon

Charlotte awakens with a start. Daylight is streaming through the window. Where am I she wonders? Why am I on the floor? Suddenly the events of a few hours ago flood back. Sidney... I cannot hear him. I cannot have slept while he passed? No let it not be so. She raises herself from the hard floor covered by the thin quilt that was her bed and looks at Sidney. He is so quiet. She leans close, please let him be breathing she prays. He looks so still and pale, almost like a statue of marble, as he lies there but watching closely at last she can see his chest rising and falling. He is asleep still. Charlotte breaths a huge shuddering sigh of relief. He is alive and there is hope.

Charlotte stands and puts a hand to Sidney's forehead. It is cool, not like it was when she came at the midnight hour and saw a man, the man who owns her heart, at death's door. As she watches, Sidney begins to stir and grimace with pain. He does not open his eyes but she sees that he hurts. Charlotte speaks softly to him saying, 'Sidney are you awake. Can you hear me?' He does not respond. She decides to call for Mary. She goes to the door and opens it. She sees Morgan who appears to be asleep in a chair in the hallway. But he raises his head at the sound of the door and says, 'Miss Heywood, how can I be of assistance?' 'Oh Mr Morgan,' Charlotte cries, 'were you here all night?' 'Yes, Miss,' he replies. 'I could not leave if perhaps you should call for help in the night.' 'Thank you, Mr Morgan,' she replies, 'pray if you could summon Mary for me if she is awake?' 'Yes, Miss,' he replies and goes down the stairs returning in a few minutes with Mary. 'Is there improvement,' Mary asks? 'Yes, I believe so,' replies Charlotte, 'but Sidney is in pain from the cutting I think. Perhaps you can help me trickle a little water into his mouth and some of the laudanum that Dr Kniepp left here for the pain.' Mary raises Sidney's head slightly from the pillow and Charlotte pours a few drops of the laudanum mixed with water into his mouth. Sidney swallows and groans a little but does not open his eyes. 'I shall send Morgan to summon Dr Kniepp soon,' says Mary. 'Then Mr Morgan will need some sleep,' replies Charlotte. 'He spent the night outside this door.' 'I know and he shall have the rest of the day at leisure because of it; after he fetches Dr Kniepp,' replies Mary with a smile. Morgan goes out on his errand.

Mary then pulls a paper from a pocket on her night gown and says, 'Charlotte, I must bring this to your attention. Sidney brought it when him when he came yesterday morning and he had begun to discuss its contents when his illness manifested itself. I fear that Tom's anger at what Sidney said about this letter contributed to Sidney's collapse and if so I shall never forgive Tom for it.' 'What is it,' asks Charlotte? 'I shall read it to you,' replies Mary and begins;

Mayfair

8 June 1818

Dear Sidney:

*I have had a troubled mind since I came to Sanditon in my
effort to recover you, to restore you to me. I loved you as I love
you now when I chose to marry another ten years ago, but my
security is very important to me. I watched my Mother suffer as
my Father lost the bulk of his fortune to speculation and poor
management. I know you made your fortune in Antigua, but you
were so young with uncertain prospects when we were to be wed.
My Mother knew of a older gentleman who had a fortune and
no serious vices who was searching for a bride. So I married him
and with his passing, I am secure in my fortune.*

*So now that I am free, I want you, I want you back. You have
been in my heart all of these years; you are the only man whom
I truly have ever loved, and since you have not married, I harbor
hope that I remain in yours still. Yes, I know, that if we marry,
you will be marrying me for my wealth although it is my hope
that you will love me again after we are wed. And you will have
my wealth for Sanditon Town including the loan that I bought
which you can forgive. But there is a price to be paid. I have
seen how you look at that young woman, Charlotte Heywood;
it is how you once looked at me. If we are to marry, you must
promise me to never see her again under any circumstance. That
is the price for my fortune; you must banish Charlotte Heywood
from your life. And if I should so much as gain a hint that you
have ever violated my trust with regard to her, she will be ruined,
I shall bend my utmost efforts to ruin her. There will be scandal
and she will pay the price.*

I shall await your reply,

Maria

When Mary stops reading, she says, 'Charlotte, Sidney told Tom and me he cannot marry Maria. He begged our understanding and said he will find a way, he said he would even take Tom's debt upon himself and go to debtors prison in his stead. But he wanted us to know above all that when he read your letter, Charlotte, your letter releasing him from his obligation to you so he could marry Maria to save Tom and me, that the thought of losing you was unbearable. Then as he read Maria's letter a day or two later while yours lay in his pocket close to his heart, he said he knew he could not and would never marry her nor any woman who would threaten you with scandal or harm. Tom, to my shame, tried to protest that they were just words but Sidney would have none of it.' Charlotte stands with tears in her eyes looking at Sidney lying still on the bed. Then she says quietly, 'Sidney shall get well and, Mary, there is a way to realize Tom's dream and save both Sidney and Tom.' Mary looks at Charlotte with surprise. Charlotte continues, 'An investor has been found and the loans, including the one Mrs Wickham bought shall be expunged. Sanditon is saved and so are we all.'

Charlotte sees Mary's face relax. How beautiful and young she is thinks Charlotte. I had not thought how worry makes a face old before its time. She too has borne the burden of Tom's mistakes and now she can put her concerns where they belong, with the raising of her children and the health of her family. 'Oh, Charlotte,' Mary says, 'that is wonderful news; what have you done, where have you found that investor?' 'I am not at liberty to disclose that as yet,' Charlotte replies, 'but rest assured that concerns with financing and debt will soon be banished to history. But now, we must turn all our efforts to restoring Sidney to health. When he is able, I can discuss the how of it with him and also with you and Tom.' 'Yes, of course,' responds Mary, 'Sidney's recovery is the most important issue at hand.'

They are interrupted by the arrival of Dr Kniepp. 'How is the patient,' he asks? Without waiting for an answer, he goes to examine Sidney. 'Excellent,' he says. 'Fräulein, I confess now I had great concerns that Mr Parker would survive the night but did not wish to worry you. This morning, Mr Parker seems to be doing very well and as long as we do not see signs of infection, I think he will recover. He should only be given water and laudanum for the pain for the next few days then perhaps he can have a little soup to begin his recovery to full health. I shall remain in Sanditon for several days to watch over him, and it also will give me time to discuss further my arrangements to open my health spa clinic with Mr Tom Parker.' Mary interjects, 'Dr Kniepp, perhaps you should discuss your clinic plans with Charlotte as well. She will likely be one with whom to discuss the future of Sanditon alongside Tom.' As Dr Kniepp looks to Charlotte, she says, 'Well, Mary, that subject will have to wait for a while until Sidney is on his feet again, but Dr Kniepp, I shall always be grateful to you for saving Sidney's life.' 'Do not get the cart ahead of the horse, Fräulein,' responds Dr Kniepp. 'Mr Parker will be in danger for a few days yet. He should be watched around the clock during this time for any signs of relapse.' 'Yes, and so he will be,' agrees Mary. 'I shall watch over him for a while and give Charlotte time to organize some additional nurses.' 'I shall do that forthwith,' replies Charlotte. 'My sister Anne will help as will Georgiana and I am sure there will be others.' 'Sehr gut,' says Dr Kniepp. 'I shall call again in the evening to check on Mr Parker, but for the moment, I wish you good day.' He goes out. Charlotte says to Mary, 'While you watch over Sidney, I shall make those arrangements we discussed and I must also call on Lady Denham and let her know that Anne and I have arrived in Sanditon. She is expecting us.'

Charlotte goes downstairs leaving Mary with Sidney. Tom is nowhere to be seen and Charlotte goes into the kitchen to see if she can scurry up something for late breakfast before walking to Mrs Griffiths'. She finds Mrs Morgan in the kitchen with Mr Elkins who sitting at the kitchen table with tea and toast slathered with jam. 'Good Morning, Miss Heywood,' says he. 'Good Morning to you, Mr Elkins, did you rest well,' asks Charlotte?' 'I did, thank you, Miss' he responds. 'I was well provided for. But I must begin my journey back to Willingden forthwith. Mr Heywood needs me and the horses back as soon as I can get there.' 'Of course,' agrees Charlotte. 'Let me prepare a note for Papa for you to carry to him and then I shall let you be on your way.' She runs to Mary's desk in the drawing room, takes pen and paper and quickly dashes off;

Sanditon

18 June 1818

Dearest Papa and Mama:

Anne and I traveled safely to Sanditon with Mr Elkins' and Mr Stringer's assistance and there is good news about Sidney Parker. A wonderful physician, a Doctor Kniepp, came soon after we arrived to find Sidney in very dangerous condition, but he has done surgery and now this morning we have great hope that Sidney will recover his health.

I shall write more later when we know more. There still is Sidney's recovery to watch over and we pray that there will be no setbacks or impediments to his full return to health.

Please know that all is well with Anne and me.

Your loving daughter,

Charlotte

Charlotte returns to the kitchen as Elkins is finishing his breakfast and puts the note into his hands. He promises to place it in Mr Heywood's hands as soon as he arrives back in Willingden. Charlotte thanks him for his help then he says his goodbyes and goes out.

Now feeling herself more than a bit peckish, Charlotte realizes that she has had nothing to eat since the few nibbles Mama had sent with her to sustain her on her journey to Sanditon. She asks Mrs Morgan who provides her with tea, bread, cheese and jam along with some freshly picked early strawberries of the season. Oh she thinks, these berries are delicious and Sidney must taste them when he is able. With her hunger satisfied and her spirits lifted by the strawberries, Charlotte goes out, quickly walks the few steps to Mrs Griffiths' and goes in to find Anne and Georgiana together with Victoria and Rose. They jump up and all ask at the same time about Sidney. Charlotte reports that it is early days yet, but Sidney seems to be holding his own and asks if there are volunteers to sit with him when she cannot be there. She very quickly has four volunteers joined by a fifth, Mrs Griffiths, who comes in as they are discussing the arrangement. Charlotte explains that Mary is with him now but she will need spelling soon. Mrs Griffiths promises to go immediately to Mary to discuss scheduling her charges each to sit with Mr Parker for a few hours. Charlotte expresses her thanks and then says, 'But now Anne, you and I must call on Lady Denham. She is expecting us and we should inform her of our arrival in Sanditon.' Mrs Griffiths promises to call at Trafalgar House with Georgiana to spell Mary while Charlotte and Anne make their call on Lady Denham.

Chapter 51

As Charlotte and Anne walk toward Sanditon House to make their call on Lady Denham, Charlotte asks, 'How was your night with Georgiana, Anne?' 'Wonderful, she is most amenable,' Anne replies. 'I like her very much and I think we shall be fast friends. And she is most complimentary of you, Charlotte. She said she considers you a sister.' Charlotte smiles and says, 'Georgiana is a wonderful young woman and I am sure you cannot have a better friend as I myself have discovered.' Charlotte then asks, 'Mr Stringer seemed to be finding ways to stay close to you on every occasion, Anne. What do you think of him?' Anne looks down then back up at Charlotte saying, 'He is very kind. We talked of the world and of our dreams on the journey from Willingden and I feel as if I have known him forever. He told me about how he and his Father have worked to help build Mr Tom Parker's Sanditon Spa Town and his interest in becoming a builder and perhaps even an architect that he has realized after becoming engaged with the Sanditon bathing town project. He also mentioned the coming High Summer Ball that you told me about when you returned to

Willingden, Charlotte, and asked if I would have him first on my dance card and for two sets too.' 'And what did you say,' smilingly asks Charlotte? 'I said, I would strongly consider it,' laughs Anne. 'Of course, I shall have him first on my dance card. He came all the way to Willingden to fetch you and ...,' Charlotte finishes for her, 'and he is very handsome as well.' 'Yes, that too,' replies Anne with a blush.

Their conversation carries them to the gates of Sanditon House. Anne is properly impressed with the grandeur of the place. She says with great excitement, 'Oh, Charlotte, this looks like the palace of a King or Queen!' 'Well, it almost is,' responds Charlotte. 'Lady Denham certainly has the power of a Queen in Sanditon or at least demands the fealty of everyone as if she thinks she has. She knows everything that goes on in her fiefdom and she makes no bones about showing anyone who questions her that she rules it. But inside that formidable creature that you shall soon make the acquaintance of, you will find that she has a heart, perhaps even a soft one, although she is very careful to keep it well hidden.' They reach the door and ring to soon be greeted by Hawkins, the footman. 'Welcome back to Sanditon, Miss Heywood,' he says, 'Lady Denham is expecting you.' 'Thank you, Mr Hawkins,' responds Charlotte. 'It is good to see you again. But why is the Lady Denham expecting me? I did not know that she knew I was back in Sanditon.' 'She knows everything, Miss Heywood,' Hawkins replies with a smile. He shows them in to the drawing room where Lady Denham sits with Clara. Clara jumps up at Charlotte's and Anne's entry and runs to them. 'Oh I am so glad to see you back in Sanditon, Charlotte. I was lost when I heard that you had left and without a goodbye. But you are back.' 'Yes, Clara and please allow me to introduce my sister, Anne.' Civilities are exchanged then Clara leads them over to Lady Denham.

'Well, Miss Heywood,' Lady Denham says, 'it is good to see that you have remembered your civilities and called on me this time unlike the last when you left. And I presume that this is the sister that you wrote to me about?' 'Yes, My Lady,' responds Charlotte, 'this is Anne.' Anne curtseys shyly and Lady Denham says, 'You look to be sturdy and of fair appearance. I am sure that you will find Sanditon pleasing. We shall have to put you to work. And with regard to that, Miss Heywood, when do you expect to take up your position here at Sanditon House. Clara has plans to leave me for London to take up a position in Mr Nisbet's household just after the High Summer Ball. There is very little time for you to become competent to assist me before she goes so I shall expect you to begin your work here today.' 'No, My Lady, I cannot,' answers Charlotte. 'I shall be engaged over the next few days at least with the care of Mr Sidney Parker as he recovers from his illness.' 'Yes, I have heard that he was ill but surely the Parker family can care for him. I need you here,' responds Lady Denham. Clara speaks up. 'Aunt, you know very well that Charlotte must be with Sidney and you know the reason why!' 'Yes, I know the reason very well. Miss Heywood told me a while back and I have heard it from you and Esther too. But, if you cannot be here now, Miss Heywood, perhaps your sister can begin to work with Clara so that we shall have made some progress toward someone being ready to help me with my needs before she goes. What do you think about that?'

Charlotte looks to Anne and waits for her to respond. Anne looks back at Charlotte then says, 'Well, perhaps I can help at least for a while since Charlotte needs to stay close by Sidney until he is well again.' 'Very well then, Miss Heywoods, as I wrote in my letter of some time back to Willingden, I have had sleeping chambers prepared for you. You may occupy them immediately. I presume that you have your trunks somewhere and if you wish, I will send you back to Trafalgar House in my landau to fetch them.' 'Thank you, My Lady,' responds Charlotte, 'that will work very well for us. But I shall be spending most of my time at Trafalgar House until Mr Sidney Parker is on his feet again.'

'And if I may,' Charlotte continues, 'I have another request. I have my horse, Lady, in the stable at Trafalgar House but I would strongly prefer that she be stabled here where she will have the fields and grass on which to graze.' 'Yes, Miss Heywood, you may bring her here. But tell me,' Lady Denham asks, 'how did you come by a horse of the breeding and cost found only in the most famous stables of England?' 'I'm sorry, My Lady,' puzzles Charlotte, 'what do you mean?' 'Come now Miss Heywood, don't be coy,' responds Lady Denham. 'Stable hands do talk you know, and already your horse, Lady, is the talk of the alehouses and such talk never takes long to come to my ears. By all accounts, she is of a standard found only in the royal houses of the Regency.' Charlotte hesitates while thinking to herself that nothing gets by this formidable woman, then says, 'She was a gift, My Lady.' 'A gift,' snorts Lady Denham, 'and from whom may I ask? And what have you done to deserve such a "gift"?' Charlotte stands nonplussed for a moment, then says, 'I am not a liberty to say, Lady Denham, but she is mine and I love her.' 'I should guess not, Miss Heywood, but I have to say that you continue to amaze me and until you came along in my long life, I had thought to have seen it all. No matter, get yourselves away from here so I do not have to wait 'til I am in my grave to see Anne here at work.'

Lady Denham then calls Hawkins to ready the landau and while they wait, sends Clara with them to show them their bed chambers. Anne is properly impressed with the size and luxury of her bed chamber and whispers, 'My bed chamber is sufficient to put all of the Heywoods together in comfort, Charlotte. I do believe I shall be quite comfortable here.' 'Well,' responds Charlotte with smile, 'perhaps you may wish to see what kind of taskmistress Lady Denham is before you determine that.' Turning to Clara, she asks, 'Clara, will we see Mr Nisbet here for the Ball?' 'Oh yes,' she answers, 'both he and Somerset will be here. I think Somerset and Esther plan to be wed in Sanditon just after the Ball. Esther said that Somerset had procured a license from the Archbishop and that the wedding will be on 1st July. 'Wonderful,' replies Charlotte, 'and we certainly must talk more later, but now I must hasten back to Trafalgar House to see about Sidney. I have been gone far too long.' She starts for the stairs and the front door and Anne follows. They go out to the waiting landau and Hawkins hands them up into it.

They wave goodbye to Clara, the coachman slaps the reins and they are on their way back to Trafalgar House. After a short ride, they find themselves at the door and go in without ringing followed by the coachman who is to carry their trunks to the landau for transport back to Sanditon House. All is quiet in the house. Where is everyone wonders Charlotte? She goes into the drawing room to find Mary sitting with a bowed head along with Tom, Arthur and Diana. Mary looks up at Charlotte's and Anne's entrance. Charlotte sees that Mary has tears in her eyes. Mary stands, comes over to her, clasps Charlotte's hands in hers and says, 'I am so sorry, Charlotte.' What... Charlotte thinks, what is she saying? Mary continues, 'Georgiana is with Sidney and The Reverend Hankins along with Dr Kniepp. Sidney is...!' No..., I shall not hear those words ricochets through Charlotte's mind. No, no, no... as she turns and runs for the stairs. She passes Morgan who is standing outside the door and runs into her bed chamber, Sidney's bed chamber. She sees Georgiana standing by the bed and Reverend Hankins behind her with his bible. Dr Kniepp is leaning over a still figure under a quilt on the bed. Charlotte stops and takes in the scene. No, no, no is all she can think. I cannot bear it if he is gone, if he has gone whilst I was not with him. Dr Kniepp turns his head, sees her and beckons for her to come toward the bed.

With her heart in her throat, Charlotte steps forward to see what she dreads to see. Dr Kniepp stands and moves back so she can see Sidney, her Sidney. Charlotte feels as if she is walking in treacle; an awake nightmare. She looks down at the face of the man she loves and sees him smile at her. Her legs will not hold her as her knees buckle and she falls to them beside the bed. 'Charlotte,' croaks Sidney, 'my darling Charlotte, I am so happy to see you. You saved me you know, when you came last night. I would have given up had you not come. My life is not worth living without you. You can never leave me again.' Charlotte bursts into tears and when they have subsided enough for her to talk, she says, 'Oh Sidney, I thought you had passed when I came into the room. Everyone downstairs is in mourning. Forgive me, my dearest for ever leaving you.'

Dr Kniepp speaks up and says, 'It is understandable that there were concerns. I think perhaps Mr Parker had received a little to much care if you will, a little bit too much laudanum, but it is of no concern now. I shall make it very clear the quantities to be administered going forward so that we do not have a scare like this again. 'So,' states Charlotte, 'Sidney is on the mend?' 'Well,' replies Dr Kniepp, 'it is a bit too early to say that with certainty but all looks good for Mr Parker. There are no signs of infection yet, his lungs are clear and his heart beats strongly in his chest. Perhaps,' he continues with a smile, 'Mr Parker will even be in condition to attend the ball next weekend though he may not be up to his usual standard on the dance floor. A week should be sufficient for a substantial recovery bar-ring any setback which frankly I do not expect of someone like Mr Parker here who has the constitution of a fine horse or perhaps a very stubborn mule.' 'Oh, Dr Kniepp, I shall never forget your indispensable role in saving

Sidney and we shall find a place for your clinic here forthwith so that you may work your miracles for others going forward.' 'Thank you, Fräulein,' he replies with a laugh, 'but now I must go down and save the rest of the Parker family from their thoughts that the grim reaper has visited.' He goes out as Charlotte turns back to Sidney. Georgiana says, 'I thought Sidney had passed when I came to sit with him. He was so still and pale. And The Reverend Mr Hankins came in and thought the same so we sent Morgan to call for Dr Kniepp who was downstairs with Mary and Tom. When he came, he was quick to say that it was just too much laudanum and after a while Sidney opened his eyes and you see that all is well. But I shall never forget this day.'

'Well,' says the Reverend Hankins, 'it seems that my services are not needed here and I have other calls yet to make this day so I will depart,' and he does. Charlotte tells Sidney and Georgiana that she will be back soon and goes out to Morgan in the hallway. She says, 'Mr Morgan, you still have not had your rest, have you?' 'No, Miss,' he replies, 'but I shall now that I know that Mr Sidney is recovering and you are here with him.' Charlotte then remembers that Lady Denham's coachman is waiting for her and Anne's trunks. But she goes to her own first and takes out the necessaries for a few days so that she can remain with Sidney then asks Morgan to fetch the coachman to carry the trunks out. It is all taken care of and then leaving Georgiana with Sidney, she goes down to find the Parker family in a relieved and celebratory mood. She sees that Mr Stringer has come while she was upstairs and is standing near Anne. She smiles at that then goes to Anne and asks, 'Anne, are you amenable to go and be by yourself at Sanditon House without me. I feel that I must stay here for a few days.' Anne hesitates then says, 'Do you think Georgiana would join with me? Then I should feel like I have a friend in that strange place.' 'Shall we ask her,' replies Charlotte. Diana who is listening to the conversation rises with Arthur and says, 'We shall go up and visit with Sidney for a bit and send Georgiana down to you.' They go out and in a few minutes, Georgiana comes in. 'Georgiana,' Anne asks, 'would you accompany me to Sanditon House and stay with me for a few days while Charlotte remains here to be near Sidney?' 'Yes, of course I shall,' replies Georgiana. 'I am sorely tired of my small room at Mrs Griffiths' and I should fancy staying in new surroundings for a few days.' It is settled. After jotting down a quick note to Mrs Griffiths detailing her approval of Georgiana's stay at Sanditon House, Charlotte walks them out to the landau followed by Robert Stringer where she directs the coachman to make a stop at Mrs Griffiths to allow Georgiana to inform Mrs Griffiths of the arrangements and to fetch a few necessaries for her stay at Sanditon House. Mr Stringer volunteers his services as escort which is accepted by Anne and Georgiana and they set off.

Charlotte goes back in to Trafalgar House and up to Sidney's chamber where she finds that Diana and Arthur have been joined by Mary and Tom. They are talking and as Charlotte comes in, she catches a few of Sidney's words. '...and I shall ask for her hand again.' As she enters all heads turn to her, with smiles on every face except Tom's. Charlotte continues on to the bed where she reaches down to find Sidney's hand. He smiles up at her and says in a weak voice, 'Charlotte, this is not the way for a gentleman to ask for the hand of his lady. I should be on bended knee, but since this is my second proposal and given the circumstances, I hope you will forgive the informality of it. Will you marry me?' Charlotte looks down into his pale but smiling face, lightly presses his hand and says, 'Yes, Sidney, I shall marry you.' Mary quickly comes and hugs Charlotte. Diana smiles and offers her congratulations while Arthur joyfully dances a jig around the sickroom. But Tom just nods stiffly, says 'My felicitations, Miss Heywood,' and leaves the room. Mary calls to him and when he does not stop or return, she glances at Charlotte whispering, 'Please forgive Tom,' then goes out after him. Well, thinks Charlotte as she goes to sit beside Sidney, Tom's temper will improve no doubt once he knows that Sanditon is saved without dependence on Mrs Wickham. But now all attention must focus on Sidney's return to health.

Chapter 52

Wednesday - 24 June 1818 - Sanditon

A week has passed. Charlotte has rarely left Sidney's side except as necessary to deal with her own personal requirements. Sidney has improved each day and sat up on the third day. Charlotte has kept the healing wound in his side clean and he has not needed the laudanum by the third day after the surgery. Dr Kniepp has called each day and been happy to see and report additional progress toward full recovery on each visit. On the fourth day, Sidney rises from his bed and demands a bath which Dr Kniepp sanctions with the proviso that the wound is kept dry. Charlotte who by now is no stranger to the secrets of Sidney's body assists him along with Morgan who helps him into and out of the bath and assists him with his night shirt. Charlotte's happiness soars with the improvement she sees each day as the man who owns her heart is slowly restored to the Sidney she knew before the illness with the sparkle returning to his beautiful eyes, especially when they are turned on her.

Charlotte has made regular visits to Sanditon House to see Anne and Georgiana and on this day, decides to call on Lady Denham whom she has only seen in passing during her short visits. She is ushered in by Hawkins to find Esther and Clara with Lady Denham. 'Well,' challenges Lady Denham, 'you finally deign to again find a few minutes to call on me, your benefactor, after all of this time. Here I have offered you a fine position in my household and this is how you treat me. Perhaps you have determined that I am not of your station and you can treat me as you wish?' 'Oh no My Lady, I should never wish to show you any disrespect. I simply have been fully engaged in the care of Sidney Parker about whom I am happy to report is well on the road to full recovery of his health,' replies Charlotte.

Lady Denham smiles, 'So all is well with Sidney Parker and I presume with you too, Miss Heywood, as a result of it. Well, I have several matters to discuss with you. First, I do not believe that I will require your services as my companion!' 'What,' replies Charlotte with shock! 'You heard me, Miss Heywood,' says Lady Denham. 'I have determined that my needs will be well served by another who does not have so many demands on her time as you.' Charlotte sits abruptly and looks at Lady Denham while she waits for her to continue. She does. 'Yes, your sister Anne suits me very well as a companion. I have found her to be highly competent. Clara has found her to be quick of mind and learning and I expect that she will entirely suit my requirements and, she is not so strong in her opinions as sometimes you are.' 'And have you inquired of Anne if she would be amenable to accepting the position,' asks Charlotte? 'I have,' replies Lady Denham, 'and she said she must await your opinion and approbation before making the commitment. Shall we call for her and ask the question? She and Georgiana went for a stroll this morning but they should have returned by now.' Turning to Clara she says, 'Clara, please go and see if you can find and fetch her to us. And Esther please go with her as I have matters to discuss for Miss Heywood's ears only.' Esther looks to Charlotte questioningly then rises with Clara and they go out.

'As I said,' Lady Denham continues, 'I have other matters to discuss with you, Miss Heywood. The first has to do with my investment in Tom Parker's Sanditon Town. It has come to my attention that another investor has taken interest, in fact that investor has bought the loans outstanding from the banks except for the one owned by Mrs Maria Wickham and may have advanced additional funds to the project. What do you have to say to that, Miss Heywood?' Charlotte shakes her head and marvels at Lady Denham's ability to nose out anything and everything that happens from Sanditon to London and indeed probably in the whole of England as well. 'Yes,' Charlotte replies, 'that has come to my attention, My Lady.' 'And...,' snorts Lady Denham with a soul piercing stare. 'Well, I see you are not going to be helpful in this regard, Miss Heywood. It is of no matter, I shall find out soon enough and I must say that I feel much more secure with my own investment as a result of it. Now to another matter, that of your horse, Lady, I believe you said her name was. I have had several inquiries about her, how I happen to have her in my stables and two offers to purchase her. That last caused me to make a rare visit to my stables to view her and I must say that I have never seen a better bit of horseflesh and even I was surprised by the amounts offered for her, and as you know Miss Heywood, I am not easily bowled over. Because of that, I now do not allow her to graze in the fields without a groom present and I have a man posted with her in the stables at night to guard against her loss. Do you still wish to keep the secret of your possession of her to yourself?' 'I must,' replies Charlotte. 'You are a conundrum, Miss Heywood, but never fear, I shall unravel the mystery of you,' Lady Denham concludes with a smile.

At that point to Charlotte's immense relief, the inquisition is interrupted as Clara and Esther come back in with Anne and Georgiana in tow. Anne and Georgiana come to Charlotte and greet her as if they haven't seen her in months even though Charlotte has made daily calls on them at Sanditon House while caring for Sidney. 'Enough of this folde-rol,' snaps Lady Denham. 'We have business to discuss. Sit down Ladies. Anne,' she continues, 'please ask your question of your sister to resolve the matter of your becoming my companion.' Anne looks to Charlotte and says, 'Charlotte, this position as companion to Lady Denham is yours but now she has asked me to declare my interest in it.' Charlotte asks, 'Anne, would you like to serve as Lady Denham's companion?' 'I am amenable to it,' replies Anne 'but it is yours to accept or decline first.' 'Then the position is yours, Anne. I shall have other matters to engage my attention going forward.' Anne jumps up and comes to hug Charlotte who stands to receive her attentions while Lady Denham smiles and says, 'Well then, it is agree-able to all and we thus are agreed. And when,' she concludes with a laugh, 'are you to be married, Miss Charlotte?'

As Charlotte stands blushing, tongue tied and unable to look into any of the rapt pairs of eyes looking at her, Lady Denham continues, 'Esther, it seems this summer will see more than one wedding. Tell the young ladies about the arrangements of yours to Lord Somerset about which by the way I am most pleased.' 'Yes, Aunt,' replies Esther. 'Somerset and I are to be wed next week on 1st July, Wednesday next in fact, here in Sanditon. We have engaged the parson, the Reverend Mr Hankins to conduct the cere-mony. And following our wedding, we shall take part year residence here as well, at least through the end of the summer. I expect that we shall pur-chase one of Tom Parker's new apartments here in the new town. I shall know more about that after Somerset arrives back in Sanditon tonight. He has been addressing some matters in London.' 'Then you will attend the High Summer Ball this Friday, two days hence,' asks Charlotte? 'Yes, I shall, and what of you, and Sidney,' returns Esther? 'I do not believe that Sidney will be recovered enough to attend the Ball,' responds Charlotte, 'but if he should be, then we shall be there.'

'You will not attend without Mr Parker,' interjects Lady Denham! 'No, My Lady, 'I shall not,' replies Charlotte. 'So, Miss Heywood, you will attend with your love or not at all on the day of Venus,' exclaims Lady Denham! 'I cannot say that I am surprised...! Well, look at me, Miss Charlotte, what do you see?' 'My Lady...,' puzzles Charlotte? Lady Denham continues with a laugh, 'Miss Heywood, you are looking at yourself, in about fifty years, should you be so blessed with years as I have been. I see more of me in you every time we make our acquaintance. So get yourself back to Trafalgar House and your Mars, because I know that "only Venus dominates Mars, and he never dominates her" as Marsilio Ficino said several hundred years ago, and we shall wish to see the two of you married forthwith. Go now and cure Mr Parker of both his afflictions and leave me and your sister to get on with the mundane of our lives.'

Chapter 53

Thursday - 25 June 1818 - Sanditon

The next morning, Charlotte rises and goes to Sidney's chamber. She knocks. There is no answer so she quietly opens the door and peeks in. The bed is empty. Where is Sidney she wonders? She hears the sounds of children downstairs and goes down into the dining room. Sidney is sitting at the table with Mary and Tom and smiling at the three children who are gathered around his chair, clamoring for Uncle Sidney's attention. They all look up at Charlotte's entrance as she quickly walks over to him. 'Sidney,' Charlotte asks, 'should you be up and about? Are you healed enough?' 'Yes,' he says, 'I am well on the road to recovering my strength. Dr Kniepp came early this morning before you rose to examine me. He told me he had to go to London to see some patients there, but first he wanted to be satisfied that all is well with me. He concluded that I am no longer in need of his services, but I did need to be up and about and so here am I. Perhaps we can take a short walk after you dine, if you are willing, Charlotte?' 'I should like that very much,' replies Charlotte.

Tom whom Charlotte notices has been sitting quietly looking at her suddenly blurts out, 'Miss Heywood,... Charlotte..., Mary has told me that you have found an investor or investors to repay the loans outstanding against my project thereby relieving our financing problems, but she could not tell me the how of it. Will you now deign to tell me, tell us whence those funds shall come..., and when?' 'Tom,' responds Charlotte, 'I yet do not have the liberty of telling you the source, but you may be assured that that the funds will be forthcoming. Perhaps we shall talk this afternoon, in the quiet of the drawing room, without the children!' 'Very well, Charlotte, if that be your preference,' Tom returns.

At that moment, Morgan comes in to announce a caller. It is Lord Somerset. Tom quickly rises followed by Sidney a little more slowly to greet him. 'Sidney,' Somerset says, 'you look somewhat worse for wear. I did not know that you were so ill until I saw Esther this morning and she advised me that you were near death's door last week. Who has worked this miracle on you, Sidney? Certainly, Miss Heywood had a hand in it,' he concludes with a smile. 'Yes,' Sidney replies, 'with a little help from Dr Kniepp, Charlotte is almost entirely responsible for my recovery. It would not have happened without her. She is my very own angel.' 'Yes, I know how that is,' replies Lord Somerset. 'I have one of my own soon to be my bride in Esther. I shall expect to see you, Charlotte and Sidney, indeed all of the Parker family at our wedding Wednesday next.' Then turning to Tom, Somerset continues, 'Esther is bound and determined that we have our honeymoon here in Sanditon rather than Italy as I had proposed so we shall be in need of one of your new houses or apartments for the rest of the summer at least and thanks to Miss Heywood's expected continued presence here in Sanditon, Esther is demanding that I buy one. What do you think of that?' Tom jumps up out of his chair with eyes shining and shouts with glee, 'What a capital idea, if I do say so myself, is it not Mary!' As Tom prances around the room, Somerset turns to Charlotte and says, 'Miss Heywood, I almost forgot in the moment, but I have a letter for you. Here it is,' placing it into her hands. 'But now I must be going. We shall undoubtedly meet again tomorrow at the Ball and perhaps at other times between now and the wedding next week as I do not plan to return to London until after the wedding. Oh, and Francis..., Mr Nisbet is here at the hotel as well and will have Miss Clara on his arm at the ball. I do expect that our jaded Mr Nisbet has met his match and we shall see a wedding there as well before the new year. But, now I must be off.'

He goes out leaving Tom Parker in a celebratory mood with the news of Somerset's interest in purchasing an apartment or house. 'I knew that all would be well,' says he. 'It is a step to the better, Tom,' returns Mary, 'but you cannot throw caution to the winds with your expenditures. Let us first hear from Charlotte this afternoon after she and Sidney take some air.' 'Yes, Mary, of course you are right as usual,' responds Tom, 'but you must admit that we have in hand some very good news.' Mary just glances at Charlotte and Sidney then shakes her head with a smile.

Sidney turns to Charlotte and says, 'Shall we try my sea legs and see how far we shall travel on these strangers I have attached, my legs are a bit uncertain, perhaps too much time in bed, but I should certainly enjoy taking the air.' Charlotte responds, 'I wonder if we might borrow the curricle, Mary, to transport us to Sanditon House and back. There is someone there I wish Sidney to meet that should require walking enough on his first excursion after his illness without adding the journey from and to Trafalgar House.' 'Of course,' replies Mary, 'Morgan, will you please see to it.' 'Yes, Mrs Parker,' he replies and goes out. After a bit, he comes back in and announces that all is ready. Charlotte and Sidney go out and board the curricle. As Sidney drives, Charlotte opens the letter that Somerset has delivered to her. She quickly glances over it then says, 'Sidney, there is something that you should be aware of with regard to the debt for Sanditon Town.' He looks at her and says, 'Somerset's talk about purchasing an apartment or house was a bit of good news, Charlotte. But I am afraid that I was unsuccessful in saving Tom and me with my efforts. And perhaps I was precipitous in again asking for your hand, as I quite forgot the debt in the throes of my illness. How can I marry you if I am to go to debtor's prison? I would not and should never subject you to being bound to me as a penniless man.' 'Sidney,' Charlotte replies, 'Mary read me the letter that Mrs Wickham sent you and told me what you said before your illness took you down. You should not concern yourself with the debt.' 'How can I not, my darling Charlotte,' he asks? 'Sidney, did you not hear my reply to Tom at Trafalgar House just a few minutes ago, that funds to save Sanditon Sea Bathing Town are coming? Allow me to read the letter that Lord Somerset just placed into my hands moments ago, please Sidney,' she replies and begins;

Grosvenor Square 1

23 June 1818

Dearest Charlotte

I was very distressed to hear from Philip Stanley about Mr Sidney Parker's illness as he reported to me on his return to Warwick Court after accompanying you to Willingden. I trust that all is well with Mr Parker by now and of course with you.

I had hoped to remain at Warwick Court for a few more weeks but it was not to be. There was a matter having to do with the investment we discussed before your departure back to Willingden that required my attention in London. Without going too much into the heart of the matter, suffice it to say that the holder of one loan was reluctant to relinquish her hold on it. However, the matter has now been resolved along with the other two loans of which you were aware and I am pleased to tell you that the debt hanging over Sanditon Sea Bathing Town, with the exception of Lady Denham's investment has been extinguished. With that, I am now the major investor in the project. Going forward, although I am advised that construction is substantially complete, I expect that future outlays of funds will be decided by you and Mr Sidney Parker as we earlier discussed, not by Mr Tom Parker.

I shall look forward to seeing you later this summer to discuss in more detail these matters with you.

In the meantime, I remain

Your affectionate friend,

Susan

When Charlotte stops reading, she looks up and over to a silent Sidney who she realizes is staring at her. 'Sidney, what is it,' she asks? 'That letter; it is from the Duchess of Kent and she has decided to invest, to become the major investor in Sanditon if I understood it right?' 'Yes, Sidney, you understood it right,' replies Charlotte. 'And you and I are to determine how the funds are to be spent?' 'Yes,' returns Charlotte. Sidney continues, 'And Sanditon Sea Bathing Town has been saved. Tom and Mary have been saved. I have been saved...! How did you accomplish that, Charlotte...? Who are you?'

'That you know already, Sidney, and now there is someone I want you to meet,' Charlotte responds with a smile as Sidney drives the curricle into the Sanditon House courtyard whence Charlotte directs him to continue on to the stables. On arrival, she says, 'Let us get down. Oh look, Sidney, there is Georgiana and Anne and Mr Stringer too.' Their arrival is noted and the three came over to them as Charlotte steps down and helps Sidney with his more gingerly dismount. 'Sidney,' cries Georgiana, 'you look almost well. It must be the influence of Charlotte. The last time I saw you, I thought you at death's door. But to happier matters, has Charlotte told you of her horse, Lady?' 'Her horse,' questions Sidney with a puzzled look on his face, 'no she has not. She did say that there was someone here she wanted me to meet.' 'Well then, follow me,' laughs Georgiana, 'and meet.' She leads the way through the stables and out into the paddock behind. Lady who is standing in the middle of the paddock nickers when she sees Charlotte and trots over to her. As she lowers her head to have her ears scratched, Charlotte turns to Sidney and says, 'Sidney, I would like for you to meet my Lady.' Anne says, 'You know that Lady Denham keeps a watch day and night of this horse because she fears theft.' Sidney just looks back and forth between Lady and Charlotte and shakes his head.

'Well, Sidney shall we take that walk now,' asks Charlotte? 'It is but a short distance to the cliffs looking over the sea. The path should not be too difficult for you.' She extends her hand and Sidney takes it. They begin their walk and Sidney struggles a bit, but as they continue along the path and the sea comes into view, Sidney gains his stride and begins to walk more surely and purposefully while still holding tightly to Charlotte's hand. They reach the chalk cliffs and look toward Sanditon rising on the shore in the distance then back at each other. Sidney turns to Charlotte and takes her into his arms. As he lowers his face to her upturned one, he whispers, 'I ask you again, Charlotte, who are you?' As she closes her eyes in anticipation of the kiss to come, she replies, 'I am the woman who loves you, Sidney Parker. I am Charlotte Heywood of Willingden.'

End

Epilogue and Author's Notes

"Oh! write, write. Finish it at once. Let there be an end of this suspense. Fix, commit, condemn yourself."
- Jane Austen 'Mansfield Park'

Charlotte and Sidney marry on 1st September 1818 in Sanditon. The Reverend Mr Hankins officiates. Even before marriage, they take over the management of the financial side of Tom Parker's Sanditon Sea Bathing Town project. With proper discipline in handling the funds and paying suppliers and workers, construction is completed quickly. And with the influence of Lady Susan over the London Beau Monde, a substantial number of summer residents are attracted from Brighton and other spa towns on the south coast to the great benefit of Sanditon. Sidney rarely leaves Charlotte's side in Sanditon, turning over more and more of the management of his London based business to his partner, Charles Porteus, as his confidence in him grows. Charlotte's happiness knows no bounds and when she and Sidney move into their own house in Sanditon near the sea, she is the recipient of regular visits from her Willingden family as her Papa expands his willingness to travel away from the Willingden farmstead from five miles to five and twenty to allow for frequent visits to Sanditon.

And when Charlotte gives birth to her first child, a girl whom she names Susan around the time of the High Summer Ball in late June 1819, there are other special visitors who just happen to be present on the occasion including Papa Stephen and Mama Jane Heywood and the Lady Susan herself. Charlotte and Sidney eventually have five children, three girls and two boys.

Tom Parker at long last finds escape from his "obsession." At first, he is indignant at having lost control of the funds for "his town", but as he realizes that he can dream and plan and, yes, build, without the burden of worry over how to pay for it, his attitude begins to change. He sees his dream for Sanditon coming true with the help of Charlotte and Sidney and Robert Stringer as the foreman of his now well paid workers. Mary is happy to have a loving husband again who rediscovers his role as a father to their children. They take long walks on the beach, enjoy the growing number of Sanditon amenities and watch their children grow. The children themselves enjoy the almost daily contact with their beloved Aunt Charlotte and Uncle Sidney.

The Duchess of Kent, Susan as she prefers to be known to her familiars, maintains her close relationship with Mr and Mrs Sidney Parker as her Sanditon investment managers, purchases a house and becomes a frequent presence in Sanditon during the summer season as she finds it distinctly superior to Brighton in all respects. And she also finds it necessary to be present in Sanditon on other occasions, particularly it seems when a new addition is expected to Charlotte's and Sidney's growing family.

Lady Denham is rewarded for her "patience" in maintaining her investment in the Sanditon Sea Bathing Town seeing it develop into a substantial moneymaker. She is less pleased by the regular presence of the Lady Susan as her star is dimmed a bit by by the Duchess. But her joy in her increasingly close relationship with Charlotte Parker and the opportunities their meetings offer to engage in verbal swordplay grows by the year. She sees Charlotte as her only equal and never loses hope that one day she will manage to trick the truth of who Charlotte really is out of her. She lives to the ripe old age of eighty-nine and enjoys every minute of it.

Georgiana is taken under Lady Susan's wing and moves to London where she blossoms under her guidance and tutelage. She becomes a sought after presence in London Beau Monde circles and upon attaining the age of 21, she determines to purchase an estate. Sidney becomes even more of a beloved brother after his marriage to Charlotte as he seems to better understand the requirements of young ladies under Charlotte's influence. While still protective of her, Sidney allows Georgiana her freedom to engage more with Charles Porteus under proper supervision of course and after her 21st Birthday, she determines to begin working with him to promote the abolishment of slavery throughout the British Empire. Charles becomes quite influential in guiding the political debate about slavery working closely with abolitionists in the House of Commons until slavery is abolished in 1833. And during that time, his business acumen turns Sidney's London based business into a roaring success. Sidney rewards him with a part ownership in 1821. Georgiana and Charles toy with the idea of marriage, but ultimately decide that their feelings for each other are more sister and brother than love and marriage. They do marry, not to each other, but maintain a close family relationship all of their lives.

Mrs. Maria Wickham never receives a response to her demand letter to Sidney. She does however hear via London gossip that Mr. Sidney Parker has taken as his wife a certain Miss Charlotte Heywood at Sanditon Town on 1st September, 1818. Shortly thereafter, she decamps with all her household to the south of France whence she returns to London from time to time. But she finds happiness and a title as the Countess Nevers with her marriage to a French Count in 1821.

Robert Stringer finishes building Sanditon Town and moves on to London where he apprentices as an architect to John Nash, Architect to the Prince Regent, with the support of Lady Susan. Anne continues in her role as Lady Denham's trusted and increasingly influential companion. She and Robert marry on 1st September 1820 in Sanditon when he is financially secure which comes more quickly than either he or Anne expect. They name their first child, a daughter, Charlotte.

Sir Edward finds that his conspiracy with Mrs Wickham is rewarded with the back of her hand rather than money or marriage after Sidney rejects her efforts to bribe him into marriage and instead marries Charlotte. And after a time, with the support of sister Esther and her husband, Lord Somerset and a degree of rapprochement with Lady Denham, he stops his drinking and turns over a new leaf. He becomes a citizen of good standing rather than a ne'er-do-well, gradually takes a greater role in overseeing the Denham estate and eventually marries. On Lady Denham's death, he inherits her fortune.

Lord Somerset and Esther Denham, who marry on 1st July 1818 in Sanditon, to be known as the Earl and Countess of Tewkesbury, spend increasing amounts of time in Sanditon Town. They become investors as well and join Sidney and Charlotte as co-managers of the Sanditon Spa Town Enterprise. Lord and Lady Somerset also establish a carriage horse breeding farm near Sanditon and their Sanditon Blacks as they are known become sought after status symbols among the London Beau Monde. They also determine to rival the Heywood family and embark on a production that ultimately results in seven children. Their first child, a boy, is named Sidney.

Clara Brereton and Francis Nisbet become a pair of social butter-flies among the London Beau Monde and ultimately decide to wed as it is vexingly inconvenient always to part to separate bed chambers. They surprise themselves by finding marriage to be quite agreeable and in addition purchase a Sanditon apartment where they enjoy the sea air from time to time and never miss the Sanditon High Summer Ball which Charlotte and Sidney always lead off unless the birth of a child interferes.

Diana and Arthur never marry. They do however invest a great deal of time in Dr Kniepp's popular health spa in Sanditon enjoying daily or almost daily treatments for their many imagined and real humors and other assorted complaints. They also become favored Aunt and Uncle to Charlotte's and Sidney's eventual five children.

Mrs. Griffiths and The Reverend Mr Hankins marry to great celebration in Sanditon and live Happily Ever After.

Background to Charlotte's and Lady Susan's relationship

Mr Stephen Heywood was a trusted member of the Duke of Kent's staff, in line to become the House Steward as was his father and his father's father before him. When Lady Susan's short 1st April 1795 marriage (annulled by the King) to Prince George, who became the Prince Regent in 1811 and then King George IV on his father's death in 1820, resulted in a child, Mr Heywood moved back to ancestral land and was given a stipend to establish himself as a gentleman farmer in Willingden. He and his wife, Jane, moved there with a young son, Benjamin, and the baby, whom Susan named Charlotte, shortly after she was born on 18 February 1796. Stephen and Jane Heywood subsequently had ten more children of their own; Anne, Elizabeth, Thomas, George, Harriet, Annabella, Henry, Sarah, Ellen and John. Although Charlotte was raised with the freedom and lack of pretense that country life offered, she was tutored from a young age and well educated to allow her to take her place in the world when the opportunity offered it. The happenstance of the carriage on the "very rough Lane" opened the door to Sanditon and Charlotte found her love and life there. Lady Susan of course kept a close watch from afar as Charlotte grew into the beautiful young woman she became and when Charlotte went to Sanditon and fell in love with Sidney Parker, the debt troubles of Tom Parker's Sanditon Sea Bathing Town required Lady Susan to come to the rescue of the love and happiness of her daughter. And so she did because Jane Austen's heroines always find Happiness Ever After (HEA).

And finally, may I offer you some of my favorite Jane Austen Quotes taken from the headings of my own earlier Spring 2020 Season 2 writings to savor and enjoy if you should be so inclined. Miss Jane Austen had a incomparable way with words that penetrate the heart and the mind, did she not!

"There is a stubbornness about me that never can bear to be frightened at the will of others. My courage always rises at every attempt to intimidate me." - Jane Austen 'Pride and Prejudice'

"A woman, especially if she have the misfortune of knowing anything, should conceal it as well as she can." - Jane Austen 'Northanger Abbey'

"Seldom, very seldom, does complete truth belong to any human disclosure..." - Jane Austen 'Emma'

"How wonderful, how very wonderful the operations of time, and the changes of the human mind." - Jane Austen 'Mansfield Park'

"I do not think I ever opened a book in my life which had not something to say upon a woman's inconstancy. Songs and proverbs, all talk of woman's fickleness. But perhaps you will say, these were all written by men." - Jane Austen 'Persuasion'

"If I loved you less, I might be able to talk about it more." - Jane Austen 'Emma'

"Time will explain." - Jane Austen 'Persuasion'

"I have no talent for certainty." - Jane Austen 'Mansfield Park'

"None of us wants to be in calm waters all of our lives." - Jane Austen 'Persuasion'

'If I could but know his heart, everything would become easy." - Jane Austen 'Sense and Sensibility'.

"You pierce my soul. I am half agony, half hope." - Jane Austen 'Persuasion'

"It is particularly incumbent on those who never change their opinion, to be secure of judging properly at first." - Jane Austen 'Pride and Prejudice'

"Let us never underestimate the power of a well-written letter." - Jane Austen - 'Persuasion'

"Her affection would be his forever." - Jane Austen, 'Persuasion'

"He..........was beginning a new period of existence, with every probability of greater happiness than in any yet passed through." - Jane Austen 'Emma'

"The very first moment I beheld him, my heart was irrevocably gone." - Jane Austen 'Love and Friendship'

"I offer myself to you again with a heart even more your own than when you almost broke it." - Jane Austen 'Persuasion'

"Do not give way to useless alarm…though it is right to be prepared for the worst, there is no occasion to look on it as certain." - Jane Austen 'Pride and Prejudice'

"How quick come the reasons for approving what we like." - Jane Austen 'Persuasion'

"To be fond of dancing was a certain step towards falling in love." - Jane Austen 'Pride and Prejudice'

"When once we are buried you think we are gone. But behold me immortal! By vice you are enslaved…" - Jane Austen 'When Winchester Races'

"If adventures will not befall a young lady in her own village, she must seek them abroad." - Jane Austen 'Northanger Abbey'

"I can feel no sentiment of approbation inferior to love." - Jane Austen 'Sense and Sensibility'

"It is not time or opportunity that is to determine intimacy;—it is disposition alone. Seven years would be insufficient to make some people acquainted with each other, and seven days are more than enough for others." - Jane Austen 'Sense and Sensibility'

Well then! Thank you for reading.

D B Thomas

Authors bio

Thomas Hamby, writing as DB Thomas, is an actor and writer who shares his time between Finland and Florida USA. He is a great fan of all things Jane Austen and British Period Drama. You can discover more about him through his Instagram account at https://www.instagram.com/db_thomas_hamby/ and his IMDB account at https://www.imdb.com/name/nm9362545/. You can read his step outline entitled *Sanditon – HEA Found* written for possible development into a Sanditon Season 2 screenplay which also includes analysis and comments for the 2019 ITV/MasterpiecePBS production of Sanditon Season 1 at: https://www.booksie.com/users/db-thomas-288777 .